BATTLE CREEK

BATTLE CREEK

SCOTT LASSER

Perennial

An Imprint of HarperCollins*Publishers*

A hardcover edition of this book was published in 1999 by Rob Weisbach Books, an imprint of William Morrow and Company, Inc.

HarperCollins books may be purchased for educational, business, or sales promotional use. For information please write: Special Markets Department, HarperCollins Publishers Inc., 10 East 53rd Street, New York, NY 10022.

First Perennial edition published 2000.

Designed by James Sinclair

The Library of Congress has catalogued the hardcover edition as follows:
Lasser, Scott
    Battle creek / Scott Lasser. — 1st ed.
        p. cm.
    ISBN 0-688-16785-3 (alk. paper)
    I. Title.
    PS3562.A7528B3   1999
    813'.54—dc21   99-12607
                                                                          CIP

ISBN 0-688-17763-8 (pbk.)

00 01 02 03 04 ❖/RRD 10 9 8 7 6 5 4 3 2 1

For my dad

Winning is a habit. Unfortunately, so is losing.

—*Vince Lombardi*

BATTLE CREEK

MAY

I

Before the screen door can slap shut, the smell of grass hits him. It is the very odor of youth and freshness, and it makes him come to a stop on his porch. By any measure it is a glorious day. The sun shines, the air is warm, the sky is the robin's-egg blue of spring. Though Gil Davison is not normally the type of man to appreciate the natural world, he notices that the buds have opened on the large oak that hovers over his driveway. Across the street his neighbor, Tom Foss, is dropping clear plastic bags of lawn clippings along the curb.

"Beautiful day, Gil," Foss says. Gil has now moved out in front of his house, as this is a neighborhood in which men commonly talk from their lawns.

"Beautiful," Gil repeats.

Foss waves, as though from a great distance, and goes back to work.

Gil then remembers what he has set out to do: fire a player. Though he has coached baseball for nearly thirty years, he still dreads letting people go. Every year he has to do it ten times or a dozen; it doesn't get any easier. This year, though, he is taking no chances. He has made up his mind that this will be his last season. He wants to go out on top. In previous years he kept some people on board out of loyalty, or because he liked them, or because he liked their wives or girlfriends, or just to avoid having to fire them, but this year he won't do it. This year a player has to produce, or he's gone. Hitters have to hit; pitchers have to get people out. He isn't going to have any shenanigans, any lackadaisical grab-ass. For four years running his team has made the national finals only to lose. No other amateur team has the national reputation of Koch and Sons, no other team has ever made the finals four years, in a row or not. No other team has placed so many players in pro ball, or has had so many go all the way to the bigs. Koch alumni have played in the World Series, are making big bucks in Anaheim, Baltimore, and Osaka. Last year one of the Battle Creek papers called the team a dynasty. Gil thinks of last year, when he left Mercer in so that the kid could get the championship win, left him in even though he knew Merc was tired, and when San Antonio rocked him and all was lost, Gil could think only that again he'd let his heart rule his head. Football was the game of emotions. Baseball required clear-headed logic. In baseball you played percentages and made your own luck. So this year emotions will have nothing to do with it.

Jerry Callicotte does not think Gil is soft. Callicotte has played on the fringe of Koch and Sons for three years. He has found ways to make himself useful. He has played every position—even catcher—and once got a key out while pitching in an early-season game. Really, he's an infielder, and dead weight. The squad can no longer afford two-fifty hitters who play all positions adequately but none exceptionally. True, Callicotte has an exceptional love for the game, and enthusiasm goes a long way with Gil. Gil has given him tickets to Tiger Stadium, which Callicotte eagerly uses, going early to watch batting practice. He's a good kid and likable enough. Callicotte has even sent Gil a Christmas present. Gil considers all this, but his mind is set.

They are to meet in Ann Arbor. The University of Michigan is playing Wisconsin. Callicotte went to school at Michigan. Gil wants to check out the Wolverine second baseman, and thus he can knock off two jobs with one trip. He convinces himself he can be hard and efficient. He has told Callicotte to meet him behind home plate, Gil's favorite place to sit.

Gil steadies himself as he drives down M-14. His Continental is freshly washed, a moving spectacle of shiny deep-green clear-coat paint. Gil is content for the moment, a feeling borne, unconsciously, by the smell of leather and what he sees out the window. Here, then, is the comforting landscape: rows of corn barely sprouted; trees quaking with their new leaves; the roadside Queen Anne's lace bowing in the breeze; the now milky-blue sky stretching out endlessly toward Chicago and beyond. On the radio the WJR jockey chatters on about a human interest story a step above the supermarket tabloids, and then comes a Frank Sinatra song sung by Tony Bennett. Gil glances at the car's clock. In seventeen minutes the Tiger pregame show will begin.

Perhaps it's the music or the sky or even the drive along M-14, but suddenly Gil remembers waking this morning certain that his two sons were standing at his bed. Rick was about eight and Laurence five. They were in their pajamas, their short hair matted from sleep. They looked so innocent, especially Laurence, that Gil thought he might cry. They wanted to play, to roughhouse on the bed. This was before Gil's two disks were removed, before the second knee operation and the cholesterol watch. Downstairs he could hear the radio; there was the long-ago smell of bacon. When he invited the boys up, they jumped, but instead of landing, they disappeared. The sensation was overpowering. Gil staggered to the bathroom, where in the mirror he saw his tired, sixty-four-year-old face lined with tears.

Later that morning, at the barber shop, he again had a memory, this one only of Laurence. Gil places the year around 1970. Rick refused to get his hair cut and after the crying and a fight with Susan, Gil grabbed Laurence and whisked him off to the barber. Laurence was about seven, still obedient, not yet surly. Gil watched the barber work on the boy's head and this gave Gil the feeling that he had done something lasting and tangible, something he could point to and say, Hey, that's mine. I made that. When Stan, the barber—indeed the same barber these twenty-odd years—wheeled him around Gil was again surprised to see his old face, not Laurence's.

Something wrong? the barber said.

Gil stared a long time into the accordion mirrors, back and back through the images, as if he expected one of them to be different.

Behind the backstop sit the regulars, men Gil's age, men whose
company he enjoys. They are big, American men. They sit by
spreading their legs wide on the aluminum benches, forearms
resting against thighs so as to buttress barrel chests and bulbous
stomachs, weight accumulated through seasons of spectating.
They cover their bulk with Michigan paraphernalia: baseball
caps with block M's, blue-and-gold sweatshirts, pins. Several of
these men have football season tickets. The others are on the
waitlist. They come to trade stories and eat. Each is supposed to
watch his weight; none does, except that a Diet Coke is now
considered acceptable to wash down a hot dog or ice cream
sandwich. They talk about baseball and sometimes local politics,
if the subject—such as the possible demolition of Tiger Stadium
and the bond issue to fund its replacement—has some direct
relevance to their lives. Not one of them is a Michigan alumnus,
but there is little they do not know about Michigan baseball.

When they see Gil they wave him over. "Where have you
been?" asks John, who took early retirement from GM and lives
what he calls the good life off Social Security and his UAW pension.

"Busy, I guess," Gil says. This is only the fourth home game.
He sits. Callicotte is nowhere in sight, which is expected. He's
not due for another forty-five minutes.

Michigan's team runs onto the field to brief and restrained
applause. The pitcher, a lanky redhead, starts throwing, the ball
popping the catcher's glove. Gil doesn't have to look to know
the kid has a live arm. But he's a sophomore and the nongradu-
ating players play in the Cape League over the summer, which
Gil doesn't think is so great for their baseball.

In the on-deck circle the Wisconsin batter is swinging in time, as if to hit the pitcher's warm-ups.

"You hear about Clement?" Roger asks. Gil looks for Clement, realizes he's missing.

"Ain't that something?" says one of the regulars.

"What about him?" Gil asks.

John takes over. "He's got this daughter, see. Lives down in Miami. So, Clement figures, why not go for a visit, see her and the grandkid, and then, hell, catch some of spring training. Something he's wanted to do all his life. The spring training. So, he goes, gets there, and the daughter? She's got a black eye."

Gil nods. The men watch the pitch, a ball outside.

"So, anyway, she sees her ol' man and starts in crying. Takes about a minute and she's telling him it was the husband, some Cuban." Pause for a foul tip. "Montez? That's Cuban, right? Anyway, turns out the kid's got bruises up and down his backside. Kid's only three, mind you, and it's Clement's grandson, right? So he goes off to where the guy works."

A ground ball to short, one away.

"He works at this Nissan dealership. It's bad enough for Clement that his son-in-law sells Nissans for a living, right? And you know Clement, never what you'd call a diplomat. Ol' Clement, he walks up to the guy and tells him what for. The guy claims he never touched either the daughter or the grandkid."

First pitch pop-up, two away.

"So, that night Clement is in a stew, and Linda, his wife, she calls me. So I call him. At his hotel, long distance. I say, forget about the spic, get your little girl and the baby and bring 'em up here. I mean, a guy's a hitter, he's a hitter. People say men change, but I ain't never seen it. Hitters don't change. Am I right?"

John looks to the regulars, who nod, then turn their heads to the pitch, a called strike.

"Clement, though, he's a Marine. Guadalcanal. Did you know that? Anyway, he's beside himself and so the next day he goes to get his daughter and bring her up here, but she's really a mess. I guess the guy got home the night before and let her have it. The kid's got a broken arm. Can you imagine?" Pause, a ball, low. "I'm not making this up. Broke his own kid's arm. Clement, he just goes berserk. Drives to the dealership, walks up to the guy, takes out his old service revolver—the thing's been under the front seat of his car since Truman was president, he showed it to me once—and so he takes his gun and shoots the husband in the face. Except you know Clement, not so good with faces. We all know he needs new glasses all the time. Took him a season to tell me from Gene. So . . ." A ball, away. "You guessed it, Clement shoots the wrong guy, just some poor bastard trying to sell Nissans. I guess they all wore blue blazers." Pause for a foul down the third base line. "Anyway, Clement gets so excited, he has a stroke right there in the showroom."

Pause, ball three.

"That's it?" Gil asks.

"What else is there?"

"The daughter, the kid? His wife? Clement?"

"Got me. The shooting part and all I got from the papers.

But I tell you what, you raise 'em and they marry assholes. What can you do? I'm with Clement, though. 'Cept you got to get the right guy."

"Hear, hear," says one of the regulars.

The batter hits a fly to center, end of the inning. Michigan trots into its dugout.

"Good inning," John says, and the other regulars agree.

It is the third inning and still Gil is thinking about Clement. Jesus, he thinks, it's a crazy world if Clement can shoot a man in the face. Soft, doughy Clement, never said but a word or two during a whole doubleheader. Gil is thankful he has no daughters. Boys. Boys he can handle. He wouldn't have known what to do with a daughter. But even boys can be trouble. They can take their mother's side or not speak to you. They get fooled by curve balls and misinterpret your remarks, turn everything you say till you can't speak at all. In your own home. And they can be careless, so careless. When you can't imagine how they can go wrong, they go out and get drunk, take drugs, rob stores, beat up women, crack up cars, get hit by them. Gil has coached through the generations and seen it all. Fathers have called him, begging for answers. *He was such a fine ballplayer, how could he do this?* Gil has no answers. You never know sadness till you've buried a son, he told one father, hoping some perspective might help. It didn't.

"Hi, Coach," says Callicotte, who has managed to surprise Gil. The young man wears a Michigan sweatshirt and cap, like the regulars. Gil gets up and moves down the bleachers, for privacy. Callicotte sits next to Gil, who glances at the player's ruddy cheeks and close-cropped hair. Callicotte is an insurance salesman by day. Gil thinks he must have a hard time of it, looking, as he does, as though he's not old enough to drive.

"What do you think of this Kukla?" Gil asks. He means the second baseman. Gil has already decided he wants the kid. He's got a quick, compact swing, and good range and glove, and he's a base stealer. Everyone says Kukla's got speed, that he can fly for a white boy, which Gil figures is about as nice a compliment as a person can give a white boy these days.

The conversation pauses for the pitch, a ball inside.

"How's work?" Gil asks.

"Good."

"And Carol, your girlfriend?"

"Cheryl. We broke up." Another ball inside.

"Sorry to hear that."

"Don't be. She wanted to get married, have babies. I'm not ready for that."

"What have you been doing with yourself?"

"Getting in shape. Been throwing, going to the batting cage. Weights."

This isn't going to be easy, Gil thinks. For a moment he wonders if maybe he can use Callicotte after all. He thinks of the year when he was thirteen, when someone made a spot for him. Then he thinks again and says no. No dead weight. Be tough. Do what has to be done.

"Listen, Jerry," Gil says, sotto voce, so that the regulars can't hear. "I'm not going to be able to use you this year."

"What?"

"I'm not going to be able to use you this year . . ." The Wisconsin batter drives the ball deep up the alley in right. The center fielder, a wide receiver on the football team, sprints for the ball, dives, and misses. The right fielder retrieves it and throws it in. The batter stops at third to delirious cheers from the Wisconsin bench. It's the first hit of the game.

Everyone sits down. Be tough, Gil tells himself.

"Listen, Jerry. I'm not going to be able to use you this year," he says for the third time.

"What?"

"You heard me."

"You're firing me?"

"Yes."

Callicotte takes a deep breath. "Gil, I've been with you three years. I contribute." He looks down at his throwing hand, spreads his fingers, then looks up into Gil's eyes. "You yourself called me just to tell me that this winter."

Gil remembers. Lonely, with nothing to do in February, he made that call, praised Callicotte. Jesus, he thinks. How could I have done that? That was the old, soft me. That person? Long gone.

"You've been a big help," he says, "but I can't use you this year. There are too many young guys coming in. Why don't you devote more time to your career? You can't play baseball forever."

"Mercer is thirty-three. Jefferson is thirty-four!"

"But, Jerry, you're not Jefferson or Mercer. Frankly, they are better players."

Gil is surprised to hear himself speak this simple truth. It is a hard thing to say; there's a meanness to it. Gil feels sorry, even embarrassed, for Callicotte, whose face is turning the scarlet of Wisconsin's uniforms. He seems to be trembling, as though he might shout or cry.

"Try not to take it hard," Gil says. "Every player has to stop eventually. It's normal. And most kids don't have the run you've had. They stop in Little League, or junior high. My own son stopped in high school. Even me, when I came back from—"

Suddenly, Callicotte jumps up. "You're a bastard," he says. Callicotte stares at Gil with a look of hatred that startles him. This blond, all-American Dennis the Menace hates him. *Hates him.* Callicotte begins to leave, then stops. "A bastard!" he yells again, then tromps off.

Gil turns toward the regulars. They are staring at him. Not one even glances at the field.

"You're brutal," says John. The others chuckle. "You brought the poor guy out to his alma mater, then let him go." The men shake their heads, smiling.

Gil smiles. You're all losers, he thinks. This year I'm going to get it done. This year.

II

Late that night, Ben Mercer stands in his kitchen breaking plates. He takes them by the edge, and with a quick movement of his pitching arm he brings them down on the corner of the kitchen counter. Ceramics fly. When he finishes with the dinner and salad dishes, he goes for the bowls, smashes a set of eight.

He feels no better. He is in love, in love in the gut-tugging, sweaty-back, all-encompassing way, as if some terrible fever has overtaken him. All other women he sees only in comparison to her: one has her walk, another her tilt of the head, or her hair. He thinks about her at work and on the ball field. Every pop song on the radio seems to speak to the desperation of his position.

Her name is Emily. She is twenty-four, five-nine, with the body of a goddess. When they make love, at the moment of her release, she cries and then laughs uncontrollably. He wants her all the time, wants to have her, to possess her. He wants to marry her, though he will not admit this even to himself. Also, she dates another guy, someone she's been going with since she got to college, which was a long time ago, six years. His name is Doug, and she complains to Mercer about him. In her stories Doug is weak and pathetic, a puppy, but then she goes off and sees him, spends the night at his place. When Mercer thinks of them sleeping together he is driven to lunacy. And so now he has bolted upright in bed, run to the kitchen, and broken everything in sight. He stands in the harsh light, wading in broken crockery, amazed by his madness.

The next morning, a Sunday, he wakes early and goes for a run. He runs every morning. He is by build and disposition a pitcher: long, lanky, and intense. He has played baseball around the world, from Glens Falls to Caracas to Tokyo and Manila. He earned a subsistence wage to play ball into his late twenties, then landed back in Michigan, signed up as a trainee at Merrill Lynch, and signed on with Koch and Sons. He once played for Baltimore. He spent only two weeks in the bigs, but the mere fact that he'd pitched from a professional mound was qualification enough for Merrill and Koch.

He lives in Ann Arbor, not far from the Huron River, and his typical run takes him into Nichols Arboretum, where the trees have blossomed and the earth smells loamy. He runs east, through Gallup Park to the dam, then back, up the hill, past a couple of frats and into the subdivision where he is renting. He has college professors and two light manufacturing tycoons for neighbors. Roughly a quarter of these people are now his clients.

He showers, takes his Sunday *New York Times* under his arm, and drives into town. He is playing a game with himself. He knows where he is heading but pretends to be just another guy out for a Sunday cruise. He drives a 1987 BMW 325, a car he loves but one that causes him a good deal of grief in the domestic car country of southern Michigan. He gets to Packard and cruises through the student ghetto, where old family homes have been converted into apartment houses, a magical land where bicycles hang from trees, refrigerators rest on porches, where eaves sag and paint chips float on the wind, where there is more street traffic at three in the morning than at nine. Party detritus—plastic block-M beer cups, Cottage Inn pizza cartons—lies abandoned on the lawns. He notices late-model Beemers with New York plates parked on the street and thinks, I've got to get myself some rental property. Then a coed comes swinging out of one of the homes, her wet hair billowing in the breeze, and he remembers why he has come.

This is Emily's street. There, in the third house in, is her apartment. Emily is something new for him. She wears sandals, eats brown rice, no meat, smokes cigarettes that she rolls herself. She is fairly well convinced that cattle and automobiles, especially the expensive models of each, are at the heart of human troubles and discontent. She thinks violence against very young boys—by which she means circumcision—is the cause of all violence against women. She votes Democratic, demonstrated against the Gulf War, cares nothing for baseball or the stock market. Also, she likes expensive wine in fine restaurants, and will spend any amount of Mercer's money on her bohemian clothes. At the natural food store he has bought her shampoo the price of molten gold. He thinks of the way her hair tumbles over itself when she tilts her head, and it makes him wild with desire.

He has the *Times* under his arm. She likes the *Times*. One of his fondest memories is of a Sunday morning of lovemaking, sections of the *Times* read when resting. They didn't finish the paper till almost two that afternoon, and he got her to Angelo's for thick slabs of raisin French toast just before they locked the door.

Somehow his feet have brought him under her window. She lives on the top floor—the third. He can see that her shade is drawn—it is only ten-thirty—and he wonders if he should go up. What if the puppy is there? The puppy doesn't know that Mercer exists. At first Mercer liked this, but now he knows his situation is untenable. The puppy can go on forever in ignorance, while Mercer is about to get an ulcer. He would like to bust upstairs and throw the puppy out the window, but Emily would not forgive him for this. She likes him with his clothes off and his wallet open, and because he will argue politics with her. He has found no limits to her passion but suspects that he skirts around the border of what she finds acceptable. She likes to have a little fight before lovemaking, so for now the relationship works.

To go up or not to go up. He looks skyward for guidance. Clouds float by—it will not be as nice a day as yesterday—but still he is paralyzed. Is the puppy there or not? It's impossible to tell.

He seizes on a bold plan: the fire escape. It is wooden, built on the back of the house as a sop to the fire inspector. Last summer, late on a night as hot and steamy as they come, Mercer and Emily made love on the flimsy, rotting structure, then rolled cold bottles of beer over each other to cool down. He walks now to the back of the house. Here old newspapers and magazines, socks, beer bottles litter the yard. There is a compost heap directly below the fire escape, so that tenants can throw their biodegradables over the rail and still feel ecologically correct.

Mercer begins to climb. The steps creak and groan. The neighborhood is as still as a school at midnight. He tiptoes, imagines himself light, lighter than air, wills away the noise. Jesus, he thinks, the original backdoor man.

He is floating across the second-floor landing, looking in the window to make sure he isn't seen (he feels he's invisible if he's looking, as if he's operating behind a one-way mirror), when he puts his foot through a rotten board. He starts to tumble and feels his ankle wrench. He lets out a cry. He frees his foot, watches the paper spill from his arm and fall to the backyard.

Still trying to regain his balance, he bangs into the handrail, and it gives. For a fleeting moment he feels as though he were a character in a cartoon, hanging off a precipice. Then he drops the twelve feet into the compost heap.

His ankle is on fire. He rolls about in the rotting grapefruit rinds and coffee grounds, an organic ooze of squash and potato skins, egg shells, long-forgotten tomatoes, and newly formed mold. A primordial swamp. He tries to stand, but can't. Not yet. It's his right ankle, his push-off foot. Bad news.

Eventually the pain eases and he does what any man in his situation would do: he rises to his feet, wipes himself off (as much as possible), and heads for his car. He drives with his left foot and marvels at his situation. He is crazy with jealousy of a twenty-four-year-old kid who works in a coffee bar. But this is old news. The admonitions of dozens of coaches come to him, all the warnings of his youth suddenly turned true, a moment as powerful as the one in which he realized—not long ago, he's not that old—that most of what his father had taught him was right. Finally, he has found a woman who is bad for his baseball.

III

Vince Paklos sits in his backyard and sneaks cigarettes. His wife is reading the Sunday paper in bed and so Vince can count on a moment of peace. He sniffs the breeze, strains against the emphysema. There are times—now is one—when he feels he is suffocating and only a cigarette will pull him through, that only the smoke can navigate the clogged and coated byways of his lungs. To Vince cigarette smoke is the life force, the one little bit of pleasure still afforded him. Pulling the cigarette from its pack, the match strike, the first drag—he thinks, when I die I'm going to miss this.

He is, he thinks, also going to miss baseball. Cigarettes and baseball. These are not unusual vices. Vince has no need for or patience with unusual vices. Baseball and nicotine he can understand. Women he can understand. Cars, food, gambling. Drink. What gets him is the weird stuff he reads in the paper. Just last week they found a pair of brothers dead in a house in Northville. The house was literally stuffed with trash. They never threw anything away. One brother was seventy-four and the other eighty and infirm. When the younger one keeled over, the other starved to death. Weird.

Today Vince has one task: he has to sign a player for Gil. The kid plays at Central Michigan, so this requires a drive to Mount Pleasant and a meeting in a restaurant of the player's choosing. This is almost always a bad idea, letting a college kid pick a restaurant. Often they're nonsmoking. The food is little better than fodder, sandwiches too thick, stuffed with vegetables, or there's nothing on the menu but pizza. No one serves good meat loaf anymore. He reaches for the sports pages. The Tigers are not doing well. Already, and it's only May. At least this year there will be no false hopes. Next year Vince won't have to endure the misery of a Tiger season, if his doctors are right. He thinks, I'm going to miss that, too.

He hears the creak of the screen door and swiftly snuffs out his cigarette on the round arm of the lawn chair. He puts the dead butt in his pocket. Ellen is coming. He turns in his seat to see her walking in her typically small, tentative steps. She stops five feet away.

"Vince, dear, aren't you cold?"

"Now, if I was cold, would I be sitting out here like this?"

"I don't know," his wife says. The look on her face displays honest concern. He turns back straight in his chair and waits for her to walk back into his view. He tries to picture her in 1947, the year they were married, but to do that he needs to think of a different woman. We have grown into different people, he thinks. No, we have just gotten to know each other very, very well.

It's the fluffy slippers he notices first, pink against the grass. Then the robe. He looks to the trees he planted ten years ago. In another decade they might shield a scene such as this from his neighbors.

"How 'bout some coffee?"

"Great," he says, thinking it will warm him up.

"Come in, then. I'll make some."

"I prefer it out here."

She humphs. She doesn't approve of his sitting outside in the mornings. She thinks it's not healthy. I'm dying of emphysema, he once yelled at her, but for Ellen a cold is more palpable. She heads back to the house. He wonders what in God's name will happen to his wife. The woman simply refuses to acknowledge the inevitable. They have a son, but he happens to live in Boise. Idaho! He went off to live in Idaho. A lot of help he'll be to his mother.

Vince feels the anger rise within him. He gasps, grabs a gulp of morning air. It is barely enough, this air. He longs for a cup of coffee, and it isn't long till his wife provides it.

The restaurant in Mount Pleasant is really a sports bar, the kind of place where the patrons throw peanut shells on the floor, the kitchen overstuffs the sandwiches, and silent TV screens blink at the crowd. Vince takes a table in the smoking section, thankful that they've got one.

The kid arrives. Tommy O'Rourke. Vince normally doesn't have much faith in Irish ballplayers, but there have been exceptions. John McGraw, for example.

O'Rourke is six feet three, 220 pounds, and twenty-two years old: a big guy with a boy's face. His cheeks are pimply and his voice high, but he hits with power, runs well, and has a cannon for an arm. He'll be drafted into pro ball in two weeks, but he wants to get his degree before he signs, which makes him free for the summer. Gil wants him for center field. They've made a deal on the phone. Gil is very good on the phone, all gravel and certainty in his voice. Especially certainty. Gil believes he can win, and when players listen to him they hear that vision. Eat it up. So now Vince is just running an errand. There was a time when Vince would have helped with the recruiting part, too, but that was ten thousand cigarette packs ago.

Vince stares across the booth at O'Rourke. They toss small talk back and forth beneath the replicas of old advertisements—soaps, patent medicines—that are nailed to the wall.

"I've been thinking about going pro," O'Rourke announces, after a silence. "I thought I should tell you that."

"What's that mean?" Vince feels his chest tighten.

"Just that maybe I should go this year. There's a lot of money now. It may not be as good in the future."

"What about your degree?"

"I can get that anytime."

"You won't," Vince says. "You leave now, you'll never get a degree." The kid starts to speak, but Vince cuts him off with a raised hand. He uses the time to catch his breath. "Don't even consider dropping out."

"But the opportunity is there now. That's all I'm saying. I didn't say I've made up my mind. But I may go pro, is all."

"The opportunity is always there. But you get older, you won't go back to school. Look at me. I played minor-league ball from New York to California. I was good. Winter ball, too. Venezuela, Cuba. Once I got called up by Branch Rickey. Said he was going to make me a Dodger pitcher. Oh yeah, those were good years. Owned five suits." Vince pauses; slowly he feels the air finding its way into his body. He fishes around for his cigarettes. "Yes, fine times. Good years. Even made the bigs for a month, mid-August into September, 1949. You got any idea what it's like to play in front of thirty thousand people?"

The kid shook his head. His eyes are glossy dreaming about it. Red base paths, grass like green velvet. Exploding scoreboards, his picture in lights.

"Forget it, Tommy. It'll never happen." Vince lights a cigarette, feels the surge of smoke. "Yeah, by 1952 I was selling textiles. Fabric. You know what that is like? Driving from here to eternity. That's what I did. 1952 till last year. Never got an office. Never got my own desk. Never made forty thousand dollars a year. That what you got in mind?"

"Today they pay . . ."

"Today they don't pay. Sure, you're Barry Bonds, you make money. You think you're gonna make millions in the minors? Think again. Then, when you get out, what are you going to do then? Can't be a fabric salesman—got foreigners doing that now. My old company's almost as sick as I am."

The food arrives on the table. Vince pulls a piece of corned beef from his sandwich. Hey, he thinks, I feel pretty good.

"We got a guy who pitched for Baltimore," Vince says. "But he never made any money at it. Got his degree first, though. Now he makes over a hundred K. Drives a German car."

"I still gotta think about that draft."

"Think—that's fine. Nothing wrong with thinking. But don't go. Play for us, then go back to college. And get your degree. Here, I brought the papers."

Vince puts the contract on the table. It is one sheet and it means nothing. The kid could still play for a pro team and Koch and Sons would lose a roster spot. Vince figures that if he signs, though, he'll choose to stay amateur. The kid hesitates.

"If you play for Koch and Sons," Vince says, "you'll have pro scouts in the stands practically every game. You will play with players who have been where you want to go. And you'll get three uniform jerseys, two types of pants, practice shirts, undershirts, shorts, duffel bags, satin jackets, and spikes. No other team outfits like we do. And no other team wins like we do. We're a class operation."

"Cincinnati was talking a six-figure signing bonus."

"And a low-five-figure salary. Sign the contract, Tommy. Stay in school."

O'Rourke signs. Vince pays for the lunch. He keeps the receipt, so that Gil can reimburse him.

IV

Sunday morning Gil is back on M-14, this time driving to see his father. The man is ninety-eight years old. When he was born, in a tiny Lithuanian village, baseball was still in its childhood. Now the old man seems to care about nothing but his checking account balance. He is convinced that his money is evaporating.

Gil is at his wit's end. He is the only person left to look after his father. He has nursed him through serious illness. He has driven thousands of miles to sit by the man and prove, by his very presence, that Morris Davison is not alone in the world, that his name lives and will continue to do so.

The elder Davison is housed in his own apartment, which is part of a complex that contains a nursing station and a common dining facility. The home is called Pineridge, a nod to the row of white pine the developer planted at the front of the property. The word "ridge" is either hopefulness or false advertising; the home sits in a profoundly flat glacial lake bed. From the building's center three spokes spread out onto what was once a cornfield. The apartments lie along these spokes, which experience semidaily round-trip migrations. The first, usually at noontime, begins with the residents shuffling with their canes and walkers to the dining room. The second, late in the afternoon, finds the nurses starting out in the opposite direction. By checking on everyone every afternoon, the facility can guarantee that no one will be dead and undiscovered for more than a day. For Morris, undiscovered death is a serious concern. His brother died in a bathtub in Chicago and lay floating in cold water for two weeks before someone found him. Not that Morris can bathe alone. Gil pays one of the nurses to help him, ten dollars per bath.

Catty-corner to Pineridge sits Mapleshade, a traditional nursing home. The residents of Pineridge tend to think of Mapleshade as a stopping-off point on their way to the great beyond, though many go the direct route. Mapleshade gives Gil the willies. The nurses there place the wheelchair-bound residents in the sunlight of the glass-fronted foyer, as though they were houseplants. Many of these residents are palsied. Their eyes roll up, their tongues wag erratically, their bodies give up swampy noises and smells. There is one woman whom Gil remembers because she always cried when he walked in. Tremendous heaving sobs. This was five years ago, when Morris caught pneumonia and almost died. Gil still thinks of the woman, wonders who she was, if she's still alive.

Pulling into Pineridge's parking lot, Gil looks for Rick's Mustang. His son has promised to show up. Together they will take Morris out to lunch. Usually Gil has to do this alone, and when he proposed to Rick that they meet in Jackson it was as much to relieve his own loneliness as that of his father. And if Gil lives long enough, it will be good training for Rick.

Gil gets out of his car and sees his father standing behind the screen door, a short, stocky man in glasses and a golf shirt, a look of anticipation and forbearance on his face. He would wait another hour, another day, whatever it took. Gil knows that look. It was the same look he used to see when he came back into the house after a ball game.

The old man rode out the storm. Always. He has been alive now twenty-three years longer than his wife, longer than any of his younger brothers and sisters, longer than his daughter and one of his grandsons. He'll outlive me, Gil sometimes thinks, though the approach of one hundred brings on new frailties. Loss of vision and the return of afflictions of early life: incontinence, bizarre phobias.

Inside his father's apartment, Gil quickly takes a seat at the desk. "How are you, Dad?"

"Fine. Did you hear about Geraldine?"

Geraldine is one of the women in the complex. Practically all the inhabitants are women. Gil hasn't heard.

"The paramedics came. A heart attack. They got her hooked up to machines. I heard it's awful."

Gil looks up at the pictures on the wall. He sees himself in a naval uniform, his face thin and unlined. Rick is there, Laurence. Gil's mother.

"Do you want to go visit Geraldine, Dad?"

"I think I better, don't you? She's pretty old."

"How old is she?"

"Eighties."

Gil nods. Geraldine. Last month they took her out to what passed for Passover dinner. You can't have a seder in a restaurant in Jackson, Michigan. Gil found that the woman didn't have a thing to say. It is probably the reason his father likes her. What do these people have to look forward to day after day? Morris can no longer see well enough to watch television. He hasn't read for years. He takes pleasure in certain foods—beet borscht, vanilla ice cream—but these he eats in such small quantities that it is amazing that the old man can stay alive.

Gil turns to his work. This is the biweekly check-writing trip. On the desk are the bills. Unlike practically everyone else in America, Morris Davison can't sleep if an unpaid bill rests on his desk, even if the payment is not late. Bills simply must be paid. This week, a week before the end of the month, there's the rent, the electric, temple dues, supplemental health insurance, a bill for a hearing aid checkup. Also, some money is owed to one of the aides, who drives Morris to the grocery store, and to the bath nurse. Gil quickly writes out the checks, a total of about seven hundred dollars. Because the old man can no longer see or write, Gil uses a signature stamp to "sign" the checks. There is over twenty thousand dollars in the account, as Morris wants to be sure he doesn't bounce any checks. Gil has invested the rest of his money in four-year CDs at the local bank.

"What's the balance?" the old man asks.

"Twenty-three thousand, one hundred and thirty-seven dollars and sixty-four cents."

"There should be over forty thousand there."

"Dad, do we have to go through this again? Don't you remember? We moved some money into CDs so you could get some interest on it. Two years ago we did this." Gil says this to the wall, where the entire family is smiling back at him. Then he turns to look at his father.

The old man sits on the couch. Gil can see him breathing, short of air. The conversation has winded him. The walk to the car—if Rick ever gets here—will take an hour.

"Dad, your money is all there. I moved some of it. So we could put it to work. Remember?"

He nods.

"You've got more money than you'll ever be able to spend. We could buy you new furniture and a new car and it would hardly make a dent. You've got plenty of dough, Dad. Okay?"

The old man nods, his chin slumped into his chest. He'll be all right in a minute or two. Always is. Gil turns back to the wall. Gil will wait, which is mostly what he does for his father.

Gil wonders what the money means to the old man. He always cared about it, never spent it. This was something Gil could never understand, how you could want nothing. It was one of his father's European mysteries. So Gil doesn't feel guilty about the missing money. And besides, the money went to the team. It's not as if he kept it for himself.

"Where we going?" asks Rick. He's been in the room thirty seconds maybe. "What do you think, Dad?" Gil asks. "Red Lobster?"

The old man shakes his head no.

"Bob Evans? Bill Knapp's?"

"Dad," Rick says. "Why don't you pull the car up. I'll bring Gramps."

It's good to have Rick around, Gil decides as he walks out to the Continental. Not that they haven't had their troubles, but the kid understands responsibility and duty. He's a hard worker. Always has been. He used to do sit-ups before bed, and shadow swings in the basement in front of a dressing mirror. It was amazing, really. Anything you told the kid to do, he did it, when he was young. Incredible dedication, though at the time Gil hardly noticed it, since he had been that way himself.

They go to Bill Knapp's, at Rick's insistence, even though Gil knows that Rick hates Bill Knapp's. "This place definitely does not make me nostalgic for the fifties," he said the last time. Now they drive up to the white building, the green shutters, a chain restaurant in the Midwest meant to look like colonial New England.

Inside Gil watches a waitress in a hairnet drop several plates off to a table that looks as if its members might have reservations at Pineridge. One of the men is still eating his soup, a paper napkin tucked in his collar. The waitresses wear white dresses and thick-soled shoes, like nurses.

The Davisons are seated in the back room. The waitress brings water and all three men order black coffee. It is the one thing, Gil thinks, that we all have in common. He thinks that Rick looks out of place here, with his lean face and expensive clothes. Elsewhere bulk is in style. There is a person on social security at every table.

"So how's life treating you, Gramps?" Rick asks.

"Okay. Did you hear about Geraldine?"

"Geraldine?"

"Gramps's friend," Gil says. "You met her at Thanksgiving."

"Oh, right. What about her?"

"She had a heart attack," says Morris. "The men came and revived her with electricity. Now she's all hooked up to those machines they got."

"That's too bad."

"When I go," the old man says. He starts to cough. Once, twice, a third time. Finally he brings up some phlegm and deposits it in a handkerchief carried for that purpose. "When I go," he says, "I want to go fast."

"You sure you're okay?"

"I said I want to go fast."

"We heard you, Dad," Gil says.

"Sometimes," Morris says. He takes a deep breath, then another. "Sometimes I have to repeat myself. Especially this time of year."

Rick looks over to Gil. Gil knows where this is going.

"You aren't still playing baseball, are you?" Morris asks Rick.

"Baseball?" Rick chuckles. "Gramps, baseball was half a lifetime ago for me."

"That's good. You always were a smart boy."

"I don't know if smarts has much to do with it," Rick says. "I'm too old."

But Rick wasn't too old when he quit, Gil remembers. This was when he was in high school, before his senior year. Rick wasn't going to the pros, but he was about as good a player as most high school teams could hope for. By then Gil had a reputation, and Rick's high school coach called Gil and begged him to have Rick reconsider. Gil, of course, had already tried, and it embarrassed him to admit that even on baseball matters his counsel meant nothing to his son. Now Gil thinks how typical of his father, who speaks so little, to bring this up, memories better left behind.

"Your father is too old," Morris is saying. "But he still plays."

"Well, Gramps, he coaches. That's something that even old men can do."

"Men need to work at their jobs, old or not," Morris says. "They need to save, so when they are too old to work, they should have money. They should not play and spend. Children's games . . ." Morris dismisses these games with a backhand flick of his trembling hand. He is breathing too heavily to finish the sentence any other way.

"Well, Gramps," Rick says, "I guess most of us need some form of recreation."

But not Morris, Gil knows. Not Morris.

"Did I tell you," the old man says to Rick, "that your father is already helping himself to the money?"

"What money?"

"My money."

Rick looks to his father. "I put it in CDs for him," Gil says.

Rick turns back to his grandfather, his dark bangs sweeping across his forehead. "Look, Gramps, I'm sure it's all there. Besides, I've got money now. You'll always be okay."

"That's not the point." A silence settles over the table. Morris stares into his lap, as if looking there for his lost wealth.

At the cash register Gil buys a bag of glazed doughnut holes for his father's apartment. Morris does not eat this kind of food, which Gil has never really understood. There are many times when he feels his own tastes are universal.

Rick offers to take Morris to the county hospital to see Geraldine, but Morris says he's too tired. He wants to go home.

"You sure?" Rick asks.

"I'll go to the funeral," the old man says.

Back at the home they leave him on the couch. "I just need to rest," he tells them. "Now go along."

Outside Gil chats with his son under the awning.

"Why don't you help yourself to the money, Dad?"

"What?"

"It makes no sense to leave all that sitting there in a checking account, without interest. Besides, when he does go you'll have to pay taxes on it. Move some now."

"I couldn't do that," Gil says, wondering what Rick is up to.

"Well, you should. All the time you spend here. Besides, Gramps can't tell what should be there. Really, you owe it to yourself."

"Do you need some money, son?"

"No, of course not."

This makes sense, really. Rick is a lawyer. He makes more than his father already, with what they pay lawyers these days. Gil remembers when Rick announced that he wanted to go to law school. Gil was against it. Lawyering seemed an illegitimate career. How, he wondered, had Rick come up with that one? He wondered if Morris had planted the idea in Rick's head.

Morris wanted all the Davison offspring to be professionals, and this made Rick's decision seem almost spiteful. Gil thought of the long stone wall of the prison in Jackson, and of Rick defending drug dealers, holdup men, scam artists. Of course, Rick seems to spend all his time on business contracts, and Gil can't even guess at the money he makes.

"What's your mother up to?" he asks. "Still a tennis player? She still married to that guy Bart?"

"Yep, they're still living the good life in Florida," Rick says.

"Sounds good."

"You're better off here, Dad."

The flag above them snaps a staccato rhythm. They stand together, a long pause as Gil waits for the next thought to be brought to him on the wind. There's only one subject left between them, and Rick comes to it on his own.

"How's the team?" he asks.

"Shaping up, son. Shaping up."

V

"Two bits! Two bits!" yells Jefferson. In the outfield several pitchers scatter as a fly ball floats their way. One, Kindle, waves the others off, moving his arms in arcing motions, as if he's doing the breast stroke.

Kindle dances. The wind is gusty, and even the regular outfielders have been having trouble. This ball is high enough to bring rain. It hangs, as fly balls do, at the top of its flight, then accelerates to the ground. Kindle taps his feet right, left, more left. The hoots and hollers begin. Kindle moves back right, then lunges left, and misses. He is hit by a barrage of ribbing.

"Put grass in your hat!" someone yells, lest the next one hit him on the head.

"You owe me two bits!"

"Get him in here before he hurts himself!"

"That's two bits, Kindle!"

Koch and Sons is at practice.

Mercer watches. He feels like a god. Two nights ago, a Thursday, he entertained Betsy, a nurse from University Hospital, who, as if anticipating his every wish, had to be at work at 6:00 A.M. Friday the market was up thirty points. Last night he took Emily to the Gandy Dancer, a restaurant converted from a train station on the north end of town. They ate Caesar salads and pasta dishes, drank two bottles of Chianti, bought two desserts as a nod to decadence. Afterward they went back to his place, listened to Billie Holiday and made love, slept, woke at four, made love again. When he left to drive to practice she was sleeping in his bed, a bare ankle protruding from under his quilt.

Mercer is throwing batting practice. His arm is strong, accurate. He has taped his right ankle, as it is still a bit sore and his push-off isn't everything he wants it to be. Still, the hitters can't hit his curveball even though he tells them it's coming. Later, shagging balls in the breezy outfield, he watches as the dust whirls about the infield, sees Kukla fielding ground balls and O'Rourke, another new guy, hitting sharp liners. Vince smokes furtively in the stands. Gil is fungoing ground balls in between pitches. The team is a machine, one of constant motion and efficiency.

Mercer decides to jog to the bench, where he has left his jacket, a blue satin number with "Koch and Sons" in script sewn on its front and Mercer's number on its back. Gil takes a break from slapping fungoes at Kukla and comes over for a chat.

"Looked good today," Gil says. This perks Mercer up. Gil is not a man who gives unwarranted praise. In fact, Gil is downright stingy with praise. Mercer figures it's why his players play so hard for him.

Mercer doesn't respond. He is a salesman, and it's only with Gil that he sometimes finds himself without his verbal stuff. Silence is the conversational equivalent of an intentional walk, and Mercer finds that he is often giving them up to Gil.

"New guys are pretty good," the coach manages to say.

"Real good, Coach. Real good." Mercer is about to ask where he found them, but Mercer knows it's all done on reputation and that knack Gil has of making guys want to play for him. People call Gil from all over the state and beyond, tell him they've got players for his team. When Mercer washed out of the Baltimore organization, he called his old high school coach, and that guy made a call, who made a call, who made a call, and then Mercer got a call from Gil. The next week Mercer had to show up at St. James Field, behind the Y in Birmingham, which was where he first met Gil, Vince, and Brattenburg, whom Gil had brought along to catch.

Gil looked to Mercer the way a baseball coach was supposed to look: broad shoulders and barrel chest, with enough girth and age to make you think there was wisdom in the body. He had the right eyes, too, some intensity to them that Mercer associated with success. It was pretty clear that Gil ran the show. Vince was a skinny old man even then, with a wheeze and a shaky walk. Mercer figured he probably knew a lot about baseball (and, as it turned out, he did), but he was no head coach.

Mercer had been throwing for what he was sure was less than ten minutes when Gil grunted something at Vince, who said, "Okay, phenom," and Mercer stopped. The four of them walked over to Gil's Continental—a black one that year—and Mercer signed. Gil slid the contract back into the manila envelope and placed it in the Continental's trunk, which was loaded with catcher's equipment, batting helmets, two bat bags, the works, even a bleacher cushion. Mercer smiled at the thought of Gil driving all over the state with a trunk full of baseball gear. Here was a man who really loved the game.

Now Mercer thinks how he, too, loves the game, loves it for the particulars: the dance of infield practice and the pop of the ball in the catcher's mitt, the flicker of signals from the catcher with a man on second, and the lean of a ballplayer as he rounds third base. Even women and wealth don't measure up, though they come closer than anything else. Mercer knows he is captivated by athletic, sexual, and commercial pursuits. He is aware that these desires are somewhat base, beneath the higher callings of justice, charity, and art, but Mercer knows where his talents lie. He lives and plays, as the ballplayers say, within himself.

The season is closing in, what with the first game ten days

away. After practice the team drives to Gil's house to get uniforms. Vince sits at the top of the basement, the gatekeeper. Five players descend at a time. Mercer is in the first group, along with four other veterans: Kohn, Jefferson, Hagenbush, and Goodstein. In the basement they pass a refrigerator on their way to the main storeroom, where the uniforms—three jerseys, two sets of pants, warm-up jackets—hang from movable clothing stands. There are number-coded duffel bags, two sets of stirrups, five pairs of sanitary socks, caps, color-coordinated batting gloves and sweat bands, practice shorts, T-shirts, and blue-armed undershirts. Back toward the bulbous, fifties-style refrigerator is a set of recessed shelves that pushes open to reveal a bomb shelter. Inside the bomb shelter are boxes and boxes of blue spikes, each pair labeled with the proper player's name.

Mercer gets number 34, the number he's had the last five years. This year it's his age.

"Another year with the Koch and Sons Dodgers," says Hagenbush, purposefully pronouncing the name like the soft drink. This makes Mercer cringe. He thinks of Hagenbush as a six-foot-five-inch pillar of rectitude and boredom. Hagenbush is an insurance guy and a professional worrywart. A married guy. A good ballplayer, though.

"Rhymes with 'crotch,'" says Goodstein, who plays third base, the other corner of the infield from Hagenbush, and about as far away as he can get.

"Why aren't our colors black?" says Kohn. Koch and Sons is a funeral home chain, Catholic, high-end, full service.

"This team?" Jefferson says. "I don't think so." Jefferson is the team's only black player. His father, Lester Jefferson, Sr., was a Motown star. His raspy voice is still a staple of nostalgia radio. Mercer figures that Les Junior is probably his best friend on the team, though in the dugout and in life Mercer is happy enough just to be left alone.

"They still sponsor us?" asks Hagenbush.

"They help," Gil says, but Mercer hears hesitation in his voice. Mercer talks to people every day about money. His ear is tuned to the timbre and trill of a voice that speaks of its personal wealth, and he knows now that there is no more Koch money coming in.

His arms are filled with hundreds of dollars' worth of clothing. Gil is a man of adequate means, but it doesn't add up. Mercer places his gear in the duffel and carries it upstairs. Gil's house has been turned into a cross between a locker room and a sports bar. The TV is tuned to ESPN, without the sound. The ballplayers drape themselves across furniture or lean in doorways, their hands cupped around glasses of beer. There's Kindle and Booth in the corner with Hagenbush. Kukla and O'Rourke, Metz and Krauss are playing poker at the small dining table in the back of the room. Kohn stands behind O'Rourke, shaking his head. Mercer spots Goodstein and Jefferson settling in on the fireplace ledge, which is over by the TV and the coffee table. Goodstein picks up one of the coffee-table books. Mercer knows these books. There's one on America's baseball stadiums, another about the Baseball Hall of Fame in Cooperstown, and a third about Vince Lombardi called *You've Got to Pay the Price*.

A half hour later Mercer is chatting with Goodstein and Jefferson when Gil and Vince emerge from the basement. Gil comes into the center of the room carrying a diet Vernors; Gil almost never drinks alcohol. He looks around the room, then clears his throat. Mercer knows what is coming. Gil has been giving these little speeches since Mercer joined the team, and probably a lot longer. It always amazes Mercer how all Gil has to do is clear his throat and the whole room quiets and turns to him. All the guys just smiling and hanging out, they're dead serious now.

"Right here in the room," Gil says, "there is more talent than on any team I've ever had. There is more talent in this room than on any team we are likely to face, even if we go all the way to Battle Creek in August. And I expect to be playing in Battle Creek in August.

"But let me tell you, talent and winning are not the same thing. Winning is what counts. I've been doing this a long time, and there is no longer any room on my team for second place. I am sick of second place. There is only one place that matters: first place. And we're going to get there. We're going to get there with hard work, execution, and esprit de corps. You belong to a team here. Don't ever forget that.

"There can be no letup. You don't win just when you feel like winning. You win all the time. You win and you win and you win till you expect to win and won't—can't—settle for anything less. That's how we're going to do it this year. And then, come fall, and for the rest of your lives, you'll look back on this season and say, 'Hey, I was part of something once.'"

Gil walks out of the room, which slowly comes back to life. Mercer looks around and sees a bunch of guys who don't know what to do with their hands, because what they really want to do is run out and beat up on some opponent, which isn't an option now. "What's esprit de corps?" Mercer hears O'Rourke ask, and Mercer has to smile. "Esprit de corps" is one of Gil's favorite phrases. Not really what you'd expect from Gil, which is why Mercer notices every time Gil says it. Gil has other lines: "I'm up to my ears in apple crates" (I'm busy); "like Grant took Richmond" (fast); "like molasses in January" (slow); "intestinal fortitude" (guts); and "reckless abandon" (how he expects a player to break up a double play). Mercer likes playing for Gil. Not much politics on Koch and Sons. Gil is happy if you play hard, win, and act like a good team member. It's not usually that simple with other coaches, but it is with Gil.

But Gil is not a rich man, so Mercer waits for the players to finish eating their way through the fifteen pizzas and for the poker game to end and for all the chatting to die down. He waits till everyone has headed off into what has finally become the night. With the house empty he checks on Vince, who is smoking a cigarette on the back patio. Then he finds Gil loading glasses into his dishwasher.

"Coach, you're not getting any more cash out of Koch, are you?"

"We're doing fine."

"Coach, it's . . ." Mercer leans in and whispers, as when he's making a face-to-face sale. It's the best way to talk to Gil: pretend he is a client. "It's too expensive to go it alone. Why not ask the players to pitch in? All these guys would pay to play for you. I know I would."

"I can't ask the players to pay, Ben."

"Why not?"

"Well, they don't all have jobs like yours, for one thing. And it's not right. They're too good. They deserve better. Most of these guys should be making their livings playing ball. Like you did."

"But we're not. And just because we can't get paid to play doesn't mean we wouldn't pay to play. This is a first-rate operation. I mean, where else am I going to go if I want to stay at it? It's not like weekend softball is going to cut it. And where else is a guy like Kukla going to go if he wants to stay on his game? Every one of us needs this team, Coach."

Gil shrugs.

"Besides," Mercer says, "it's not about money. I never made much money. No one plays baseball for money."

"The young guys do, like you said. Kukla, O'Rourke. They've got pro dreams."

"But they don't play for money. They'd play if they never had a hope of making a dime. Like I do."

Gil frets. Mercer knows the look. This conversation is about over.

"At least let me give you some money," Mercer says. "And Les, and Kindle. The guys with decent jobs."

"I get help, Ben. Don't worry. Don't you worry."

Okay, Mercer thinks, shaking his head. I won't worry. It's not my money.

He says goodbye and heads for his car, changes his focus, thinks now of Emily's bare ankle, then of the rest of her, then of Sylvia, with whom he has a tentative date, then of the night itself, warm and pleasant, and really quite young.

VI

In theory, Vince has a pension. Eighty percent of his pay, which, because he was on commission, they figured some special way and is less than four-fifths of what he remembers making, and he doesn't remember making much. Then, to top it off, they cut the pension. It isn't right, it isn't fair, but not even the union lawyers—and Vince is not union—could stop the company from doing it. It grabs at Vince's gut. You give 'em your labor—which is, after all, all a man really has—and they tell you times are tough. Sorry.

So there's money in and money out. Money in is the skeleton of his pension, the VA benefits, and social security. Money out is the house, clothing and nourishment, what Medicare doesn't cover, and the life insurance. Money out is winning.

It's the life insurance that worries Vince. Dead he's worth almost half a million dollars. A half million. It's a number he cannot fathom. There was a restaurant over on Gratiot, a Greek place where he used to take Ellen, back when she let him smoke, back when money wasn't so tight. When it got up to forty bucks for the two of them, they stopped going. Now it's probably fifty. Fifty bucks. That goes into a half million ten thousand times. That's a dinner every night for almost thirty years.

The first time Vince let the payment slip, he expected the world to stop. It didn't. In fact, he didn't even hear from the company. That took a month. Now he's got ten days to come up with the money. And only one place left to turn.

It is a peaceful evening. The players have eaten their pizza and left with their uniforms. Gil is in the kitchen, probably folding pizza boxes and wiping counters. Vince marvels at what a fastidious man Gil is. A man of pressed clothes and manicures. A man who pays professionals to do his lawn. Vince sits now in the backyard, looking through the darkness to Gil's finely cut grass. He wishes he could help Gil with the cleanup, but he gets winded.

Finally, after what seemed like enough time to paint the kitchen, Gil comes outside and sits beside him. It is a warm evening for May. There are crickets about and the sounds of children playing. A car races its engine. Somewhere someone is using an air gun to pound nails, each punch the echo of its predecessor.

"I think it's a good team," Gil says. "The best we've had so far."

"The pitching is good," Vince says. Pitching is his area. It is better than good. He feels that Mercer and Kohn could contend in the majors. Then there's Booth and Kindle. But Mercer: the guy is amazing. Year after year.

"I want it to be this year, Vince."

"Me too."

"Did I tell you that Richardson called from Japan?"

"What did he say?"

"He doesn't like it. Says it's like the army."

"They're paying him a half million bucks." There's that number again. "What's not to like?"

"Can you imagine if they had those salaries when we played?"

"I would have stayed at it longer."

"Me too," says Gil.

They sit in silent contemplation of riches lost.

"Gil," Vince says, "I got a problem." He explains about the life insurance, finishes by saying, "So, the deal is that I pay you back whatever you put in. Outta the policy."

"Vince, don't even think about it."

"I'll put you in my will. Really. Believe me, now I know a lot about wills."

"I don't want to be in your will."

Vince wonders, Why is he arguing with me? I was at war when he was in short pants. Does he think this is easy?

"How much do you need, Vince?"

"Two grand would do for a while."

"Gimme a few days."

The men sit silently as the crickets grind, till finally they call it a night.

VII

It's ten-thirty. Gil sits in his underwear as he watches a game from the Coast. The phone rings. This can only be bad news.

"Gil, it's Fredo."

Gil says hello, wonders what Alfredo Schuster could want at ten-thirty at night on a Sunday. Gil and Schuster go way back, grew up in the same hometown, played on the same teams. Now Schuster bird-dogs for Chicago, usually calls Gil at work. Every couple of months they have a meal together.

"Gil, I got someone for you," Schuster says. "A bona fide phenom."

Gil can picture the story. Some kid got cut from AA, one who Fredo signed, and if Fredo can find him a spot on Koch and Sons, his conscience will be clear. He has done this before. Fifty years of friendship or not, Fredo doesn't know he's dealing with a new man. A hard man.

"All filled up, Fredo. Ain't even got room for a backup bat-boy."

"No bull, Gil. This kid really swings the bat. It makes you stand up just watching him take batting practice. He's a Jackson kid, too."

"No. Can't do it." Be hard, Gil tells himself.

"Gil, listen to what I am saying. This kid can't miss. *Can't miss.*"

Oh, Gil thinks, all the can't misses who missed.

"Fredo, what's going on here? Why don't you want him?"

"We do."

"So why are you calling me?"

"Because we can't sign him yet."

"Why not?"

"Look, Gil. He's a good kid. He's just made some mistakes. Been in the state pen for five years. He's on parole, just started last week. Can't leave the state. That's why he's perfect for you. You play all your games in Michigan. Even the national championship is in Battle Creek. It's perfect."

"We play over the Fourth in Dayton. I got games in Windsor."

"For Chrissakes, Gil. Take a look."

"I told you, full roster."

"I have watched more of your godforsaken players than I care to remember," Schuster says. "I'm asking you to watch one of mine. One. Come out tomorrow. Take a look. That's all. A look."

Gil weighs the trouble of refusing, calculates the cost of bad will with a scout and a friend against yet another trip to Jackson. Well, he could visit his father.

"What time?" Gil asks.

"How 'bout six, at the batting cages down by Schmidt's Ice Cream. You know it?"

"I know it. What's his name?"

"Luke James."

"Black?"

"White as you or me."

"What did he do?"

"Uh, it's not pretty. A crime of passion."

"Fredo."

"Someone got kilt. It was over a girl. Happened at the High. He was seventeen and they tried him as an adult. He's only twenty-two now."

Gil remembers reading about a murder at Jackson High. With a baseball bat. Was that really five years ago?

"Let's face it, the kid needs you. You run a good outfit, and the kid needs a good outfit. You won't regret this."

"I already regret it. Tomorrow at six."

VIII

Several hours after Gil climbed into bed, Mercer climbs out. It is not his bed but Sylvia's. She lives in Chelsea, about twenty miles from Ann Arbor, which Mercer likes, because Ann Arbor is a small town, where it is easy to run into people you'd rather not see.

Fetching. That's what Sylvia is. She's blond, not too tall, with bright eyes and a sinewy body. She makes him laugh. Right now he looks back at her. She is sitting upright in bed, the sheet wrapped around her, her eyes on him.

"What?" she asks.

"Just admiring."

She smiles. God, it's so simple. Just tell them the truth. Tell the truth. He was thirty before he realized it. This wasn't some arcane game: just tell them what you are thinking. If you think they are beautiful, tell them so. You want to kiss them, say so. As Lester J. says, you want something, ask for it. That's all I do, Mercer thinks. And it works. Then another thought comes to him. What does she want with me? Then the next thought: probably the same thing I want with her. He heads off to the bathroom.

When he returns home an hour later, there are three messages on his phone machine. One from Booth, who wants to throw tomorrow. One from Joy, whom he hasn't heard from in a month, and one from Emily. He dials her number.

"Hi," she says. "I was thinking about you. Where were you?"

"Detroit, with the ball team." A lame excuse. It's after midnight.

"You busy now? Thought I might come over." Mercer finds this to be one of her more quaint qualities, asking to be picked up in the middle of the night. Emily works in an art gallery, supplements her pay by bartending at a local restaurant a couple of lunches a week. She never has to wake before ten. Mercer is tired. Even were he a twenty-year-old, it would have been quite a day: Emily in the morning, a workout with the team, the pizza bash, Sylvia, and now back full circle.

"Hey, Mercer," she says playfully, baiting him. "You want to see me or what?"

"Sure," he says, and heads for the shower.

IX

"See?" says Alfredo Schuster.

When Gil sees Luke James swing the bat he believes, believes in the game and a God who intends men to play it. It's that beautiful. The kid is tall, with broad shoulders and lightning wrists. He gets solid wood on everything. What impresses Gil the most is the kid's poise. He stands at the plate like a man with a vision. He knows he will crush the ball. Just knows.

After ten swings Gil has seen enough, but the machine is paid for and keeps going, so the kid keeps taking cuts. Gil studies the kid's chin, his pale eyes. He puffs out his cheeks before each pitch. Veins leap from his neck and forearms. And that swing! It's grace and truth. Those words, those terrible words—*can't miss*—float up in Gil's mind, and he wills them back down, must not let them form, not on his lips, not even in the front of his mind, must will them back down so as not to jinx the kid.

"The great thing," Schuster is saying, "is that no one can draft him, on account of the parole thing. So he's yours for the season. I been watching this one since he went inside. Watched him inside. Remember we useta play there? Us Legion boys with the murderers and stickup men?"

"Of course I remember. Lefty Wardwell."

"Yeah, ol' Lefty. A curveball that fell off the table. And you hit one out when you were the team baby. Lefty's still in there, you know."

"No."

"Yep. I seen him. Helps coach now. They say he's rehabilitated but the parole people won't let him out."

"Fredo, he killed a dozen people, execution-style."

"It was his job. Besides, men change. He's an old man, for Chrissakes."

Gil could never understand thinking like that, that belief in redemption. Wardwell killed twelve people, execution-style, including three children—even a four-year-old girl, if Gil remembers right—and there is no rehabilitation from that.

The pitching machine stops. James comes over to the edge of the cage. "You want to see more, Coach?"

"No, son. Come on out here."

Schuster is smiling his I-told-you-so smile.

"Where do you live?" Gil asks.

"With his mother," Schuster says, "On Melville."

"I'll give you a ride."

James settles into the front seat of the Continental. Gil watches him. The kid looks, well, innocent. Dark hair matted from the batting helmet, wide, round, almost girlish blue eyes, high cheekbones underlined by the gauntness in his cheeks. The kid's staring at the dash, at all the styling he's missed in the last five years. Like he's never seen a leather interior before, or a digital dash.

"I like the way you swing the bat," Gil says. "You throw lefty, too?"

"I do."

Gil is silent, waits for traffic to clear so he can make a left turn.

"Look, Mr. Davison. No one's gonna work harder than me," James says. "No one. And no one's gonna play harder for the team. Mr. Schuster told me you were the best. I need a chance to play with the best. That's all. A chance."

Gil thinks of Doug Reese, who is supposed to throw relief for him and who yesterday picked up his uniform. Gil wonders what words he will find to fire Reese, now that he's going to take James. He winces.

But that's what winners do, Gil tells himself. They make tough calls.

James lives in an old brick apartment building. Gil knows this building, remembers that it was seedy even when he was a boy.

"You can't live here and play on my team. It's too far. All of our home games are in Pontiac. You'll have to move to some-place around Detroit."

"I can't leave this stinking town fast enough," James says.

Gil hears not longing in the boy's voice, but anger and inten-sity. Good, he thinks. He takes the kid's phone number.

"Okay, Luke. I'm putting you on the squad. But you've got to play by my rules. You show up on time. You always play full out. No shenanigans."

"No, sir."

Gil tries to look tough, but it's silly. This kid could eat him for lunch. James grabs up his glove and bat and trots up the walk to his building. The bricks of its facade are black with years of grime. Dandelions cover the yard.

On his way home, Gil stops to visit his father. The old man is upset. A Monday-night visit is not routine. Gil cannot convince him that he just stopped by to say hello, that he happened to be in the neighborhood.

"Sit, Dad. Tell me about your day."

"It's time for bed."

"Dad, it's only seven-thirty."

Morris does not care what time it is. He has a routine and will live by it. Gil listens from the living room as Morris struggles into his pajamas. The old man shuffles back out and closes the blinds. When he goes into the bathroom, Gil writes himself a check for five thousand dollars, then makes it official with a roll of the signature stamp.

JUNE

I

Opening day, the last inning. Vince sits in the dugout corner, the scorebook resting across his knees, and takes a count of Mercer's pitches. Eighty-seven. Impressive. Mercer's no kid, tires more easily now, but he should be good for three more outs.

"Eighty-seven," Vince tells Gil. Gil nods but does not turn around, his foot still on the dugout step, his bulk a shadow against the midday light spilling in from the field.

Vince coughs out Kindle's name. Kindle knows what to do. He stands, grabs his glove and Brattenburg; they jog down to the bullpen and begin to throw. Vince has finally convinced Gil that he wants someone ready at the end of every game, no matter how well the starter is doing. Even for Mercer. After last year, especially for Mercer.

Vince turns his attention to Jim Garbanes, who is pitching for the opposing team, Freeways Oil Change. Two seasons ago Garbanes won twenty-three games for the Tigers and was second runner-up for the Cy Young Award. Now his gut hangs a bit lower over his belt and he has the desperate look of a man who is lost. He's losing a Class A Amateur baseball game. Five runs he's given up in seven innings. Baseball is cruel that way.

Players live on a thin margin. Back when Vince was playing, a twenty-game winner could go out at ninety-eight percent and stay in the bigs. Now he loses on a dusty sandlot field in the shadow of a General Motors factory.

Jefferson lifts a ball deep to left with the clank of good metal.

"Get out! Get out!" Gil screams at the ball. He's up by four runs, but he wants more. Gil always wants more. Spikes click on the concrete as the team runs up the dugout steps to watch from field level.

The moment drags out. Vince glances at the infield, where Metz is sprinting around the base paths—there are two outs and he runs hard on everything—and then back to the outfield. The left fielder has stopped with his back to the fence. He waits, though it's impossible to tell if he's watching the ball go out or planning on making a play. Then his glove goes up and the ball drops into it. End of inning.

Garbanes walks back to his dugout, head down.

Vince hears the shuffle and click and the players take the field. Jefferson is standing out by second base, waiting for O'Rourke to jog out with his glove and cap. It's those little things—the last out waiting for his equipment, the futile sprint required to "run it out," parts of the game they don't show on television—that keeps Vince in the game.

"Okay, cham-peens," he says. "Three more. Three more."

"Let's go, let's go. Let's see some hustle out there," Gil yells in that incredible Midwesterner way of his, loud but somehow through his nose. Vince can't understand how these people can make fun of his Jersey accent, which, truth be known, he has mostly lost over the last forty years.

Okay, Vince tells himself. You have one thing to do today. You must thank that man. Yes, Gil has given you three thousand dollars and no man has ever done that for you before.

Gil sits next to Vince on the bench and pulls out his reading glasses. He reaches for the scorebook as though Vince has merely been holding it for him the whole time. "What did this guy do today?"

He means the opposing batter, standing now by the batter's box, swinging two bats in one hand. Vince knows the record: 4–3, a backwards K, 8. Ground out to second, a called strikeout, a fly out to center. Hits the ball more right than left.

"Maybe we move Metz more up the middle on this guy," says Gil. He stands, walks to the top of the dugout steps, and yells for Metz to move to his left. Instead, the shortstop moves toward the hole.

"*No!*" Gil yells. "The other way."

Gil sits back down, says to Vince, "He did it again. Doesn't he know his left from his right?"

"About half the time," Vince says.

Metz is no genius, but Vince likes the kid. He works midnight shifts at UPS, loading packages. He's the only player on the team, aside from the new one, who's never been to college. Runs like the wind, stops everything. Solid hitter. Kid's got a smile, too.

The batter grounds the ball toward Kukla, who fields it and throws to Hagenbush at first. The ball zips around the infield. Kukla and Metz hold their index fingers in the air. One away.

"Listen, Gil," Vince says. "I want to thank you."

"For what?"

"The money."

"I told you, Vince, it's nothing."

"It's certainly something."

"Don't worry about it."

"No one's ever lent me money like that."

"It's not a loan."

"Yes it is," Vince says. Mercer gets up on the batter one-and-two, then fans him on the next pitch. Krauss starts the ball around the horn: Goodstein, Kukla, Metz, back to Goodstein, and then Mercer. Now the infielders hold up their index and pinky fingers, steer's horns. Two away.

"It'll come back to you," Vince says.

"What will?"

"The money."

"Vince, forget about it."

The batter hits a ball deep up the right-center gap. O'Rourke and James run hard, two white uniforms against the light green wall of the factory. The runner is almost to second when O'Rourke jumps and gloves the ball for the game's final out. The whole team runs onto the field to shake hands with Mercer and high-five O'Rourke when he arrives in the infield. The wives, girlfriends, and parents shout congratulations and the PA announcer gives the game totals, and in this noise Vince decides to let it go. Gil is a man who won't acknowledge your debts to him, and now Vince wonders if this isn't born of a selfish desire to be owed. There's no sense, Vince sees, in wasting his breath.

||

James looks out the windshield of Metz's car at stucco crossed by stained wooden slats, Bavarian-style, the facade bathed in yellow light from the muffler shop next door. "Welcome to the clubhouse," Metz says. They're on Woodward, in Royal Oak, ten miles south of the game, at a bar called the Mountain Chalet. Inside, long wooden tables spread out below a hovering cloud of cigarette smoke. Decade-old promotional posters for Octoberfest—the real one, in Munich—cover the walls. The waitresses are middle-aged but they dress like milk maidens, and they're all smiles as the players stroll in. The players are still in their Koch uniforms, sweaty and dirty as they take their places at one of the beer-hall tables. Pitchers of beer and stacked plastic cups arrive and no one even ordered. James can see that the players' return is not unlike the return of robins in spring. It's a new season, the waitresses know, and now business will be better.

"That was some hitting, son," Jefferson says, patting James on the back. "Where'd they find you?"

"What do you mean?" James is apprehensive, Jefferson being black. Jefferson is all smiles and affability, and this makes James even more uneasy.

"I mean, where you been playing ball?"

"Jackson."

"Michigan?"

"Yep."

"Well, keep it up." Jefferson moves down to slap other backs.

James spots Mercer at the far end of the table. The pitcher is dipping his right elbow into a bus tub of ice and water. James has been watching Mercer. He finds it impossible not to. Mercer has been to the major leagues, and he stands apart in the way he acts, the quips he makes, the neat cut of his hair and the make of his car. He's pitched to major-league batters. He knows things.

"Jamesie, you want a beer, right?" Metz's expression says that there's nothing he'd rather do, right now, than to tip his right hand, which holds a full beer pitcher, toward his left, which holds an empty cup.

"Sure."

Metz pours. "Yeah, baby," he says as he slides the plastic cup James's way.

James hasn't had a beer in five years, back when he drank Miller out of cans, he and his friends sucking them down not for taste or even enjoyment, but for speed and inebriation. When he thinks back to life before prison, James can remember only things meant to take him away from the world—beer, music via earphones, movies—and baseball. Now he wants to be here. In fact, as he looks down the row, at Metz and O'Rourke, Hagenbush and Goodstein, Vince and Gil at the end, he knows he's right where he wants to be. For now. He notices that Gil is drinking a Coke. This makes James feel a bit guilty, but he still sips at his beer. He's only having one, because it proves to himself that he has both discipline and taste. The beer that slides down his throat is cool and wonderful.

Metz is again at his ear, talking up a storm. "I mean, I live for summers, you know. I finally realized it last year. Everything I do, I'm thinking about playing ball. I join a weight room, I'm thinking about hitting with power. I read a newspaper, I make sure the lights are bright enough, so I don't lose my eyes. I meet a girl even, I make sure she likes baseball, or I just don't call her once it's May. You know what I mean?"

"I do," James says.

"Yeah, baby. If she don't like baseball, well, forget her." Metz sips his beer. "Well, listen. I ought to go. One of these guys will give you a ride home."

"Where are you going?"

"Work. That's me. The graveyard shift."

"That's tough. See you Friday."

"You bet."

"Yo, Metz, don't drop my package," someone shouts.

"Won't touch your package." Metz waves, and is gone.

"Hey, helluva game." This is Goodstein, dark wavy hair and what looks like three days' growth, though he probably shaved this morning.

"Thanks," James says.

"Metz can talk your ear off."

"He's a good guy."

"Yeah, well, he can talk even faster than he runs, and a lot longer. But you're right. He's a good guy. We love him. Makes me laugh, anyway. Good shortstop."

"Definitely," says James. "Everybody here is good."

"That's Gil," Goodstein says. "He's got the eye." He puts his finger to his eyelid.

"The eye?"

"For talent. Guy missed his calling. Shoulda been a pro coach. Instead he works for a car company."

"What do you do?"

Goodstein smiles. "I work for GM. Most of the guys here work for one of the car companies, or steel, tires, that sort of thing." Goodstein suddenly stands up. "'Cept Metz, and Mercer. I gotta hit the head." He slaps James on the back. "Like I said, helluva game."

Mercer. He is down at the other end of the table, his elbow still in the ice. James looks around, notices that almost everyone is in urgent conversation. Even Gil is talking to Vince, who is dragging on his cigarette. The man is killing himself, James thinks, but he turns his attention back to Mercer, who looks either preoccupied or very bored, his head tilted back, his left hand on a beer cup. James gets up, walks the length of the table, and pulls a chair in next to him.

"Hi."

Mercer turns and James hears the ice shift in the tub.

"What's up?"

"Doesn't your arm get cold in there?"

"That is the idea."

"Yeah, but . . ."

"Wait ten years."

"It's nothing to look forward to."

"You don't pitch. Maybe you won't have to do it." Mercer

shifts the iced elbow, his brow arched in pain. "You sure beat up Garbanes tonight," he says.

"I can't believe it was really him," James says, and he can't, can't believe he got three hits off a guy he used to read about in the papers. From the sports section, not crime.

"He can't believe it, either."

"Listen. I hear you played for Baltimore."

"I did. Long time ago."

"What was it like?"

Mercer chuckles. "How am I supposed to answer a question like that?"

"I don't know. Tell me one thing, one thing I couldn't think of on my own."

"Okay," Mercer says. "I got a business card."

"Huh?"

"You know, a business card. It had an Oriole on it, and some nice raised orange lettering. Benjamin A. Mercer, it said. Still got a couple hundred. You want to see one?"

"Sure."

"I'll try to remember to bring one to the next game."

"You want to go back?" James asks.

"Go back where?"

"To the majors."

"Hey, Luke, who doesn't? Of course, it's not like you get a choice. The choice is all theirs."

"I'd like to go," James says.

Mercer nods.

"Maybe you and me could get together sometime. Have a beer somewhere."

Mercer looks at him with his pitcher eyes, gray and cold, sizing him up.

"You know," James says, "no one calls me Luke. Just my mom." James wishes he could stop talking.

"It's your name, right?"

"Sure, but they all call me Jamesie. I don't know why."

"I like Luke," Mercer says.

James is about to tell him that he likes it, too—which is odd, since he's never much liked the name till tonight—when Vince goes into a coughing spasm on the other side of the table. It doesn't seem like much at first, just some throat-clearing, but then it takes on the ferocity of a man trying to come up for air. He turns an odd color as he hacks, something close to purple, while his hands grip the table edge and his head dips and his shoulders shake. All talking stops. The jukebox pounds out Guns N' Roses' latest—James does not like what has happened to music in the last five years—and Gil stands above Vince, a meaty hand on the coughing man's shoulder, a worried look on his face. This picture sears its way into James's brain—two old men in baseball uniforms—an image he knows he will carry with him, age and baseball, a kind of nightmare.

There is a loud cough and a hack and then a voice, maybe Jefferson down the table, saying, "Should I call the doctor? Should I call a doctor?"

"No, goddammit," Vince yells, as he lifts his head and pulls his chair back to the table. "Get a goddam undertaker."

There is a long, unnatural silence. James looks to Mercer for guidance, but the pitcher is merely standing beside him, his right arm milky-white and dripping water. James swivels his head, scans the room, takes in the team, the T-shirt-and-jeans crowd, the silent TV above the bar—there's a hockey game on—before he realizes how conditioned he is. He's looking for guards to bust in and take charge.

"This is Koch and Sons, ain't it?" Vince says, laughing and coughing, but easily now. To James's great relief, the room soon fills up with noise.

III

On Saturday morning summer hangs in the air like fog. Gil's legs are heavy as he swings them out of bed, lifts them into his trousers. They are still heavy as he walks out onto his porch. The street is quiet, the sky such a depthless gray that the roofs of the houses across the street seem to sink into it.

At Stan the barber's Gil makes a five-dollar bet on the NBA play-offs. Increasingly he finds himself disinterested in basketball, especially pro basketball, which lacks the high school sounds and smells that are, for Gil, the game's main charm. Outside the barbershop, shaven and trimmed, he realizes he must feel better, for he is considering now whether this humidity will turn to rain and cancel his game this afternoon. First, though, he is going to the cemetery.

For the first ten years of his son's life, Gil thought Laurence was the most beautiful, well-behaved boy a man could hope for. He imitated his father in any way he could, to the point of embarrassment: he took *Sports Illustrated* into the bathroom, wore rubber bands around his sweat socks in imitation of his father's sock garters, said "Damn!" in his father's manner. Like his older brother, he practiced his swing in front of the dressing mirror Gil had installed in the basement, and he said "Yes, sir" and "No, sir" in an era when such words seemed wholly forgotten.

Then, without so much as a peep, he changed. Nothing loud and confrontational, like Rick; no, he just stopped listening to his parents. He left his clothes about the house, refused to cut his hair, never put more than three words together for his parents. Most frightening, he began to disappear on his bicycle. One day Gil saw him riding along Woodward at Twelve Mile Road. This was no place for a boy still shy of his eleventh birthday. Gil brought it up at dinner.

"I saw you at Twelve Mile and Woodward, on your bike."

"Where's that?"

"You know where it is. You were there."

Laurence just shrugged. So what.

"You are not to leave this neighborhood," Gil said, "or cross any major streets. Do you understand?" He looked to Susan, his wife. She nodded, thank God, for once in agreement.

Shortly thereafter Laurence didn't show for dinner and Susan called the police. The boy came home several hours later carrying his bike. He'd had a flat. Obviously this had happened far from home. Gil decided to lay down the law. If he used the bike to leave the subdivision again, he'd lose it. In the meantime, there'd be no bike riding for a week. This was easy enough to enforce. Gil wouldn't get the tire fixed.

The next day, while Gil was at work and Susan at Rick's Sandy Koufax League baseball game, Laurence carried his bike to the corner gas station, where he paid to have the tire patched with the allowance money he so parsimoniously controlled. Laurence waited patiently while the mechanic fixed the tire. The mechanic charged him a dollar and sent him on his way. Laurence made a wide lap around the gas pumps, the mechanic later reported, then rode out into Maple Road and the path of a wood-paneled 1972 Chevrolet station wagon.

Afterward sadness fell across the household, a sadness the family couldn't shake. Rick withdrew into his teenage world, and then he moved out when Susan left. Things had not been good with her for some time, and Gil saw later that an event far less traumatic than the one that had occurred would have sent her away. It was the kids who held them together, and Rick wasn't enough. Not that it was his fault, but when the three of them were together Gil began to feel that it was even worse than when they were apart, because together Laurence's absence was so pronounced.

Susan said she couldn't stand to stay in the house, and so she moved out. Gil remained, unable on the one hand to overcome the listlessness of grief and determined on the other to stay and do his penance. He got into coaching in order to be closer to his sons, but instead he found that he had to be harder on Rick than he was on the other kids, lest someone accuse him of playing favorites. When Rick went east to college, Susan went south. Suddenly Gil was alone, in the middle of the country, with their old house and its ghosts.

———

In cemeteries there is an odd competition played out with flowers. The first time Gil visited his son's grave, after the funeral, he noticed it. Flowers mean someone cares; the bare graves, or those with the weather-beaten plastic flowers (even worse), are unbearably depressing. So every Saturday a dozen freshly cut daisies are laid on Laurence's grave. Roses regularly grace graves near Laurence's and certainly roses are nicer, but they are also expensive, prohibitively so. The death made Gil look hard at who he was, and one of the things he learned was that he could no longer pretend he had the wherewithal of a rose man.

Today is Laurence's *jahrzeit,* the anniversary of his death. Gil stands, his hands in his pockets, and calculates what Laurence's age would be: thirty-one. He gathers his thoughts, not in any set order, but where he'll be able to call them up, like players from the bench. Then he speaks, not aloud, but in a voice of the mind.

"Not much has changed since last year," he says, "except that I've come to some decisions, which I'll tell you about in a minute. Your mother, she's still living in Florida and we still don't talk much. That probably doesn't surprise you, but when I think back to when we met, it surprises me.

"Some guys at work got offered early retirement, and they all took it. I'm not sure why no one has offered it to me. Maybe they've forgotten I'm there. We buy eight times the steel that we did when I started, and we do it with half the people. So maybe they need me. Of course, my boss is only forty-two, and that's hard, when you realize the people giving you orders are younger than you.

"The team, though, that looks good. I've got some new blood. O'Rourke from Central Michigan and Kukla from U of M.

Then I got this kid from Jackson, of all places. He was in prison for killing a kid in a fight. How 'bout that? Hits a ton. And fields, too. Seems like a good kid.

"I should have gone into baseball as a career. I can finally admit that mistake. I think that my whole life since the navy I've been mad about it. I knew I should have tried to play when I got back, but I didn't, and I should have tried to coach, for a living. Your grandfather never would have understood that, and I just couldn't go into baseball unless he said it was okay. Silly, right? But I couldn't. That's how it was when I grew up, and it's funny how those beginnings stay with you.

"The way I figure it, if I'd been in baseball then I wouldn't have been so hard on you and Rick. You and your bike. I'm sorry. I used to sneak out of the house to go to ball practice, back when I was a boy. My father thought I should be studying. Maybe you were sneaking out, too, so you wouldn't have to practice. I don't know.

"Vince once gave me some advice when I couldn't get Rick to change his stance. Rick wasn't hitting and I knew how to fix it and I told him, but he was stubborn. Drove me crazy.

"'Look,' Vince told me, 'sometimes, if you pitch it slow, you get more of a curve.' He was right, of course, about that.

"So that's another decision. This year I'm going to throw slow curves. And also, I'm listening to my head. Doing the right thing, instead of acting like what I want to happen is what I think will happen. Being hard. But at the same time, letting go, letting the ball float up there 'cause I have the confidence that it will go where I need it to go. I have to fight to do that, 'cause it's not like me at all.

"That's it. This year I'm going to let it happen. I'm not going to force things. I think it's going to come a bit easier, because this year I'm tired. Just plain tired. And when you're tired you start to figure out what's important. I wish you were around, because I think I would do better with you now. I could let you ride your bike. That's for sure."

Gil lays the flowers at the base of the tombstone, then walks back to his car. He looks up and sees that the sky is breaking. The sun might even peek through. He does feel tired, exhausted, really, and it's not even noon.

IV

Top of the fifth, time out. Mercer stands where the mound meets the infield grass and rubs the ball. It is white, this ball, and too smooth. He bends to fiddle with his shoe, and grabs some dirt, drops it in his glove, stands, rubs the dirt into the ball. The runner on third is standing in the coach's box. Same with the one on first, that little squirt Spellone, who runs like he talks, fast and when he shouldn't. Mercer vows that if Spellone steals second, he takes it on the chin next time up. If Mercer can still get some heat on it. Right now he can feel his elbow click with each twist he puts on the ball.

It started with his right ankle. The damn thing took so long to get better that by the time it did heal his back was a mess, as he was overextending it trying to make up for the bad ankle. The pain kept moving, up his back to his shoulder, then down the shoulder to his elbow. Mercer shudders, knows that everything in baseball is fragile, unstable, barely in balance. Little things become big things and then loss. This inning he's given up a triple, then gotten an out, then given a walk to Spellone—trying to be too cute with an umpire with no guts to call a corner—and now he's got Freddie Spatts, big fat Freddie Spatts. There was a day, about thirty pounds ago for Freddie, when Mercer struck him out three times. That was Double-A ball. If Spatts couldn't hit a curve then, he can't hit one now. No one learns how to hit a curve in his thirties.

"Okay," the ump calls. "Let's play ball."

Mercer stands at the rubber and shakes off the sign. Krauss wants a fastball, wants one because he's a catcher and all catchers want fastballs with men on first, especially when the man on first has speed. No way, Mercer thinks. I'm not throwing a stupid pitch 'cause you're worried about *your* arm.

Krauss gives him the fastball again, an insistent single finger. Mercer shakes it off. Krauss calls time. He lifts his mask and jogs to the mound with the clicking equipment and world-weariness that all catchers have.

"This guy couldn't hit a curveball on the best day of his life," Mercer says before Krauss can speak.

"Shit, Ben, he's too slow for your fast one. He'll miss it or pop up." Krauss eyes Spellone at first.

"I'll keep the bastard close," Mercer says.

"Play ball," yells the ump.

"I'm throwing a curve," Mercer says. Krauss jogs back, crouches but not too low, and doesn't bother to give the sign.

Mercer throws to first, catching Spellone leaning toward second, and the guy practically does a slapstick routine to get back to first. Hagenbush tags him hard in the face. The umpire calls him safe. He stands and calls time to brush himself off.

"Jesus Christ!" someone yells from the stands. "Throw a pitch!"

Mercer's elbow is afire with pain. Save yourself, he thinks. No more throws to first. Step off to keep him close. No, he's too far off. Another throw to first, stars of pain dance now in Mercer's head, flashes of light behind his eyes. Hagenbush holds the ball. Mercer walks halfway to first before Hagenbush returns the ball. Mercer starts toward the mound, then, without looking, he wheels and throws back to first. It's a play he and Hagenbush have, and it almost gets Spellone, who has just started to move off the bag, expecting nothing. But it doesn't work.

Mercer's elbow feels as if he's holding it over a flame.

Again Krauss gives no sign. The stretch. The pitch.

The ball starts off well. The runner goes. The ball, spinning, begins to drop, and drop, and drop, till at sixty feet it arcs into the ground as if it's been shot out of the air. Dust explodes where it lands. Krauss scoops it but has no play on Spellone, who goes into second standing up. And Spatts, the lardball, doesn't swing. Ball one.

The opposing bench is hooting and hollering. Krauss walks a third of the way to the mound, then rifles the ball at Mercer to punctuate his displeasure.

"Time!" the umpire calls.

Gil is walking to the mound.

Christ, Mercer thinks. He liked it better when Vince made these trips, the settle-down visit, when Vince would tell him to be a cham-peen, settle down and throw strikes. He talked the talk, and he knew the music, too. He would say the same thing again and again, the simple thing, settle down and throw strikes, get this guy, bear down, and Mercer could feel the wisdom of it, because what he was saying was not simple at all, but there were no words for the intricacies of defeating an opponent. Vince trusted Mercer to know how to do that. Gil never settles down, wasn't a pitcher. Every moment for Gil is urgent. Up ten, down by one, it doesn't matter. At the moment he is up by one, but with opposing men on second and third.

"What's going on here?" Gil asks. "Why curve him?"

Krauss jogs up, his shin pads rattling, and lifts his mask. There's an I-told-you-so look on his face.

"Can't hit one," Mercer says. He notices that Gil is wearing glasses.

"He can't hit your fastball."

Mercer feels his arm, a torch. He shrugs.

"Okay," Gil says. "Let's get this guy. Settle down and throw strikes. You all right? Why you holding your arm like that?"

"I'm fine. Never felt better."

Gil kicks at the pitcher-mound dirt.

Mercer says, "I can K this guy in my sleep, Gil."

Gil stares at him, then waddles back to the dugout adjusting and readjusting the bill of his cap. An old coach's walk, all gut and no fanny.

Krauss gives Mercer his told-you-so look. The next pitch, a

fastball, bounces in front of the plate. Krauss knocks it down, saves a run.

Gil climbs the dugout steps.

"I'm all right!" Mercer yells. Once Gil crosses the third base line, Mercer has to come out. Those are the rules, out on the second visit. Mercer can't believe it. Gil leaves him in, always. Lives or dies with his pitching. Mercer looks quickly around, up at the crowd. They look disinterested, just hanging out in the bleachers. He wonders, What's going on here? Is Gil really pulling me so soon? I'm in the middle of a batter here.

"Good job, Ben," the coach says.

"I told you I was all right," Mercer says, thinking, What the hell, what the hell.

"You got to get the ball up there without bouncing it."

"I'm the best pitcher you got."

"You're right about that, but not at the moment." He holds his hand out for the ball. "C'mon, Ben. Give me the ball."

Mercer slaps it in his hand. Who does he think he is? In the middle of a batter. He stomps off the field as Kindle jogs in. The umpires are jawboning by the backstop. Spatts is back in the on-deck circle, swinging a bat with a doughnut. Mercer holds his right arm to his body, where it won't swing as much. Two runs in four and a third innings. Two men left on. Pathetic. The sun is streaming in now through the clouds, long shafts of afternoon light pounding down on Pontiac. For a moment Mercer is caught up in this play of light. The hugeness of the beams is stunning. As he's about to enter the dugout he sees Kukla's girlfriend leaning against the fence. She's a looker, too.

V

James spots Mercer in the parking lot. The pitcher lumbers over to his car, spikes rattling, an ice bag tied to his elbow with Ace bandages so that it appears that a hornets' nest is growing on his arm. He opens his trunk, pulls out a pair of shoes, sits on the edge of the trunk cavity to change out of his spikes. James moves in.

"Nice game," he says.

Mercer looks up. "What?"

"Nice game."

"Luke, you were there, right?"

"You got the win."

"Kindle did that. And you and Jeff and Goodie."

"Win's a win."

"Wisdom for the ages," Mercer says.

James asks Mercer if he's going to the clubhouse, but the pitcher says he wants to go ice his arm at home. James asks for a ride. He wants it to be a simple question, *Hey, how 'bout a ride,* but it comes out serious, as though he's asking Mercer to lie for him, or give him money.

Mercer takes him in with his pitcher's predator eyes. He tells James to take off his spikes, brush off his pants, and get in the car.

They drive silently at first. James drops his head back to smell the leather of the seats.

"You enjoying yourself, Luke?"

"Sure."

"Good," Mercer says. "Just keep doing what you're doing. Don't press."

A long pause.

"Must be nice to be out of prison," Mercer says.

"The best."

They hurtle down Woodward Avenue, a river of autos, a community of fast-food chains and gas station/convenience stores on its banks.

"You married?" James asks.

Mercer laughs.

"What's funny?"

"Me married."

"Girlfriend?"

"Sure."

James would like a girlfriend. He's only slept with one girl in his life and it brought him nothing but grief. He loved her so fiercely that he didn't know it was love, and it manifested itself in a constant rage. Lately he finds himself totally taken with women, all women. The cashier at the grocery store, another walking down the sidewalk. A kind word from a fifty-year-old diner waitress can just about bring him to tears. He would like to meet a girl, one to have around, to go to the movies with, to sleep late with when there's no work or game.

"So, Luke, you got a girl?"

"No."

"Then you got to meet one."

"How?"

"What do you mean, how? Do I take Maple here?" Mercer asks, looking now for directions. He makes the turn.

"How?" James demands.

"Women are everywhere. Meet them in the street, in a restaurant, food stores, malls. At the ball games. A guy like you, oughta be easy. Girls like guys who get hits."

"All the girls at the games are taken."

"I guess that's true. Did you see Kukla's girl?"

"Oh, man," James says. His vision blurs with the thought of her. How does a guy find a girl like that?

"I tell you what, Luke. I'll see what I can do. Maybe we'll double-date. I'll bring the girls."

"Really?"

"I think I can set it up, but you've got to do something for me."

"Sure."

"Tell me why you spent all those years in prison. Did you really kill a guy?"

"Yeah, I did."

"Why?"

"Stop here."

They pull up to a simple house, three stories, with white aluminum siding, fake shutters. James lives in the third-floor apartment. Gil found him the place, one of the only cheap apartments in Birmingham, close to the practice field, close to Gil. James doesn't want to say anything more—and wants to tell Mercer everything.

"I was seventeen," he says.

"So was I once. I didn't go to prison."

"I was dating this girl. Lucy," he begins, thinking, Here we go. "She was like the best-looking thing around. I just couldn't

think of nothing else. Then we started spending all our time together, 'cept when I was playing ball. She gave herself to me on
the third date. I mean, I'd never had any woman before, and I'd
been trying, and now I got the best-looking girl in the school
tearing off her clothes. I mean, it sounds stupid, but no one ever
did much for me. That really meant a lot. You understand?"

"You bet I do."

"I woulda done about anything for her. Promise you won't
tell anyone this."

"Promise."

"I would have quit baseball for her. At the time. It sounds
sappy, but it's the truth. Would have stopped, would have
worked sweeping floors just as long as she'd be there when I
was done. I mean, it was like, I don't know how to explain it.
She was religion."

Mercer turns off the engine.

"Okay, so every day after practice she'd be there, and we'd go
back to my house, which was really where my mother and me
lived, this dinky apartment. Lucy and I would shower together,
make love, then just hang out in bed, just lying together. I know
it sounds weird, but we were really good friends. And I was seventeen, getting it every day. Every day. Okay, so about seven-
thirty, my mother would come home from her job. Lucy would
be in the kitchen by then, making us dinner. She liked to cook.
It was like we were married or something.

"You got to understand. We had plans. People thought I was
a bad student, on account of I was a good athlete, but actually I
did all right, B's mostly, and I figured I'd graduate and go pro.
There were scouts, you know, sniffing around. I was going to

get a chance. Lucy was gonna come, move to whichever place I ended up. We had plans. We were getting out of Jackson as soon as we could."

James stops, troubled by the memory. The car is quiet, except for the metal ticking as it cools.

"That can't be the end of the story," Mercer says.

"No, there was this guy, John Burton. I never thought much about him. He played track, ran like the mile or something. Anyways, he was a friend of Lucy's. They were just friends. That's what Lucy said, and why should I not believe her? She was spending all her time with me. But there were rumors, mean ones. People would see them at night sometimes. I stayed at home most nights. 'Cause I had plans, you know. And ball games. Didn't need any night trouble, and there wasn't nothing I needed to chase.

"So, this one night, late Friday, my friend Bobby Chladek comes over. I figure he wants to go to the cage and hit. He carried bats in his car, we did this all the time, but he wants to go to the A&W. He's a friend, and I figure, why not? So, we're there and I look across the little aisle the waitresses use, with the cars on the other side, and I see Lucy and this guy Burton. And it looks to me like they're more than friends. I mean, he's taking these french fries and one by one putting them in her mouth. And she's sticking her tongue out and slowing lapping them up. I mean, c'mon.

"I'm like crazy. Crazy. Sitting there, feeling like the world is exploding or collapsing or something. And then they pull out.

"I tell Bobby to follow them. They go to the high school. It's past eleven on a Friday, springtime. No one's there. Burton, he drives his Camaro right onto the fields. Back then nothing was fenced in. Drove right out into the outfield of our ballpark, center field.

"I mean, in high school I played center field.

"Now, all the while we're following these guys out there I'm thinking I don't know what. I can't tell you 'cause I don't know. I don't know 'cause I was insane. That's what my lawyer said. It didn't work, that defense, but I tell you what, it was true. I mean, really. The truth.

"Anyway, all this time the bats are rattling around in the backseat, you know, rolling together on the floor, metal clacking. Like I said, we went to the batting cage all the time. Bet I took at least fifty swings a day even back then. More, lotsa times.

"So, I grab a bat. I don't know what I was thinking. Burton and Lucy, maybe they thought we were cops or something. Me, I start in whacking that Camaro. Knocked out the taillights, the headlights, worked my way up and back, went to work on the windshield—which is hard to smash—hit the sides till it looked like it had hailed bowling balls. Eventually Burton got out of the car. When he did, I started in on him.

"I mean, he was like there. I hit him in the ribs—I didn't know what I was doing, just whacking, but man, the picture came back to me soon enough. I got a problem with that. I see something, I never forget it, but it's like I'm not there, too. Anyway, the rib shot doubles him up, and I hit him again and crack his head open. Then again. I'll never forget the feeling of that second hit, 'cause it was soft. The first one gave me vibrations, but the second was like hitting a melon.

"So Burton and his brains are spilled out on center field and Lucy is screaming and Bobby is trying to stop me without getting killed himself. And I just dropped to the ground and looked at Burton's eyes. They were all glazed—you could see that in the light of the night and the headlights from Bobby's car—and his head was all mush there on top and he was breathing. Still alive, but not for long. And then I started crying like I never cried. I can't even remember how they took me away."

A long silence. James feels that no matter what happens now, he can't move. He's never told the story all out to anyone, he carried it with him, but now it's outside and he feels exhausted. He's never told anyone because he couldn't, because he is sorry and he knows that sorry is not good enough.

"Jesus, Luke."

"You asked."

"I did. And I'm glad I did, and that you told me. That's the true story?"

"I couldn't make that up."

"No, I guess not. What happened to the girl?"

"Moved away. I mean, she was doing it with that Burton guy. Came out later. Do you know what that was like? I mean, I'd've done anything for her. But it saved me, too, 'cause then it was like, you know, a passion crime. Reduced the charge, and the sentence."

"You still did hard time. Isn't that what they call it?"

"Yeah, for a reason."

"Luke, you can't take your women so seriously."

James thinks that it's easy for a guy to say that when he has women. He likes Mercer the best of anyone on the team, precisely because Mercer is so serious. He thanks him for the ride.

VI

Mercer pulls away from the curve, comes around the block, and heads east. He tries to picture James out in a dark center field, beating some guy's head in. Mercer has, at times, tried to hit batters in the head, but with a baseball from sixty feet six inches, and they were wearing helmets.

The amazing thing is that James did it for a girl, and that he, Ben Mercer, understands it completely. He has fantasized numerous times about smashing the puppy's head into blood gravy, always with the safety of distance from a weapon and a victim. But he knows now that he can do it. If James did it, he can, too. He thinks of Emily, of the look of her, the curve of her body, and he feels it, knows he can kill. No doubt about it.

He circles back toward James's house. He wants to tell James that he's with him, that James is the most natural hitter he's ever seen, ever, and that includes all the guys in the show, and Triple-A. He pulls back up to the curb across the street and looks up to James's window. The light is on behind the thin yellow of the shade, and behind that is a shadow, a man swinging a baseball bat.

Unmistakably this is James. Left-handed, tall stance, and all the grace of his swing. Over and over, the shadow swings. Mercer is struck by the silent beauty of this and the feeling, for the moment, of watching something private. Then he remembers that it's a twenty-two-year-old kid up there, a killer who's so earnest he's vulnerable, who needs protection. He's also a guy who hit the ball hard three times today, and who goes home to practice a swing that is already perfect. Mercer knows hitters, knows there is a dressing mirror up there, and that James is standing in front of it, checking his swing, his stance. Mercer waits and waits, but after ten minutes James is still swinging and shows no signs of slowing down. Mercer turns off the engine and decides to wait and watch.

The ice on his elbow melts, sloshes around when he moves his arm. A person walks down the sidewalk, oblivious. Above, the swinging continues. As Mercer watches, a thought comes to his mind, almost forms into words, fades, then comes back to his lips: *Can't miss.*

VII

The third weekend in June, with his team sitting on fourteen straight wins, Gil finds himself driving with Vince down M-14. First they've got to stop in Jackson and write checks for Morris. Then it's on to Battle Creek for a doubleheader on the very same field where two months hence they hope to win the national championship.

It is a sunny day, the sky Dodger-blue, the trees full and quaking in the breeze. The cornstalks now stand two feet high. As the Continental scoots north of Ann Arbor and picks up I-94, everything seems pretty much right. Gil's outfield is hitting .363, thanks to James's .426. Jefferson, too, is doing well, perhaps in response to the two new additions. The infield is solid; Krauss is having the year of his life, and Kindle, Kohn, and Booth have pitched well. Mercer is still a cut above, when he's on. At those times he belongs in a higher league. He's had some bad outings, but mostly Gil marvels at his cool, his control, the heat he can still bring at thirty-four. Sometimes he wonders how Mercer failed to stay in the bigs. Can there really be that much talent out there? It doesn't seem that way, but then again Mercer hasn't been facing big-league hitters. Gil wonders what Vince thinks.

"Mercer's still doing well," he says

"Yep," Vince replies. Gil can hear him breathe.

"You think he's big-league material?"

"Been there."

"For about two seconds. I mean again."

"He's old. Too old. No one would sign him now."

"Forget that. You think he's got the stuff?"

"I don't know. Why?"

"Just wondered. We count on the guy."

"You also have yanked him twice, at the first sign of trouble."

"Sure. I got Kindle to come in fresh. You think I'm pulling him too fast?"

"No," Vince says, pausing to catch his breath. "I think you used to leave him in too long. I told you that, but you never listened."

"I listened."

"Not well enough."

"You okay?" Gil asks.

Vince nods, breathing heavily. His chest rocks, mouth gapes open like a fish on deck. Jesus, Gil thinks. Look at that.

They drive into Jackson in silence. At Pineridge, the car parked but still running, Gil says, "My dad has gone crazy. I mean, not crazy, just, you know . . . senile. Paranoid. Thinks I'm stealing from him. Don't pay it any mind. He's got more money than you or I put together."

"I don't got any money, Gil. You know that."

"You know what I mean."

Gil turns off the engine, extracts himself from the car, waits for Vince. They walk inside, two grown men in baseball uniforms. Gil is hit by that familiar smell, something like formaldehyde, the smell of memory and loss, of his mother's last days, which stretched across one summer and halfway through a football season, continuous pain and then death, by then a reward. Now Gil sees an old man driving a walker by the entrance. The man looks up. "You boys play ball today?" he asks.

Vince and Gil look to each other, then at the old man, owl eyes behind dense glasses, the neck of a turkey.

"Yes," Gil says.

"Beautiful day for it." He pushes the walker on, following it with slow baby steps.

Gil finds his father's room empty. He is about to head for the office when a nurse appears.

"Oh, I'm so glad you're here. We've been trying to call you, Mr. Davison. Your father, we had to rush him to the hospital."

"What's wrong?" Gil feels his stomach tighten. Okay, he tells himself. The old man can't live forever. You knew this was coming.

"He couldn't breathe. The paramedics gave him oxygen. Took him in." She pulls out a slip of paper. "Here's the nurses' station at the hospital."

Gil takes the note, sits at the desk and dials, stares at the smiling faces of his family. He talks to the hospital nurse. Shortness of breath is not only the symptom, but apparently the diagnosis. The old man is under watch, resting, the nurse says.

Gil asks if his father is awake. The nurse believes not. He tells her he will be in later, hangs up the phone.

"I'll take you to the hospital," Vince says. "Get you on the way back."

"I'm going to the games."

"Gil, your father. Don't you want to be there?"

"He'd say I should go to the game. Besides, he's asleep."

"You told me he hates baseball."

"Baseball, yes. But not duty."

"It's not duty to coach a game if your father is dying."

"He's not dying."

"How do you know that?"

"I don't," Gil says.

He opens the drawer and pulls out the checkbook and the signature stamp. The bills are neatly stacked on top of the desk. "Give me two minutes," he tells Vince, and starts to write out the checks.

Gil's path seems clear to him now. He'll go to the hospital and look after his father, that squat little body beneath the hospital blankets. There will be the awful smells, the sounds of hospitals, and the people in waiting rooms, sitting heads down in grief or back in boredom. There is blood and death in hospitals, and false alarms, and he hates all of it. He will go, of course, but why go now and sit behind a window with its shade drawn and watch his father sleep? The old man will not know if he shows or not, probably wouldn't care anyway. Gil knows that he is too late, that whatever visits he has with his father, whatever connections might have been made are gone, lost during the Eisenhower years, or maybe even before, rooted back in the man's decision to walk—he actually walked—away from his home in Europe and catch a boat to the new world. Gil had a buddy in the navy who liked to say that it was a whole new world every morning. Hardly. There is history and duty and lessons learned, till the present for a man is more past than anything else, if he's not careful. So Gil will move on. Today is a beautiful day, full of light, and a man should be out on a ball field.

VIII

Mercer has taken a short jog this morning, trying to get loose, in preparation for pitching the second game. He's got time till he has to leave, so now, showered, he slides back into bed, spoon position with Emily, a leg scissored between her two.

"You're cold," she says.

"Not for long."

She reaches behind, pulls him tighter.

"Let me ask you a question," he says.

"Hmm."

"You know that friend of yours? Barb."

"What about her?"

"I got a friend. I'd like to set them up."

"Since when did you ever care if anyone else gets any?"

"C'mon, Em."

"C'mon, what?"

"He's a friend of mine. Just a kid. But he's a nice guy. Good-looking."

"Okay, Mercer." She kicks his leg out, turns, rolls on top of him, and he forgets all about James. "What is this?"

"Huh?"

"This friend."

"He's a friend. He's had a tough go of things. He's stuck living by Detroit, doesn't know a soul. I just thought . . ."

"A stockbroker?"

"Right fielder."

She laughs, then runs her tongue from his navel to his sternum. His heart jerks.

"What are you doing?" he asks.

"You seem to know." She takes him in her hand.

"Let's just . . . finish up this topic."

"I'll talk to Barb. She's always had a weakness for . . ." She is moving up and down him, rubbing, as though to scent him. "You're gonna need another shower."

"That's okay," Mercer says. "That's okay."

IX

Vince thinks, This, too, I'm going to miss.

He is standing behind Kindle, who is warming up with Brattenburg. It's five minutes before the game. The sun is bright and intense, the air warm. Breaths come easy today. The stadium stands are filling up, each new body covering one of the new baby-blue folding seats. Here in Battle Creek people come to watch Koch and Sons as though the players were professionals. The newspaper and radio station send reporters. Battle Creek is almost as proud of its baseball tournament as it is of its cornflakes and raisin bran. Every year Koch and Sons arrives in August to represent the Midwest, and always they disappoint. Vince has seen this phenomenon before. All that losing right at the end has made the team an object of devotion for the local baseball fanatics, as people are fanatics in Boston, or once were in Brooklyn.

At present little boys are proffering baseballs into the dugout for the players to sign. "Why you want my autograph?" Vince once heard Mercer ask. "Because," the kid said. "Someday you might be famous." Mercer told the kid that he would never be famous. "Well," the kid said, "you struck out my cousin twice."

Vince turns his eye back to Kindle. "Let me see you take a little off," Vince says, and the pitcher kicks that high knee of his and throws a beautiful change-up.

"Now the heat."

Brattenburg's mitt pops with a fastball. Kindle rolls over his glove, signaling a curve, and then snaps one off. Good stuff. When Vince met Kindle he was pure power and wild. The players called him Scud Missile, or just Scud. Since then he's picked up some finesse. He turns now to Vince.

"You look good," the coach says. "Stay warm."

"I don't know."

"What don't you know?"

"I don't know, Coach. Don't know if I got my best stuff today."

"Sure you do. Never seen you throw the ball better."

"Yeah?"

"Hell, yeah. You'll make us cham-peens. Mow 'em down. Throw easy now, if you're warm, just enough to keep the juices flowing."

Vince walks back to the dugout. What he won't miss is holding pitchers' hands, the ones with complexes. He swears they're worse than women.

Vince studies Gil for a sign, but there is nothing. Gil stares at the field, checks the scorebook, shouts encouragement and instruction, is utterly focused on the game, as usual. To Vince it seems that for Gil coaching is like one of those bodily functions that happens naturally, without thought, like digestion or (for most) respiration. Certainly the man seems to have forgotten completely that his father lies in the hospital.

Vince sneaks out and goes to the pay phone, in the dark underbelly of the stadium, where they sell Cokes and hot dogs just like in the bigs. This phone call is expensive and he really shouldn't, but he punches in his credit card and calls the hospital in Jackson. He asks for Morris Davison.

There is no answer. He is transferred to the nurse station.

"He's resting nicely, Mr. Davison," says the nurse, thinking him Gil. "I'll be sure to tell him you called." Vince puts the receiver back in its saddle.

It's cool in here, and Vince feels good, ready for the day. He pulls out a cigarette pack, taps it in the time-honored way, extracts a smoke.

"One more," he says aloud. "One more won't kill me."

He comes into the dugout in time to see James bat in the first. James is Ted Williams–tall and lean, and Vince is starting to believe. He's different that way from Gil. Gil's a romantic, in his own gruffy way. He sees a guy, believes, and then he's all hope. Vince likes to watch them for a month or two. Anybody can go on a tear, hit .500 for a couple weeks and never again.

James, though, is somehow enlightened. He is never fooled, gets a good cut at everything. Even the balls he fouls off are done with style and purpose. The thing that impresses Vince the most, though, is the kid's expression. When he gets to the plate he's dead cold. Nothing. The blue in his eyes goes gray, as hard and cold as mountain granite.

Vince was a pitcher and so is not moved to emotion by fine batting the way some men are, but watching James at work gets to him deep inside. In the end, he loves the game for its moments of still beauty, for its snapshot memories, and James, standing now, arms back and bat high, provides these, too.

X

Mercer stops at the gate, where the ticket seller/ticket taker sits on a stool in the stadium's shadow. It's the same guy who's always here, old and thin, in an ancient American Legion jacket that's two sizes too big.

"You're late," he says to Mercer, meaning, How come?

"Not late. Pitching the second game. Where are we?" There's a radio on his card table, tuned to the local public station, which is broadcasting the game.

"Third inning," the man says. "You're ahead, like always."

"We've lost more than our share in this place."

"Not in June." The old man smiles and waves Mercer past.

Rather than go to the dugout, Mercer climbs into the stands and makes his way midway up, directly behind home plate. It's between half-innings, with Battle Creek coming up in the bottom of the third. Mercer feels conspicuous in his Koch and Sons uniform, feels that everyone is watching him as he sits. Three women, young—Mercer's age, or younger—are chatting in front of him, a show of curled hair and a glittery mix of bracelets and rings.

"She ate Slim Fast all week," says the loudest one, "just so she could go to that Sunday buffet they got down at Lanahan's."

"I did that once."

"Ate Slim Fast?"

"You drink it."

Down to the right Mercer can see the diehard Koch and Sons

fans. Hagenbush's wife and kids, Krauss's and Kohn's fathers, O'Rourke's mother. Hagenbush's brother-in-law, who lives in Marshall, has come to the game with his son. Jefferson's mother is chatting with Kindle's wife. Barney Covner, Fred Smith, and Tom Carpenter are in their usual spots, high in the stands. They have no relation to the team other than attendance; Mercer doubts they have missed a game since he started playing with Koch, even the ones way out here in Battle Creek. There are a couple of men who might be scouts, and there is a random assortment of people who happen to be at the park, having paid their three dollars admission. Those three bucks, Mercer figures, get more people to the games. People will come if you charge, thinking it must be worth it.

Then, low in the stands, Mercer spots Goodstein's girlfriend, who is sitting in front with Kukla's girl. Those two, Mercer thinks, it's enough to take your mind off the game.

Mercer remembers that when Goodie met his girl it was all the team could talk about, though never when Goodie was around. It happened last summer, on July Fourth weekend, in fact. Goodie and Jefferson and Metz were driving back from the Dayton tournament, high from winning the thing and looking for something to do. So they stayed on I-75 right into Detroit, then through the tunnel and south into Canada and a strip joint in Windsor.

"We got a table and a few of those nine-dollar Labatts," Jefferson told Mercer, "and we changed about twenty bucks into ones. They got a special place at the bar where they give you ones, twenty Canadians for an Andrew Jackson. Most nights there's a line there, but the place is pretty much empty, no one coming over from Detroit on account of it being July Fourth. There's, like, four or five guys, probably Canadians who don't seem to know that on the Fourth everybody's at some family picnic or up north or something. Anyway, there's ol' Sandy, swinging her stuff over our way, and Goodie just starts stuffing the dollars. I tell you, the guy's got, like, no sense of pace. But she was good. Like she liked it. Wasn't long till we were outta ones, so we got some more, burned those up, almost all on Sandy. She's over on the table, over our laps, so close to Goodie that his eyes are tearing. So then it's break time and she saunters over covered in this Chinese robe thing, with the lights you can see she's got this sheen of sweat, and she goes up to Goodie and whispers in his ear, stuffs a piece of paper in his pocket. Her phone number."

A girl that can do that once can do it again. Mercer wonders if Goodie ever thinks about that.

She's loyal to the team, though. She's at every game, except when she's working. Right now she's sitting there in one of those shirts women wear, tight around the front and neck, bare across the shoulders, so that anyone can see the shamrock tattooed on the back of her right arm. She sits with her chin ever so slightly tipped up, as if she's ready for whatever might be thrown her way. Mercer has to admit, he sees the attraction.

Mercer turns his mind to the game, watches the Battle Creek batter take a pitch low and away, but with poor movement toward the ball, as though he couldn't get a ball there if he had to. In front of him the women are telling a story about a guy from their high school who just proposed to their friend. Mercer picks up that the guy is now a wealthy doctor, but had been a nerd. The girl said no.

A foul straight back.

The batter hits a foul down the left field line. Strike two. This batter is toast. Mercer leans forward, smelling for weakness.

A fastball outside, swing and a miss. Two away. Kindle is getting to be a smart pitcher, Mercer thinks. Finally.

The next batter hits the first pitch, a curveball, hard to the right side, but Kukla has been shading that way, having no doubt adjusted because he knew it would be a curve, and he dives, knocks the ball down, throws the runner out from his knees. End of inning.

Mercer thinks, That Kukla is a hell of a ballplayer. Mercer bends his arm, hopes he has his good stuff today. He wishes his elbow weren't so sore. Sore arms tip the balance of the game. He needs an edge. He looks to the outfield, where the flag hangs from a white flagpole, just beyond the center field fence, just before what's left of a Christmas tree farm. The wind is picking up. Okay, he tells himself. Keep the ball low. Make 'em hit it on the ground. Mercer has just the pitch to do that, too. A new one, one he's been working on.

XI

Gil watches Vince, the greenish pallor, the smoker's crags in his face. Gil would like to tell him about his father, why he came here ignoring all the rules of the family road. All his life his father has stood between him and baseball, even in Gil's most glorious moments, rounding the bases after his second home run of the day during the Olympics, another ball he hit, in high school, that sent the team to the state championship tournament. Even at those times Gil felt his father standing there at home, not with his hands out for a shake or a slap on the back, no, but on his hips, disapproving. And so now this year he will not be deterred. This is the year. He's too old to be ruled by his father. This is the year to be hard. This year he is going to win.

The team is good enough to frighten him. He can't find its weakness. Krauss has never played better behind the plate, and he's hitting the ball, too. Hagenbush and Goodstein, Kukla and Metz, it's a perfect infield. And that outfield. It's out of this league. Especially James.

James worries him most because James is so perfect. Gil would worry if he partied too much or had trouble with curveballs. But that's not it. This kind of worry is different, mysterious. Deep worry. James hits the ball as Gil has never seen anyone hit it. Twenty-one scouts have called him to ask about James, and Gil tells them all the same thing: he's never met a more polite, hardworking, earnest young man. He's also tall and handsome, and he looks every inch the ballplayer. The kind of guy sneaker companies put on billboards. Gil stares at him now, standing in the sun of right field, and worries that the kid has some extraordinary flaw, something awful that will strike and in an instant break him apart.

XII

Second game, bottom of the fifth. Mercer's arm feels good today, just the normal ache that Motrin won't dull, and Mercer won't take anything stronger than Motrin. They got a run off him in the third—a goddam walk and two singles—but now he's in the groove and what he's about to do they won't touch, either.

The ball in his glove, walking now at the base of the mound, far side from the batter, he touches his waistband, where he knows there's a dab of K-Y jelly, that wonderful water-soluble grease. It must have been tougher to do this a hundred years ago, he thinks, or maybe it was legal then. He puts just a dab on his index and middle fingers, then walks back to the rubber, where he loads up the ball, takes a change-up sign from Krauss, and throws the ball as if he's trying to squeeze a watermelon seed. The ball floats up there, then, just as the hitter starts to swing, it drops, like a duck shot from the sky. Krauss bobbles it, drops it in the dirt—perfect!—then stands, walks across the plate, and throws the ball as hard as he can at Mercer.

Mercer glances at the ball. Yes, he thinks. Perfect.

XIII

It's close to six, the shadows just starting to lengthen out, when the batter hits a fly high against the clouds and James jogs over to his right to get it. Easy play, can o' corn. He watches the ball spinning high above him, now coming at him, accelerating. His. The ball hits his glove and O'Rourke is there to pat him on the back. Last out, sweep of a doubleheader.

James hopes the guys are going out for beers. This is a special, singular joy, drinking beer with his teammates, with people who talk baseball and understand it. Friends. He dreads going home, where he knows no one, has nothing to do but swing his bat and dream about getting paid to play.

The team runs through the postgame backslapping, then files onto the field, walks single-file to the left of the Battle Creek club, all the players holding out their right hands, shaking, repeating the mantra, "Nice game."

Back in the dugout Mr. Schuster is talking to Mercer intently over in the pitchers' corner—where the active pitcher sits, alone, because pitchers are different, especially when they're pitching—except that the game's over and so James figures why not, and walks over to the pair.

"You get away with what you get away with," Mercer is saying, the hair on the back of his head still wet with sweat. "Give me a dime for every double play where second base isn't touched, for every phantom tag, and I'm a millionaire."

"This is different."

"It's not. I was just testing it out, anyway."

Something alerts them, perhaps James's breath or the grinding of his spikes. They don't look happy to see him.

"Nice game, Ben," James says. "Just wanted to tell you. And hello, Mr. Schuster."

"Call me Al," the scout says.

Mercer acknowledges the compliment in a tone that tells James to get lost, which he is on his way to doing when the scout asks him to wait by his car.

James agrees. Bobby Tasker, the batboy, is down at the end of the dugout, cinching up a helmet bag. James walks over, grabs the bag, and heads out of the dugout, through the stadium's underbelly, and into the parking lot.

James walks, his duffel in one hand, the helmet bag in the other. The day is sliding slowly toward night. James hears cars whisking along the road, the sound of movement, while closer by people stroll to their cars with easy talk and laughter. Saturday-night plans and obligatory goodbyes are shouted over the roofs of Buicks and Fords. It is a peaceful scene, one that moves James, as he is moved by simple demonstrations of camaraderie. He is then aware of someone running. He turns and practically swallows a fist, is spinning and falling, his face alight with pain, then on the ground, a blow now to the side of his head and a kick in his ribs, blinding pain that peaks and then eases slightly, so that he can taste the blood on his tongue and see the forest of shoes and shins. My parole, he thinks, my God, stay out of trouble.

"Motherfucker!" the assailant yells, but there is a policeman there, holding the screaming guy in a satin Tigers jacket, his face red, eyes bulging with rage. James is aware that people, total strangers, are helping him to stand, and he drops to his knees with weakness and the memory of being held like this before, many times, when he first got to prison, held and hit so that he would know just who made the rules.

Someone gives him a towel, and he wipes his mouth, a red swatch appearing on the towel, and then suddenly his hearing is back. There are people talking, *What the hell, just hauled off and hit 'im, look at that eye, would ya,* and then back to his feet, and over to the policeman's car, a long walk through gawker faces, also some of the team, Brattenburg and Metz and Goodie and Booth, all watching, and James, his stomach now in the kind of knot that makes him want to heave, aware that his fate will now be irrecoverably decided.

"Sit here, son," the cop says, and James sits in the front seat of the car, for the first time knows that the man who has been leading him here is Gil.

"He just hit me, Coach," James says, though the words come out funny, all thick and heavy, like a ball that won't carry on a humid day.

"I know," the coach says. "Just sit."

Again James can hear the rush of the road, maybe even of the interstate beyond. The sensations come to him now, a throbbing in his head, the rough edge of a chipped tooth, the painful tenderness of an eye that has already swollen closed, the cop's shuffling boots on the pavement.

"He says you beat him up for no reason six years ago. You are Luke James?"

"Yes," James says, thinks, Yes, I still am.

"His name is Brendan Stanz. That name mean anything to you?"

James thinks back on all his memories of flailing fists and insatiable anger, but no, he can't say the name means anything, could have been one of a hundred fights, for any or no good reason. James shakes his head. No.

Then something happens that James has never before known. Someone steps in and speaks for him: Gil. "I'm his coach. He didn't do anything. Hell, he had his hands full. But he's got a prison record, you can look it up if you want. We'd really like it if there were no record of this incident. No report. We don't want the trouble. It would just go to his parole officer, make it look like he's already getting back in trouble."

"Look," the cop says. "I've got to write a report."

"I know you do," Gil says, "but think of the kid. He just got out of prison. Been playing for me just a month, and I'm here to tell you, this kid is the next major-league, bona fide star. Were you at the game, did you see him hit? You know, there's only so much you can teach about hitting, then either a guy can or he can't. Most of us, at some level, just can't. Not this one. Just watch him play."

The cop exhales. "It's just that the law, and my partner and all."

The conversation stops and James is aware that someone else has arrived. His eyes catch a piece of wood moving outside the window of the car. It is several seconds before he can focus and see that the wood is the butt of a holstered gun. The second cop is here.

"Gil?" asks a voice. "Gil Davison?"

"Yes?"

"I'm Robert Gerth."

"Bobby! Sure. It's been a long, long time."

"We played Legion ball together," the new cop says to his partner.

Now Gil explains the situation to his old friend, his voice too low to be heard, but James knows it's Gil's voice, knows its beat, its gravelly cadences.

"I'm talking major-league baseball," James picks up. "You can't take that chance away from him."

"I'm sure he's not going to have any trouble from this," says the first cop. "Hell, he's the victim."

"Please," Gil says.

There is silence, then goodbyes are said. James is aware of the cops walking away. He tastes blood. Now the second cop is walking back, talking to Gil in a soft voice. "Take him straight home." Straight home is now 110 miles east, no beers, no camaraderie, no celebration—and a wicked headache, to boot—but, all in all, James is happy, bloodied and sore, yes, but amazed by the turn in his luck.

XIV

In the rearview mirror a dark horizon lies beneath the last embers of daylight. Ahead Gil can see only darkness, and the white and yellow lines in the headlights. Vince wheezes beside him and he can hear James in the backseat, shifting about. James has a bag of ice wrapped in a towel, and every time he moves, the cubes grind like bone. Ice or no ice, the kid's going to have a shiner.

"The guy just jumped him," the policeman said, over a fight that had occurred six years before. "The guy" seemed to feel he had a right to do this, standing there in his Tigers jacket, the orange emblem on his chest bobbing indignantly up and down. "He just hit me for no reason," the assailant explained. "See this—" He stuck his hand in his mouth, pulled out a bridge, three teeth clinging to a steel band, spittle shining in the parking-lot lights. "Got to wear this every day of my goddam life just 'cause of that bastard." He looked to the policeman, held up the bridge for better inspection, then stuffed it back in his mouth for emphasis, as if the policeman would now condone the assault.

And what if Bobby Gerth hadn't been part of that police detail? Take an American Legion team from 1945, scatter it across half a century, and what are the odds that the switch-hitting second baseman will turn up as a cop right where you need him? As soon as Gil knew it was Bobby Gerth he knew everything was all right, the way he sometimes knows, just in the way James takes a first pitch, that the kid will get a hit. Somewhere buried deep in baseball are the little signs that let you see the future.

It is hard for Gil to reconcile the kid in his backseat with the hell-raiser, with the kind of troublemaker Gil never allows on his team. He had a kid once who shoplifted on road trips, who drank too much, carried drugs in his duffel, brought heat like an oven. The guy could throw so hard some catchers had trouble handling him. He had a loud mouth and a bad attitude, and Gil would stay awake at night, pacing his kitchen with worry over what to do with him. He finally fired the guy midseason, after a third missed game in a row, one in which he was supposed to pitch. In the end the team lost that year because it ran out of pitching, and Gil knew people said then that he was crazy, that you never throw away an arm like that, no matter what, but he had never regretted it till maybe now. The guy did go on to get busted for cocaine and play three seasons for the Padres, keeping their legal staff busy. Gil thanks God that James is different. Then again, this year is different.

Gil passes an emerald sign that tells him he's twenty miles west of Jackson. Cornfields stretch out beside the highway. James shifts again. I'm going to win with this guy, Gil thinks. This time I'm going to win.

Gil stands in the hospital elevator with Vince and James and a nurse, feels silly to be dressed up in his Koch and Sons uniform. There are times when baseball makes him feel like a little boy, and this is one of them. He wishes he'd thought to bring a change of clothes, dreads what his father might say when he appears with a fellow coach and a player in baseball drag.

"You sure you don't want to wait this out in the cafeteria?" Gil asks now that they are standing outside the elevator. In the distance Gil can hear the faint but awful beeping of some medical machine.

"Not unless you want us to, Gil," Vince says. James nods, his right eye puffy, the color of eggplant.

Gil enters the room and sees his father lying on his back, the man's Adam's apple and nose in profile, a tube of oxygen taped beneath the latter, an opening beneath each nostril. A machine records the mountain-skyline beating of his heart, the beep that Gil heard back at the elevator.

He walks all the way to the bed, sees the outline of his father's small body beneath the blanket, just as he remembers it from the last illness, the sheet folded over the top and stamped with the words "Angelica Supply." Gil doesn't have to look: he knows his father's eyes are on him.

"How you feeling, Dad? You look . . . comfortable."

The old man blinks his eyes, slowly, then lifts his right arm, the one with the IV, the one closest to Gil, and he closes his fin-

gers into a demi-fist, does this again and again. Gil understands—*lean closer*—and so he leans over the bed till he is atop
his father, where he can feel the cool oxygen and the awful staleness of the man's breath. When Morris speaks it's a dry whisper,
faint and raspy.

"I didn't play ball today," he says.

Gil stands and takes his father's hand, loose and bony, a bag
of marbles.

"I know you didn't, Dad. The nurses say you can go to
Mapleshade in a day or two, and if all goes well, you'll be back
in Pineridge in a week."

This news does not impress the old man.

A long time passes as Gil stands at the bedside. Why can't
you let it go? he wants to ask. Why can't you acknowledge what
I am? Just once you could ask me if we won the game, maybe
even congratulate me. Just once. Once.

Morris motions again with his hand, and again Gil leans over
the bed.

"The boy," the old man says.

"Oh," Gil says, standing. "This is Luke James. He's from
Jackson."

Morris motions him over, but James looks first to Gil, then
glances back at Vince, who is sitting in a chair by the bathroom.
Only then does James move forward and lean over the bed.
Morris's hand comes up, tubes dangling, as if to put his arm
around James's back.

James stands and moves back stiffly, heads out to the hall,
where Gil asks him what his father said.

"He told me that I shouldn't waste my time playing ball."

"That's it?"

"He told me to get a good education, to study hard."

Gil can see the confusion in James's battered face. Why, the kid must be wondering, did he tell me that?

"That's the old world, kid," Vince says. Gil couldn't have explained it better himself.

XV

When he can stand it no longer, Mercer jumps from his car, leaving it double-parked, and runs up the stairs of Emily's building. He has been home to shower, where he found a message from her, one breaking their date. He is certain that the puppy is behind this, and he's out to do whatever it takes, whatever he has to do. He can't stay home. This he knows.

The stairs creak and the railing wobbles as he makes his way to the third floor and pounds on Emily's door. There is a sign that reads, PROPERTY IS THEFT. C'MON IN! He tries the door. It's locked.

He has a number of credit cards to choose from, so he picks a little-used Visa, and jimmies the lock on the second try. Emily's living room is clean and bare in an extreme way, with only a lavender yoga mat in one corner and several large orange pillows in another, set up to look across the bare wood floor to the television and VCR. There are posters of Bob Marley and the *Mona Lisa* on the walls.

Her bedroom is the living room's antithesis. Cassette tapes,

CDs, and books are scattered about the floor with a stunning array of billowy pants, paisley scarves, cotton panties, and two and a half pairs of Birkenstock sandals. Mercer notices, first with smug satisfaction and then with growing jealous rage, that there is not one brassiere in sight.

The descent to his car is swift. He drives to Main Street, miraculously finds a parking space in front of an ice cream parlor called the Loving Spoonful. Pulling on the parking brake sends a pulse of pain up his wrist and forearm to his elbow, where its intensity is magnified as it travels to his shoulder and then back down to his elbow, which is wrapped in Ace bandages and a bag of melted ice. He needs ice, he realizes, but instead unwraps the bandages and leaves them tangled with the ice bag on the floor of his car.

He heads down the street, through the sidewalk tables, studying the Saturday revelers, staring in restaurant windows, searching for a blond-haired bohemian with a sorry-looking, overfed, cow-eyed excuse of a man. He enters and walks the smoky lengths of their usual watering holes: the Old Town; the Full Moon; Washington Street Station; Del Rio. His right elbow is throbbing, his mind racing, looking for an answer to the question now pricking at his mind: What do I do when I find her? There is no answer. He tells himself that he'll know when the moment arrives.

After desperate long-shot searches in Gratzi and the Icehouse—high-end joints where Emily wouldn't spend her own money, and the puppy doesn't have a dime—he decides to take a seat in the Old Town and wait it out. He knows that when she's out on the town she has to move, that by running he could miss her forever but if he stays still she will come to him, drawn in by the four bars that are the base camps of her migrations.

He orders a neat Scotch with a water back, the latter used to down five hundred milligrams of Motrin, plus three aspirin for good measure. On the walls are pictures of long-gone graduating classes, the wide-skirted nurses of 1907, the high-collared engineers of 1913. John Lee Hooker is on the stereo and Mercer is not sure if it's the music or the Scotch or the sight of the smoke under the tin-plated ceiling, but his mind wanders, first to Sam Cottleburn's portfolio—unfinished business at work—and then, now and always, to baseball, to Triple-A ball, where Don Bailey tried to teach him the split-finger, and when that didn't take as it should have, the spitter. Mercer hadn't much been interested—it was an illegal pitch—but in two afternoons Bailey had him dropping the ball off the table, squeezing the ball out with Vaseline and K-Y, and watching it move as he'd never seen a pitch move. Mercer always had heat and a good slider, and a curve and change-up that set up those pitches if he could remember to subtract on the slow stuff, throw with hard motion and slow speed. It took a patience of mind and spirit to beat the batter not with power but with the batter's own overuse of it. This was always hard for Mercer to do and still is, because the satisfaction of watching a hitter, even a George Brett or Jim Rice, jump out of his uniform trying to hold back a swing that cannot be held back was and is never as great—for Mercer—as the simple unadulterated feeling of joy and power of throwing the ball by somebody. Anybody.

"You got the stuff," Bailey told him as he threw. "And, you're a college guy. A smart guy. But being smart and being smart at baseball are two different things. Smartness in baseball is strength, strength to subtract, to change up, go slow, go fast. Strength to do what it takes. That was good motion, now squeeze it harder . . . nice."

Mercer caught the ball as it came back from the catcher. He felt weird, like he didn't want the catcher to know he was learning the spitter. "Even cheat?" he asked.

"Cheat? Hell, cheating is a baseball tradition. You get away with what you can get away with. You think Gaylord Perry stays awake at night worrying about his soul? No, and I'll tell you why. In baseball, cheating ain't cheating. It ain't cheating till you get caught. You're supposed to cheat. That's why they got umpires, to make sure you're good at it. You want to make the show or not?"

He did, and he did make it, briefly, and he might have stayed if he had mastered better the art of concealment. He simply was not good at loading the ball, and as such was scared to death, in front of all those people, the professional umpires, the television cameras, to throw a spitter. He used it twice. It worked both times, but the fear it caused him wasn't worth it, at least not at the time. Only later did he see that his career had slipped away, not for lack of talent or even desire, but for something worse, the thing that every athlete fears most: a lack of guts.

Later, much later, after two more Scotches and another round of analgesics and a turn of all but the most diehard tables, after David Bromberg gave way to Lyle Lovett, who gave the air to

10,000 Maniacs, who faded into Chet Baker, when the only drinkers left were there not to pick or be picked up, not to jostle with friends or laugh at bad jokes or eat bar food but only to sit over drinks, with smoke hanging four feet below the tin ceiling and six feet from the wooden floor, then Emily strolls into the bar with a pouch of tobacco in her hand and her friend Barb in tow. Emily almost passes Mercer's table, then spots him and turns a square corner, like a cadet, and sits as if she knew all along that this is just where he'd be. Barb, long hair covering her face, starts for one of the free chairs, changes her mind and goes for the other, then changes her mind again and sits.

"Hi!" says Emily. She pulls out a small box of papers and starts to roll a cigarette.

Mercer says the obligatory hellos, to Emily, to Barb, his attention all the while on Emily. She is wearing a thin scarf about her shoulders. The scarf is a barely sufficient cover for her breasts, which are pushing, urgently it seems to Mercer, against a white singlet.

"We've been looking for you," Emily says.

"You have? I thought there was an emergency."

"There was. Barb broke up with her boyfriend."

"Sorry 'bout that, Barb," Mercer says, having had no idea that Barb had had one boyfriend of whom she could have claimed possession.

"So," Emily is saying, "she's all ready to meet this Mr. Right you got locked up in some attic in Detroit."

"C'mon, Em," Barb protests.

"Hair of the dog that bit ya," Emily says. She turns to Mercer. "What have you been doing? You look lonely."

"Sittin' and drinkin', drinkin' and sittin'," Mercer says. He wants to ask where the puppy is, but it's taboo.

"Getting a jump on the hangover?" She points to Mercer's pills.

"My arm."

"You win today?"

"Why, yes." He hears the surprise in his own voice. Emily has never asked about baseball. He tells them about James, about his now-disfigured face.

The waitress comes over, announces last call, gets no takers. Mercer promises Emily and Barb a ride. When Barb excuses herself, Emily stays at the table, a quality Mercer finds endearing, that she does not run off to the bathroom with other women.

"Come back to my place," Mercer says.

"Oooo," she teases. "An order."

"I've got others."

"I know."

"Is that a yes?"

"Do your girls ever say no?"

"What girls?"

She smiles at him. She won't tell him what she knows, probably nothing. He is careful, very careful.

Outside the air is warm. The women walk ahead of Mercer, and the swaying, his head full of Scotch and Motrin and the smell of exhaust and trees and the click of the women's heels on the pavement, it all fills him with desire for Emily. He is possessed with it, with the kind of animal spirits he has felt since he was a teenager, when all that was good and desirous in the world came to him as a woman. He can't wait to get her home, to roll about his bed, to test wits and trade quips, to feed his own desire by satisfying hers. "You're not selfish," she'd told him the first time, and why should he be? The whole point was not to do this alone. The memory of that night he can call up at will. Not selfish. He wants to get to a place with Emily where selfishness would be impossible.

"So how 'bout next Friday?" Mercer suggests when he drops Barb off at her home, a tall, cement, Soviet-style high-rise a stone's throw from the Huron.

"Can't. Going home for the Fourth. The next week."

"Done," Mercer says. He steps on the gas pedal and the BMW squeals out of the parking lot. It takes five minutes to travel along the Huron, cross a bridge, and ascend the glacier-made riverbank to his neighborhood. They enter Mercer's house through the side door. Their shoes and Emily's scarf hit the floor there, in the mudroom, the singlet in the next room (the kitchen), Mercer's golf shirt in the living room, pants left for the bedroom. It isn't long till Emily's laughter fills the house, till Mercer is gently running his left hand (attached as it is to his good arm) up and down her side, feeling the skin tighten, waiting for the second time. Even after that, he knows it's not enough.

"Aren't you tired?" she asks.

"Not of this."

She chuckles.

Later, they lie still. He looks over at her, her eyes closed, half her bangs dark and damp against her forehead, lips curled into a faint smile. The vein in her neck is pencil-thick and beating.

"I'm starving," he says, realizing that he has not eaten since the morning.

"So get something to eat." Eyes closed, smile still there.

"Let's go out. There's no food here."

"It's the middle of the night, Ben."

"Silverman's is open."

"Go." She rolls on her side, meaning he can go without her. He nuzzles in, prods. She tells him to go away, but ten minutes later they are again in the BMW, racing toward the Howard Johnson's by Hog Back Road, then pulling into the delicatessen next door, its booths filled with teenagers drawn there not by hunger or thirst but a desire not to go home. Mercer feels their eyes on him and Emily as he follows her to the table. He is aware of his age, that he is old, and he is briefly uncomfortable about it.

Settled in the booth, with the bounce of the cushion beneath him, his good elbow on the table, Emily looking disinterestedly at the menu, he realizes that he likes his situation, mostly, that he has done well with his life, made good and necessary decisions, that he can trust his instincts. And right now his instincts tell him to tell Emily that he loves her, but he checks them. Luckily, the waitress appears. He orders a club sandwich, french fries, a dinner salad, a bowl of soup, extra rolls, and coffee. Emily orders coffee.

"Big appetites tonight," she says.

"Why don't we agree not to see anyone else," he says.

"Are you seeing someone else?"

"Nothing serious."

Her lips turn down, then her mouth goes hard. "You're seeing someone else?"

"*You're* seeing someone else," he says.

"That's different," she says. "And you know about it. You've known about it from the beginning."

"Why does that make it okay?"

"It's different. It's not—" She leans over the table and whispers, "It's not like it is with us."

"You don't sleep with him?"

She shrugs.

"I have nothing like this," he says.

"That's different."

"It's not different," he insists.

"It is," she says. "You pick up some stranger on the street. That's different. I've known Doug for six years. We're friends. I can't just drop him away. It would devastate him."

"What about what it's doing to me?"

"You're so much stronger than he is. And *you're* screwing around."

She looks as if she's about to bolt from the table, but she stays in her seat. And now Mercer realizes she won't go anywhere without him. It's a long walk home, and in her own fashion Emily is a very practical girl.

"I mean," Emily says, "I don't see how you could even want anyone else. If what you say is true, how could you?"

"I don't see how you could want anyone else."

"I don't."

"Well, then, what about the puppy?"

"I explained that to you!" She pauses. "And I told you not to call him that. You think you can have whatever you want, however you want. I'm sick of it."

"I'm sick of it, too," he says. "I don't see how you can go out with someone else and expect me not to react to it."

"You make it sound like we stay up boffing the whole goddam night."

"Maybe you'd like to say that louder, so they can hear it in the kitchen, too."

"Don't change the subject," Emily says.

"How do I know what you do?"

"Doug is like family. I don't expect you to understand. You can't just walk away from family."

"You don't sleep with family."

"It's not like with us," she says.

"Stop seeing him. Just stop."

"You're so selfish."

"That's not being selfish! I'm talking about loyalty."

"So am I!"

She screams this line so loudly that Mercer is sure everyone in the restaurant—the boys in their Ypsilanti letter jackets, the young smokers in black, the two waitresses, the line cook whose head can be seen through a slit in the wall, the unseen dishwasher—is looking at them. He keeps his eyes on Emily, who is staring at her silverware, the line of her jaw hard and pulsing from clenched teeth.

"Look, Em," he says. He reaches out to touch her.

"Don't touch me." She jumps up from the table, almost knocks over the waitress, who has just delivered the salad and soup. "Take me home," Emily says.

Mercer fishes in his pocket for a twenty-dollar bill. The waitress is back suddenly, this time with the sandwich and fries. He drops the money on the food-laden table as she places the sandwich where he would have been. She looks at him as though he's done something incredibly stupid, and he feels that look on his back as he walks for the door.

They drive in silence to Emily's street, where there is life, as though it were early evening. Mercer sees students sitting on their front porches and steps, beer bottles set at their feet like so many bowling pins. Music floats out the various windows, the high fidelity no doubt chipping more paint, crumbling foundations. Emily jumps from Mercer's car and runs inside. Back in his home, the house and his stomach empty, Mercer stands in his kitchen, pulls out a paper plate, stares into his fridge. He could cook something up, but decides against it. He wonders what Emily is doing, then goes to the television and puts on a game, tape-delayed from the Coast.

XVI

Gil knows he should be asleep, but instead he is sitting up in bed watching a replay of a game between Houston and San Francisco. Expansion cities. He would rather watch teams that existed before he did, before television—Detroit and Cleveland, Cincinnati and Chicago—when New York could support three teams and Boston (imagine it!) two. This is silly, he knows, just more of that odd sense of nostalgia that seems to affect all baseball devotees by the time they are, say, eight years old. In truth he doesn't care all that much about pro ball, unless one of his guys is playing. He'll watch California all night on the chance that Bobby Greco will pinch-hit. And that, he knows, is a kind of nostalgia, too.

During the commercials he picks up the day's scorebook and goes box by box through the entire doubleheader. The team has played well and is capable of better. It is a fine team, full of skill and promise, and if he holds it right, keeps them together, playing for each other, they can go all the way. All the way. That's all he wants. One time. That, and that his father will live to see it.

JULY

I

James pictures the team driving south. They are probably at the border now, heading over the line into Ohio, where the Dayton tournament is played, where people on parole can't go. James even asked his parole officer just this week if maybe some exception could be made, and the guy looked up through his shaggy hair and for the first time, James realized, really looked at him, at the person and not the problem, and said nothing with his mouth and everything with his eyes. And so here James is now, alone, on a long, long weekend, sitting at his table wearing Koch and Sons shorts, a Koch and Sons T-shirt, and a pair of white sanitary socks. Saturday, quarter to eight in the morning.

He has allotted himself ten dollars for the day and twenty-five for the full holiday weekend. Fun money. He will ride the bus—the bus, here in Birmingham, the money suburb in car country, where only black domestics from Detroit and white people on the margin ride the bus—out to the batting cage at Koch and Sons' home field in Pontiac, then come back, catch a late breakfast at the Edsel diner, where he'll linger over the sports page—people leave papers lying around, that's forty-five cents saved—and then home to catch a game or two on the tube. He has been working for the school district, repairing play swings, lining ball fields, spraying weed killer. Each day brings the slow accretion of money—five and a quarter an hour, a fortune he thought at first, though Gil must still give him a hundred a month toward the rent—and a constant daylight reminder of one night in the past. I was crazy then, he tells himself. This is meant to calm him, to mean that he is not crazy now, that he is in control. He needs to be in control, wants desperately to stay on this side, the light side, where people give you money and like you because you can hit, where you can lie around after work or go out for a walk—out for a walk!—and smell the trees and watch the girls drive by in their late-model cars and no one can tell you otherwise.

He decides to shadow-swing in front of his mirror, two hundred times, for warm-up. He begins, but the sight of his eye still badly swollen, the eye seeing but not visible behind the purple, makes him stop to consider himself. Bruise excepted, he looks no different now, really, from five years before, except that somehow he is seasoned, harder-looking, and he is not displeased with this conclusion. But he is anxious, stuck at home without anything to do for a whole three-day weekend, his ball team in the midst of competition. He spent five years dreaming of baseball. It kept him alive inside the walls. Focused. Everyone needs a reason to live, and it was as good a reason as any.

What bothers him now, then, is that he has dreamed of days like today, shiftless Saturdays when he can just hang out and not answer to anyone, not worry about getting the stuffing beat out of him, days in which he can just live. But all he can think about is baseball and getting back to it. He starts to practice, pictures the ball and takes a swing, hears the sound of the air cut by the bat, a quick puff, like a short breath. He is hungry and feels like skipping the warm-up and the long bus ride to the cage, but he knows he will go. "Concentrate," he says aloud. He swings and swings, dreaming of being so good that everyone everywhere will know his name.

II

"Okay," Vince says. "Let me see you load it."

"What?"

Mercer gives him a look of denial, raised eyebrows, as though he has no inkling what Vince is talking about.

"Load it, throw it. But with deception, like in a game."

"Vince, I don't know what you're talking about."

A squinted look of innocence. Behind him wavy heat lines rise off the outfield. It's even hotter here in Dayton than it was in Detroit. When Vince can get a breath it feels as if he is swallowing a blowtorch. He watches the sweat drip down Mercer's face, notices the matted hair on Mercer's forearms.

Vince forces raspy words up into the heat. "Load it, throw it. I know you heard me. I want to see more."

Mercer stares. A long time.

"I'm not prepared to load it. I'd have to go to the dugout."

"Go then. Don't let anyone see, especially the big guy."

Vince knows Gil won't like it, would not let his pitchers throw spitters. He's a by-the-book kind of guy. Mean and surly at times, a real terror, dies to win, a real organizer and general, but a Harry Hairshirt, too.

Mercer returns, hitches his pants, throws.

"Very nice," Vince says. "Where'd you learn that?"

"Triple-A. Makes me nervous."

"Why?"

"Getting caught, I guess."

"Where else you load from, 'sides your pants?"

"Besides my pants?"

"You need a few spots. Try the wrist there, by your glove. Maybe right on your shoulder, like you're loosening your jersey. Use the pitch only on the good hitters. With them, don't save it. Get ahead with it. Get 'em worrying. You can beat them with your other stuff. Let 'em see it, though. Okay, let's see it again."

Mercer loads and throws. Another big drop, all at the end. A money pitch.

"Why you wincing?" Vince asks. "Your arm sore?"

"No. I'm fine."

"That pitch will get people out."

"I know."

"Okay, then. Get together with your catchers and that's all. Don't tell anyone else. That means no one on the team. Not Jefferson, not Kohn, nobody, even if you think you can trust 'em. They'll figure it out, at least some will, but don't ever admit it. It's better for them if it's an unspoken thing, so they can pretend it's not there. And don't let Gil know, whatever you do."

Mercer nods. He's a smart kid.

In the first inning, Mercer strikes out the side. From what Vince can tell, he used the pitch twice. When he comes back to the dugout he looks at Vince, holds his eyes just long enough to say, Hey, it's working.

"Way to work. Way to look out there," Gil barks, oblivious.

Gil. Vince breaths his name, a strain in the heat. Gil. Doesn't seem to know if I'm alive anymore. Never calls, never asks me to do anything. Now I'm going to make him a winner. That he'll notice. He'll thank me for that.

Vince thinks back to a couple winters in Cuba, '51 and '52, figuring out how to squeeze the ball and get people out, how for one glorious winter he pitched like a big leaguer, all on the basis of a pitch that no one had thrown legally since 1919. That was the year they fixed the World Series. One game Vince took into the bottom of the ninth, ahead by one with a no-hitter on the line. The other team had only Cubans and they were screaming all day at the umpire, who wouldn't even give them the benefit of looking at the ball. Vince's catcher would throw the ball back so gobbed up with grease that it was hard to throw a straight fastball. Still, the umpire did nothing. It was that way in Cuba then. Well, the last batter was their best hitter, a huge man with skin the color of an old penny. Vince threw him a spitter on the first pitch and the guy almost broke his back swinging at it. Then he rushed the mound. Vince still has nightmares about it, 240 pounds of rage rushing at him, the sixty feet six inches from home plate collapsing into a couple of strides, Vince ducking and rolling forward, a cross-body block, and the benches emptying, and the stands, too. Vince got twenty-seven stitches in his leg from being spiked in the melee. They sent him home that way, with credit for the win but not the no-hitter, and he never played organized ball again. He was thirty-one then, and still hadn't made the bigs, knew he wouldn't, though usually he tried not to think about it. No one likes to think about the end. Baseball was and still is full of people who stay too long. Vince was younger then than Mercer is now, and not in nearly as good shape. He figures that the spitball bought him two seasons. There's very little in life or baseball that can buy that kind of time. There was also the art of deception, the thrilling rush of getting away with something.

He loved the spitter. Still does.

III

The sky out the driver's side window is a fading glow as Gil's Continental scoots across the border, past the sign welcoming him to his home state and another advising him to SAY YES! TO MICHIGAN. It is late on Monday, the nation's birthday, and traffic northbound is light. People from Michigan tend not to vacation in Ohio. Gil seems to remember reading, back when he was a boy in Jackson, that the two states had actually once gone to war, though tonight, cruising the highway, he finds this hard to believe.

He passes signs for Blissfield, Temperance, Tecumseh; he is aiming north now, but also west, to Jackson, to visit his father. The old man is still in the hospital, with pneumonia, it turns out. The doctors keep promising to send him to Mapleshade, then change their minds. The Medicare bills are outrageous. The out-of-pocket expenses are adding up. Just this past

Thursday Gil had to hire a private nurse, his father was complaining so, causing so much disruption on the floor. There's money, though—that's not the problem. What bothers Gil is going to the hospital. He hates hospitals, hates their sounds and smells, hates the utter helplessness of the patients, hates not knowing the intricacies of the rules, hates the blasé way the staff treats illness. Last Friday he drove all the way out after work, more than four hours round-trip. The whole visit his father never woke up. On his way to his car, Gil passed a man bent over on a bench. He held his head up with the heels of his hands placed over his eyes. Doubled over in grief. Gil doesn't like to see that, either. He is ready, he thinks, for his father's illness, but he needs an outcome. If it's death, okay. The man is ninety-eight years old. If it's not death, great. Let's get him home.

Gil stops at a filling station by Milan, parks at the full-serve pump, and changes out of his uniform in the rest room while the attendant pumps the gas. He then stands on the station's brightly lit tarmac with the uniform rolled into a ball and held under his arm. He listens to the buzz of the enormously high road sign and wonders why he isn't happier.

Gil often thinks of himself as a reasonably happy man. Sure, he wants to go out a winner and he wishes he were wealthier (who doesn't?), and his father can drive him up a wall even when the old man is unconscious with a tube down his throat, but he's not dying (like Vince; please God, make that happen fast and easy) or poor (like Vince) or driven to insanity (like that guy Clement, who busted a screw and tried to shoot his son-in-law, and couldn't even do that right). Gil has few regrets. He wishes he knew Rick better. Any man would be happy to have a man like Rick as a son, a handsome, professional man, someone successful and at ease in the world. The kind of son Morris wanted. Gil remembers a visit he made to Morris when Morris still lived in the home where he'd lived with Gil's mother, a home with pink carpeting and plastic slipcovers. Rick had just passed the Illinois bar. Gil and Morris were just sitting without speaking, as they often did, when Morris let out a deep, satisfied sigh. "Well," he said. "At least Rick is a lawyer." For Morris this was, and is, enough, but Gil wants to know Rick, wants to know what he does at his job and what he does for fun; wants to know why Rick has had so many girlfriends but never found one to marry. Gil would like to share a laugh with Rick about old times, which they never do because Laurence still lurks in the past and this makes laughter difficult.

Gil tells himself to brighten up. He tells himself he's just won the Dayton tournament against stiff competition, and easily at that, without his best hitter. The baseball season is only half over. He should feel like a guy who's just gone four for four and will face the same pitcher again.

"Cash or credit?" the attendant asks, having walked over to Gil, who didn't hear the approach. Gil hands over his credit card.

The old man seems to be shrinking with every visit, but probably it's just that the equipment is growing. There are machines for IVs and EKGs, an oxygen tank, and two gizmos Gil can't name. Morris is awake. He lifts a hand, as if to say, Oh, it's you.

"Hi, Dad."

A nod.

"How are things?"

"Water," he says. He looks over at his side table, where a Styrofoam cup sits, a straw bent out of it like a wilted flower stem.

Gil takes the cup and leans over the bed, reaches through the tubes and hookups, holds the cup even as his father grasps it, helps him steady the straw and guide it to his shriveled mouth. He sees his father's throat bob. He watches the water descend, is filled with the horror of life up close. The old man takes another sip, then releases the cup and leans back into his pillow with a loud exhalation.

"Well, Dad, it's July Fourth," Gil says. He turns to put the cup back on the side table. "We won today. A big tournament."

Nothing.

"Dad?"

Gil leans close, convinced suddenly that somehow, while he has turned briefly away, his father has died. Slipped away through inattention. Panic again clamps down on his stomach and lungs, and he must breathe with conscious effort. Then he notices the EKG line bouncing along, its beeping faint but clear. The old man is not dead. He's asleep.

When Gil walks from the hospital entrance into the night a bomb seems to explode above his head. The sky lights up with color. Fireworks. This is Jackson, where things are still a bit less cynical, where people take the Fourth very seriously. There was no doubt a humdinger of a parade, many picnics and cookouts, several ball games, and now this. Gil thinks again of his father's death, how he's now lived it once, of the panic it brought on not from a fear of death but because there's still so much to work out with his father. Gil thinks of Rick, of how little he knows of his own son's life. Gil wants to tell Rick that the past is okay, that his father is proud of him, that all the arguments about long hair and respect and the way to dress mean nothing. Yes, Gil wants to talk with his son. It's after ten. Rick is in Chicago. That's only a couple hours away, and besides, Chicago is on central time, an hour earlier. It's not that late at all.

IV

"You look distracted," Sylvia says. "I mean, more distracted than normal."

"I'm a distracted kinda guy."

"Like hell. You were very concentrated about fifteen minutes ago."

Mercer throws a leg out from under the sheet. "You, too," he says.

"Still am, Ben. What's up?"

"Lots of stuff. All of it boring. I always thought I'd have a more exciting life."

"Travel to exotic places? Fame, fortune?"

"Quixotic romances."

She doesn't know the word, he's sure of it, but she won't give him the satisfaction of asking its meaning. All the while Mercer feels himself compelled to move on. His mind speaks: You've got to get out of here. There are no supporting reasons, nothing waiting for him that won't wait till the morning.

"Where are you going?" Sylvia asks.

"Got to get home."

"Spend the night."

"I can't."

"Why not?"

"I got things that need to get done. The boring stuff."

"At eleven-thirty at night?"

He nods.

"C'mon, Ben. That's so lame. Stay."

"I can't."

"Why don't you ever want to spend the whole night?"

"It's nothing personal, Sylvia. I just got to get certain things done."

"Like what? Like *what?*"

"Well, the first of the month was days ago, and I still haven't had the chance to pay bills. Got a stack of 'em waiting for me at home."

Mercer watches Sylvia pout, thinks, Did I really say that?

"You're going home to pay bills?"

There is a long silence, during which Mercer calculates just how quickly he can get the rest of his clothes on.

"Stay gone," she says at last.

He drives east on I-94, stops for gas at the Shell station by Dexter—thinks, What a country, you can buy gas at midnight on

July Fourth—then enters Ann Arbor just past the split with M-14, by Varsity Ford. Traffic is light. He easily finds a parking space on Main Street, walks over to the Old Town, but it's closed, so he moves a block north to the Del Rio. The streets are calm; people seem to be heading home, the holiday stretched till it broke, time sliding now into the work week. He is carded at the door, one of the Del Rio's quaint moves. Inside Mercer checks the specials board. It advertises a Mexican tempeh burger and carrot soup. He hates the granola-head aspects of this bar. People wear tie-dye here, and it is perhaps one of the last places on earth where people talk earnestly, even reverently, about socialism. On the other hand, right now they are playing Stevie Ray Vaughn on the tape deck and they serve Dos Equis. These are two good reasons to stay. A third is that they're still open.

He needs to ice his arm. He pitched the first game today, gave up just three hits, one of them a seeing-eye dog that slipped past Goodstein's left and Metz's right. Another was a Texas Leaguer that landed in front of Jefferson. The third was a rope. Mercer used the spitter once or twice an inning, which was all he needed it. Everything is going well now for him on the field, except the soreness in his arm. It just won't go away. He pops a Motrin, washes it down with beer. He feels he's running now on borrowed time, that any day he's going to wake up with a cantaloupe growing out of his right elbow and that will be it for his pitching career. Then what? I'm only thirty-four, he thinks to himself. Where's that exciting life?

———

Around one Emily walks into the bar. Mercer is not surprised. Now that he thinks about it, it's surprising she hasn't appeared earlier. She seems intent on ignoring him, but he sees her and she him, and now she is caught, caught by his eyes. She sits next to him at the bar. He gives her credit for this. It takes a certain kind of courage. They trade two quick, hard "hi's," as boxers trade jabs.

"You treated me badly," she says.

"I was feeling aggrieved myself."

"You lied to me."

"Let's not do a tit-for-tat."

"What then?"

"Emily, I never wanted to fight."

"Why are you alone?"

"Why are you?"

"I'm not. I'm meeting Doug."

"Well, well," Mercer says. He feels a surge of anger.

"I'm not mad at you," she allows, as if this were noble. The bartender finally ambles over. She orders a Bushmills.

"Me neither."

"I miss coming over to your house. Late at night."

"That's a hell of a thing to say," Mercer says, missing it, too.

"I also miss your reactionary views. And Barb wants to do that double date. So I told her I'd make up with you."

Mercer thinks, Right. "That's mighty kind of you," he says.

"She wants to meet him."

"He just got out of prison, you know. For murder."

"Passion crime. Impulsive," Emily says. She reaches for her drink. Mercer watches her lips as she sips at the tiny glass.

"How do you know that?"

"Barb called him today."

"I never gave you the number."

"No, but the name. He's listed." She stares at him. "You've just been with a woman."

"Emily, c'mon."

"I can tell. Either that or you haven't showered since your last game, but that's not like you. Also, your lips are swollen."

"My elbow is swollen."

Okay, Mercer thinks, lesson learned. Shower before going out into public. Probably it's a lucky guess, anyway. He watches as Emily rolls a cigarette; the music changes to Bonnie Raitt. And then the puppy is upon them, a droopy smile and a big soft paw held limp for an introductory shake.

"What's your name again?" asks the puppy.

"Ben Mercer."

The puppy pulls up a bar stool so that he's wedged between Emily and Mercer. His light brown hair is loosely and badly cut, giving as a first impression a state of dishevelment, something that his untucked T-shirt and Bermuda shorts and old leather sandals do nothing to dispel. Mercer looks down and even in the darkness he can see tufts of hair sprouting out of each toe.

There is a bit of small talk and then Mercer asks the puppy what he does, as in for a living. Mercer knows there's an edge to the question. It's meanness, but he can't help himself. It's not always bad to give in to your urges.

"I work at the Daily Grind. The coffee shop." He lifts his voice on the words "coffee shop," as if he's not sure if they are adequately descriptive.

"He's a painter," Emily says.

"Houses?" Mercer asks, to chide. Emily works in an art gallery; he knows what she means when she says "painter."

"Art," she says, glaring.

"You ever sell any of this art?"

"He's very good, Ben. He's won awards."

"Oh yeah?"

"In college," the puppy admits.

"He's very good," Emily says.

"So you haven't sold any?"

"Once, for like fifty bucks."

"You don't paint for the money," Emily says.

"I didn't say you did." Mercer looks at Emily, thinks, Hey, I know all about dedicating your life to things that don't pay. I also know about dilettantes, fakes, fear, indolence.

"If the world's ever going to get better," Emily says, "then people will have to do things for reasons other than money."

"I wouldn't be too hopeful," Mercer says.

The bartender is back. "Another Dos Equis?"

"Absolutely."

"I'll have one, too," says the puppy.

"So what do you paint?" Mercer asks.

"People."

"People?"

"Yeah, people. Portraits."

"Why?"

"Every painting tells a story, if you do it right. I try to tell people's stories."

"You talk to them first?"

"Well, some I know. Sometimes I use models, when I have the money."

"If you don't know the models, how do you tell their stories?"

"It's not a word story I'm telling."

Mercer sips his beer, thinks, This guy ought to paint himself. That would be a wordless story.

"He does great nudes," Emily says.

"Aha." Mercer tries to put down the fire rising up in his belly with a swig of beer.

"I do more with clothes," says the puppy.

"How long are you going to serve coffee for a living?"

"I don't know. I'm hoping for a painting career."

"Hope is futile," Mercer says.

"Sure," says Emily. "'The hopelessness of it all.' I suppose now you're going to bring up van Gogh. Everyone does at this point in the conversation."

"I like van Gogh," Mercer says, "but I wasn't thinking of him."

"You don't hope for things?" the puppy asks.

"God, do I hope for things. I'm just saying it's futile."

"So why hope?"

"It's weakness. I can't help it," Mercer admits.

"I guess that's why I paint."

All three pause for a drink.

"Are you Emily's boyfriend?" Mercer asks.

"Yeah, I guess. Are you?"

"No. What do you mean, you guess?"

"Ask Emily. You never know with her."

"Well, Emily?"

"Of course you are," she says to the puppy.

Mercer can't tell if the puppy is coy or uncertain.

"What do you do?" the puppy asks.

"I'm a stockbroker."

"Hey, that's great."

"It is?" Emily says.

"Yeah, I love stocks."

"You do?" Mercer asks.

"Yeah, I keep a paper portfolio. I mean, when I get some money, I'll invest for real."

"What's in your portfolio?"

"Ford, Microsoft, Norwest, Citicorp, uh, the Gap, I got them, and Wal-Mart. Also, Intel and AMD, and a company called Burwell-Craine Financial."

"What do they do?"

"A bank. They've got this business of making loans for used cars to people with bad credit. Charge 'em twenty-five percent a year, or more. Plus, they get a guarantee fee from the used-car dealers, plus they get a set of keys. You don't pay, they take your car. People, they need their cars to get to work. So they make that car payment first, before they feed their kids or pay the rent, anything. Really low defaults, unreal profits."

"That's disgusting," Emily says.

"Spell 'Burwell-Craine,'" Mercer says. "Is it a Nasdaq stock?" He writes the name on a napkin.

"Last call," the bartender says. No one wants another drink. Mercer throws down a twenty to cover the bill.

Mercer lies in bed, lights off, and listens to the crickets grind outside his open window. His elbow is wrapped in ice. The phone rings.

"It's me." Emily.

Mercer thinks, *Yes.* He asks her what's on her mind.

"Do you want to see me, or what?"

"Em, it's the middle of the night. I've got to be at work in four and a half hours."

There is a long pause. Emily is breathing.

"Ben?"

"Yeah?"

"Take a shower."

"Yeah?"

"Then come get me."

Another pause. He feels the old feeling coming back.

"Ten minutes," he says, and cuts the line.

V

Cutting across northern Indiana, Gil sees four lanes of semi-trucks, an industrial wasteland of warehouses, billboards for fast food, nearby rooms, cheap gas. Suddenly Gil finds himself driving through a rock quarry, a work crew digging under enormous lights. Day or night, it hardly matters here.

He cruises north, up on a causeway, the smell of Gary behind him, Lake Michigan to his right, Chicago ahead. The city comes into view, miles and miles of lights, an electric grid. Gil sees the movement of cars, feels as if he's part of a giant electrical circuit.

Rick lives in a high-rise along Lake Shore Drive. It is now after midnight, and the streets, to Gil's amazement, are filled. He cannot remember the last time he was up this late intentionally. There is a little Toyota in front of him, a Nissan to his right, a rusted Dodge van, circa 1975, to his left. Where do all these people have to go at one o'clock on a Monday night?

Gil parks and walks into the building, a large white slab among other large white slabs, with lots of glass down below and a jungle of potted plants in the lobby. The security guard is watching a sitcom on television. He calls upstairs, sends Gil on his way. Rick meets him in the hallway, at the elevator door.

"What's wrong?"

"Nothing."

"Dad?"

"I need to talk to you. But nothing is wrong. Nothing's an emergency."

They walk down the long hallway, to Rick's door, and enter. Gil looks across Rick's living room to the window, sees the black expanse of Lake Michigan broken in the distance by the long lights of what must be an iron ore tanker. Gil thinks of ore, steel, cars. The natural order of things around here, a process to live by. He is comforted by the idea that he is part of it. He notices now that the room is draped with legal papers. They cover the coffee table, the arms of the sofa, lie spread out on the grayish carpet as though a bunch of lawyers have been playing cards with them, and all have just laid down their hands. Two long-stemmed lamps throw light at the ceiling from opposite sides of the couch. The room feels shadowy.

"Have I interrupted you?" he asks his son.

"Client meeting tomorrow. Boning up. This"—he sweeps his hand to include the papers, the living room, maybe even the view—"is the lawyer's equivalent of a batting cage."

"They make you work this late at night? On July Fourth?"

"That's the law, Dad. No rest for the wicked."

"I'm proud of you."

"For what?"

"For working hard. For all you've accomplished."

"Well, thanks, Dad. You didn't always feel that way."

"I did. I should have told you."

"How's Gramps?" Rick asks. "You haven't come all this way to tell me he's died, have you?"

"No, he's still alive. I don't know, though. He should be getting better, but he's not. I think something else is wrong."

"Worn-out parts, maybe. What do the doctors say?"

"Nothing. Even when they talk, they say nothing."

The phone rings. Rick answers, a cordless.

"Uh-huh," he says. "Got it. Been there, done that. . . . Got that, too. . . . Hey, counselor, I've done this before. In fact, I do this every day." He laughs. "Sleep is for the weak. See you in the morning." The phone beeps as he turns it off.

"Who was that?"

"The other project head on this case. A real worrywart."

"Sweats the details?"

"That's what lawyers do, Dad. But this guy, he sweats about the sweating. We're done, though. Besides, it's only a client meeting."

Gil wonders if Morris found his own life as mysterious as Gil finds Rick's. Gil remembers when Rick told him he was going to law school. Don't do it, Gil had advised. It seemed to Gil a dirty profession, like banking, yet even less useful. It never ceased to amaze Gil how impressed people would be when he'd say, yes, Rick is doing well, he's an attorney in Chicago. And he is doing well, if you consider working this late at night doing well.

Rick is shuffling papers, neatening up. Gil watches. He thinks he can see his son's mind through the arrangement of things, how he's organizing each idea. Or maybe not. Rick was always a bright kid, too bright for his parents.

"Dad, you know who I've been thinking about lately?"

"Who?"

"Laurence."

"What about him?"

"We never got to see how he turned out. For me, it was like one day he just went away, then all hell broke loose. I spent the next few years thinking sooner or later he'd come back and everything would go back to normal. I mean, you're that age, you know about death, but you don't know."

"I was at the grave a few weeks ago."

"And?"

"Just that."

"Why did you come here, anyway?"

"It's hard to explain."

"You should try, Dad. You want something to drink, a beer or anything?"

A beer. Why, yes. Gil is incredibly thirsty. Parched. Yes, Gil nods, a beer. Rick fetches two from his refrigerator. German brew, very cold.

"I didn't think you'd want one," Rick says. "You never do."

"I didn't think I'd want one either. But I do."

"Good. So, why did you come?"

"I was with your grandfather tonight. I was helping him drink some water and then he fell asleep. Except that at first, I thought he died."

"But he's okay. You said so."

"Yes, okay. Okay as he can be. The thing was, when I left I realized that when I thought he was dead it didn't matter much at all. No, that's not how I mean it. It mattered, Lord knows—it will matter to him, especially. What I mean is that there are things between my father and me that are not all right, and if he'd gone tonight they still wouldn't be all right. And I didn't want it to be like that between us, you and me."

"Sure, Dad. But they're not. I mean, I'm 'all right' with you. If that's what you're worrying about."

"I'd like to believe that, son, but I remember how things were."

"What do you mean?"

"When you were growing up, you always seemed so angry. I understand this. When I was a kid, I was angry, too. Your grandparents, they came here with nothing. They just didn't understand what it was like to be a kid here. I didn't want life to be like that for you, but I know it got bad, especially after your mother and I split up. I can understand that."

"Well, Dad, when your brother dies, there's some pressure in that, sure, with the attention and all. There's like this unspoken comparison going on all the time between you and your brother. Except Laurence is dead, so he just gets more perfect as time goes on. But it's not like I blame you or Mom for that. I'm not angry about it. It's just the way it was."

"I could have done things differently. Like when I coached, for example. I always wanted to make sure I wasn't playing favorites and I ended up being harder on you than I was on anyone else. And at home. I should have let you be more. Laurence, too. Laurence, especially. He wasn't as hard-nosed as you. Is this getting through? I could have done better. I'm sorry."

"Dad, I told you, you don't need to be sorry. You've got nothing to be sorry for."

"I could never make your grandfather happy. I didn't want you to feel that about me. I—"

"I don't," Rick says. "I'm not upset about anything. Stop apologizing."

Gil stops. He looks at Rick, at his thick, dark hair (Susan's hair), which is sticking up from his constantly running his hand through it, his one nervous tic. Gil wonders if Rick knows what he is doing. It's not easy to apologize to your adult son for a lifetime of substandard parenting, but Gil feels he owes Rick the apology. Why won't Rick accept it? Gil doubts that Rick doesn't feel that amends need to be made. It's more as if Rick wants to be permanently owed. Gil's stomach feels hollow, the way it does when he tries to reason with Morris. He takes a sip of beer, then a long, slow breath.

"I just want you to know that I'm proud of you," he says. He feels he's allowed to say little else.

"Okay, Dad." Rick adjusts himself on the couch.

Gil knows this move, this change in posture. Something new is coming.

"What's going on with Gramps?" Rick asks. "You think this is it, huh?"

"Could be. He's ninety-eight. How long is he supposed to be able to go on?"

"I don't know. Is he in pain?"

"Maybe. Hard to know, really."

"I should have visited this weekend."

"Don't worry about it."

"Let me know the next time you go."

"It's not for you to worry about. It's also a longer drive for you," Gil says.

"Have you thought about what happens next?"

"Next? He's got a plot next to your grandmother, if that's what you mean."

"Yes, but also, the doctors. Doctors only know one tune. I had a girlfriend once, I tell you, what they put her father through before he died, it was sick. Don't let them do too much."

"Too much?"

"Like operate. The man is old, too old. You think they can operate and he'll be okay? No way. Once they get him hooked up to a bunch of machines, his life is over. You just prolong the pain. Doctors don't seem to care much about that. They think if a heart's beating, it's life."

"So what are you saying I should do?"

"Just make sure he's comfortable. Let him die in peace."

"You think he's going to die?"

"Hey, Dad, I don't know. I've just seen and heard too many horror stories. And the expense. Have you thought of that?"

"I've got supplemental insurance for him, thank God. Plus, he's got money in the bank. As you know."

"If they move him out of the hospital, Medicare stops. Then that money in the bank gets sucked out. Watch it."

"What can I do?" Gil asks.

"Like I said. Keep an eye on those doctors. No heroics."

"It's like I should hope for his death."

"Well," Rick says, "slow death sucks."

There isn't much to say after that, and soon Gil finds himself in Rick's bed. Gil asked to sleep on the couch, but Rick insisted that Gil take the bed. I've got work to do, Rick said, take my room, I'll sleep out here. After a half hour Gil sees the living room lights dim. A half hour after that he's still awake. He stands at Rick's window and tries to take in Chicago. It's funny that Rick lives here. He was most likely conceived here. This was back in '59, two weeks before the wedding. Gil proposed the trip. He and Susan traveled by train, each having left their parents with a story. Gil chuckles now at what you had to lie about in the fifties.

Gil can still remember the excitement of seeing Susan at the old Detroit train station. She wore a red skirt and white blouse, her legs tanned (it was early September), a small overnight bag in her right hand. She spotted Gil, ran to him as fast as the skirt would allow, then threw her arms around him. Her bag got him in the back of the head.

She apologized so strenuously that he wondered if she'd

knocked him out, if he was just coming to without realizing it. No, she was just nervous.

He didn't care. He could see in her eyes that this sort of rendezvous was as new to her as it was to him. He didn't expect her to have the movements down.

On the train they found two seats, stared out the window, talked as the train rolled along. After they pulled out of Flint they went to the dining car, ordered, ate dinner like any married couple. Gil was a manufacturer's rep then, and he had just landed a new account. He was flushed with the excitement of money rolling in. He and Susan had a lease on an apartment in Royal Oak, but he already had his sights on a house.

"Twenty bucks a paycheck. That's all we really need to put away. Twenty bucks a paycheck. Then we'll—"

Susan had grabbed his leg under the table. He looked at her, at her dark eyes and all that dark, slightly curly hair. It surprised him that he hadn't been looking at her when he was talking.

"What?" he asked.

"Tell me about some of the places we'll go, Gil. I want to see the world."

See the world? She'd never mentioned this before. But he was a salesman, and he rose to the occasion.

"Well," he said. "There's Paris, of course. And London. Rome. We'll do them all." He could feel the hand on his knee work its way up his leg.

"Because it's important, Gil. Rome. Can you imagine it? Going to Rome?"

He couldn't. Not that Rome was that exotic. With the navy he'd been to the Philippines, Fiji, Guam, and all over Japan, each stop making him even more eager to go home, or at least someplace with a decent hamburger.

"We've got to do it soon," Susan said. "Before we have kids. Because then it's much harder to go."

Her eyes latched onto his. Those eyes, dark brown, huge, they could compel him to craziness. Suddenly, more than anything, he wanted to see Rome. He wondered if they could put twenty bucks a paycheck away for Rome. Maybe even go next summer, for the Olympic Games. And there was London. And Paris. Like he promised.

"My parents," Susan said, "they went to Rome on their honeymoon."

Gil wondered if his own parents had even had a honeymoon. He couldn't picture his father on a honeymoon. No. As for Gil and Susan, they would take five days in New York City. This was Susan's idea. Gil had agreed immediately, and it was only now, as they continued west, that he realized why: baseball. The idea of going to New York was like a pilgrimage. The place was the capital of baseball, even with the Dodgers and Giants recently departed. The Yankees were there, and what else did you really need? He hoped he could get to a game.

By the time they arrived in Chicago, they felt married. At least Gil did. All the planning and talk of the future had done it. It wasn't till they got to the hotel lobby and Gil signed in as Mr. and Mrs. Davison, for one room, that he felt any tension at all.

The bellhop, dressed in a gray Prussian-style uniform, carried the luggage, two small overnight bags that he held in one hand.

He showed Gil and Susan around their small room as if they couldn't find a light switch or a towel without his help. When Gil tipped him he felt he was really paying the man to leave them alone.

And then they were alone. Gil found himself looking at Susan and feeling a kind of gratefulness. That a woman would choose to spend her life with him: it was amazing, really. He held out his hand—he didn't know what else to do—and she took it, then stepped up on her toes. She kissed him. Then she began to pull at the noose of his tie.

A moment later, in bed, she asked him if he had brought a prophylactic. This was the word she used, and it caught him off guard, the clinical sound of it. He had to admit that he had not. This was new to him, and so his planning had been incomplete. She sighed. "It's a risk, Gil," she said, and he felt defeat slip into the room. But then she pressed her body against his and said, "A risk," by which she meant one they would take. Gil knew his performance was Texas League, at best. There was in life so much to learn. Two months later Susan's doctor set her due date forty weeks from their wedding night, but Rick was born at thirty-eight. They never got to Rome.

VI

Vince stands at his kitchen window and sees the Chalmers boy toss the *Free Press* from his bike into the hedges that run along Vince's house. The kid has a whole driveway to aim for, and even the lawn would be all right, and yet for some reason every day he throws the paper into the shrubs. Vince slides his feet into the loafers he keeps by the front door and walks out into the murky light to retrieve the paper.

Standing now, Vince looks down the block. There are lights on. God, he wishes he were going to work today. Isn't that crazy, he thinks, that I can miss something I hated so?

Inside he sits at his kitchen table and reads the sports page. By the time he finishes with the standings there is full daylight out his window. He wants a cup of coffee, badly now. First, though, he decides to go inside to fetch a cigarette. Later, he'll wake Ellen and get his coffee.

The cigarette is lovely, a clear breath. It is a balmy day already, liable to be another scorcher. He smokes a second, then a third. There is special satisfaction here. In his condition, indulgence is usually difficult. Okay, he decides, coffee. He lumbers inside, brushes his teeth, gargles with mouthwash, goes to the bedroom, and shakes his wife. She is sleeping with the blankets pulled up to her ears.

"Hey," he says. "Time to get up." He pulls down the covers. She tugs them back up. "No, it's not."

"C'mon. Make us some coffee."

"I don't drink coffee."

"You know what I mean."

"For heaven's sake, Vincent. Can't you make your own coffee?"

"Ellen, please. Be reasonable."

"Oh, all right."

Downstairs he sits at the table and reads about Congress. My God, could anything be more boring? Why do they put this on the front page? He moves to the metro section—nothing but murders and robberies here—and then past the three pages that comprise the business section, and then back to sports, which feels like home. He decides to look more closely at the box scores. How many major-league balks were there yesterday? Bide your time, he tells himself. Let her make the coffee, let her cook the eggs, the bacon—you don't have to eat it. Let her slide into the day as she always does. Then you can get her attention.

After his third cup of coffee, with the smell of breakfast still thick, he watches as Ellen allows herself a break, sits at the table, and takes up the metro section, where she'll look up the lottery numbers, something she's never stopped doing, even after Vince refused her money to buy tickets.

"El?" he asks.

"Uh-huh."

"We need to talk about the future."

She looks at him. "The future?"

Look, he wants to say. This is it, the end, kaput. I'm here today, probably gone tomorrow, and you've got to learn a few things or you're gonna starve to death. You're like a Pilgrim now, heading into your first winter in the New World. Faith alone ain't gonna cut it.

Instead, he says, "I don't want you to worry, but you need to prepare for the inevitable. You should learn how this house really operates, prepare to run it."

"I'm prepared and you're doing fine," she says. There is annoyance in her voice, though Vince is not sure if she is mad that he has again brought up this subject or if she just wants to read the metro section without interruption.

"You are not prepared, Ellen. And I'm not fine."

"You are."

"Here, look at these. They're the bills, how they look when they come to the house. That blue one, that's the gas bill. This one's the electric, it's lighter, see? This here is the phone. The paper boy puts his bill in the paper; he'll come to collect if you don't remember to leave a check for him. Now, this here, this is the mortgage book. You rip out one of these pages each month—it's got the date right there—and you send in a check to this address. There are five coupons here. Before you run out of these, they'll send you next year's book. Next year is the last year. When you pay those off, you're free and clear."

"What do you mean?"

"We own the house then."

"No more bank?"

"Nope."

"Isn't that great, Vince?"

"Well, sure. But the important thing is that you make those payments. We wouldn't want to default now, with less than a year and a half to go."

"You just make them, like you always do."

"Ellen, I'm trying to prepare you for when I can't make them. I won't be around to help."

"Don't talk like that."

"Just listen. The insurance company will give you a lot of money. You put it in the bank. The bank will give you interest and you should be able to live on that, if you're careful. Talk to Mr. Sullivan. I've already made plans with him. He'll show you how to do what you've got to do. Don't buy anything you wouldn't buy now, and you should be okay."

Ellen is pouting. Vince hates it.

"I can't, Vince."

"Can't what?"

"Can't do this. It's too much."

"Ellen, paying the bills is too much? C'mon. Collecting interest, which they put in your account automatically? All that's easier than cooking breakfast."

"I like how we have it now."

"I'm going to die, Ellen."

"No."

"Yes."

"No."

"Yes! Try to get that through your skull. I don't have much time."

"Vince, dear, you've got to think positively. Don't let those doctors get you down."

"Please, Ellen. Try to help me."

"You help me. You can't leave. You just can't."

She pouts still more. No, Vince thinks, please no, but there's nothing he can do. First there's a shake, a gasp, one tear, then another, then a stream of them running down her cheek. He hates this, God how he hates this, would do anything to keep her from crying, never feels as impotent and helpless in the world as when his wife lets loose and cries. Helpless. Yeah, he thinks, add it to the list, yet another thing I'm helpless about.

He reaches over, touches her bony shoulder, the thin fabric, his other hand on the kitchen table cover, actually a piece of vinyl from a wholesaler, a scrap Vince picked up on a factory tour. Over on the counter there's a toaster from when they used to give them for opening bank accounts—now, Vince has noticed, it's long distance—an iron skillet, an egg carton. C'mon, Ellen, he thinks, but she says nothing. He feels her shake beneath her hand. C'mon, c'mon, c'mon. Before he got sick it would have been hard to believe she could cry like this over him. If that's what she's doing.

VII

Gil is tired, truly tired. He sits at his desk, a white legal pad before him, and maps out his reasons for wanting to use zinc-coated galvanized steel in the new XR3035. He thinks through the barrier of sleep deprivation—he's had only three hours, after which he drove from Chicago to his house, showered and shaved, and made it to work a little after lunch. Now he has to finish this presentation, which he will give tomorrow. Just get me home, he tells himself. Home to bed, where I can forget about the Japanese. They have a different idea about using galvanized in the 3035. Sure, the galvanized stuff is harder to bend, and the Japanese are very much about bending metal. They're also as stubborn as can be. If they had to drive a few winters in Detroit, what with the salt baths the cars get, they'd understand why the 3035 should have galvanized.

Bob Trany sticks his head into Gil's cubicle. "How's it coming?"

"Okay. But I don't have any new information to put in this thing. We keep repeating the same arguments. How many times are we going to do this?"

"However many it takes." Trany smiles. He's not such a bad boss, has a kid who plays second base out in Sterling Heights. "How's the team this year?" he asks.

"Better than ever."

"I should get out and see a game. You play tonight?"

"Tomorrow."

"Could we reduce the galvanized if we had to?"

"Do we have to?"

"We might. Turns out there's a capacity problem. Might not be enough of the stuff to go around, the 3035 being a high-volume car and all."

"Just once I'd like to win one of these things. Who made the Japanese so goddam smart?"

"The money gods."

"I wouldn't buy one of those little 3035s."

"Then you shouldn't care if it rusts."

"Mazda should."

"We reduce galvanized by twenty percent, what's it do to costs?"

"We save some money, and quality is job two. I'd need a half hour to work up the actual numbers."

"Get your presentation how you want it first. You look beat."

Trany leaves. It's a little after four o'clock. At four-thirty Gil walks to Trany's office, through the maze of cubicles that make up purchasing, slab after slab of gray six-foot partition. Practically every product produced by almost every economy in the world is bought by someone, somewhere, on this floor. Gil is thankful, truly thankful, that he's in steel, not foam or paper supplies. Trany's not in his office. Gil finds his secretary.

"Gone to headquarters," she says.

"When will he be back?"

"He's got a dinner after. You need me to page him?"

"No, it's not that important. I'll catch him in the morning."

A dinner. Gil wonders if he's being left out of something. Trany is young, an up-and-comer, business-school type, worked Ford Europe and Australia. Gil sometimes travels to Ohio and Pennsylvania to visit mills. Once they sent him to Japan and Korea, but he was so jet-lagged and put off by the food and the girls—yes, girls, young western girls hired to spend half the night with the men, in bars, apparently just talking—that he hopes never to have to go again. There's nothing up-and-coming about Gil, and he knows it. If they think about him at all, it's for early retirement.

He's in his cubicle, putting on his coat, when the phone rings. He doesn't answer, and soon Tina, one of the pool secretaries, speaks to him through the intercom.

"Gil?"

"Here."

"Your father, line three."

Gil picks up the receiver, thinking maybe she's got it wrong, that probably it's Vince. But no, that faint, tired-out hello can only belong to his father.

"You're talking on the phone, Dad!"

"If nowadays they do anything else with telephones"—deep breath—"don't tell me."

"You're feeling better."

Gil waits for the answer, listens to the breathing.

"No." A pause. "Not better."

"Yesterday I was there, you couldn't even speak."

More breathing. "You were not here yesterday."

"Dad, I was. I gave you a drink of water. Remember?"

"No."

Of course, no. No credit, even for that. Gil again feels that old anger coming back, the anger of a young boy who just wants to go to practice, of a young man who wants not to be constantly judged and second-guessed, of a man who wants just to be recognized. It's the same rage, through the ages.

"They say I have cancer," the old man whispers.

"Cancer?"

"In the prostate. . . . Maybe it's spreading. Maybe no."

"Spreading? To where?"

"My back." More breathing now, almost a pant. "I have pain there. Oh, my back. You don't want you should get so old."

"Hang in there, Dad."

Again the breaths are broadcast by phone across the state, short little breaths bouncing along the lines west to east. It occurs to Gil that it sounds as if his father is hanging.

"This is expensive, no?"

"Dad, you've got insurance. Don't worry."

"How much . . . in checking?"

"I don't know. The book is in Jackson."

"How come you don't know. . . . I . . . I would know."

The breathing now is fast, not furious but maybe desperate. Painful and maddening to listen to. Just breathe, Gil wants to shout, then add, Are you sure you're all right? What can I do for you? Of course, the answer is nothing. The answer is that there is no answer, that whatever he feels or does, it leaves him upset. He wants to ease his father's pain, and at the same time he feels as if this illness is a deliberate attempt to wear Gil into earth.

"Dad," Gil says, softly, "I'm going to let you go now. Don't worry about money."

Gil hangs up, calls the hospital back, but there is no doctor available, no one who will answer his questions. Cancer. Gil starts jotting down the numbers on his legal pad. He adds up the costs per week—Pineridge, insurance, some extra nursing help at the hospital. Then he adds up his father's money, the $14,000 in checking, some $160,000 in CDs. He divides the weekly into the total, adjusts for social security, figures he can go on for years. Then Gil runs a worst-case scenario, the old man in Mapleshade—no medical coverage for that—and finds that the Davisons will be broke by Hanukkah. Slow death, but not that slow.

"Jesus, Gil, take it easy." It's Trapp, from glass purchasing. "You're all hunched over that pad like it's life or death. You that busy?"

"Up to my ears in apple crates."

"I'm looking for Trany. You seen him?"

"Gone for the day," Gil says. He puts down his pen, summons what strength he has to drive home.

VIII

James takes the first pitch, a slider inside, ball one. Okay, he tells himself, look for something hard, out over the plate. This late in the game the pitcher doesn't want to get behind in the count, can't afford to put him on. Then he gets the hard one, but outside, ball two. Now James knows he's got to come in with the heat, can't go to three balls. The pitch spins in, a curve that Clancy, the umpire, calls a strike. James steps out, gives Clancy a quick hey-what-the-hell glance, bangs his cleats. Whoa, James thinks, curved me on two-and-oh, knowing I'm looking fastball all the way. That's gutsy pitching, sure. Got to hand it to him.

Okay, it's still two balls and one strike, and 2–1 is still a hitter's count. James steps up, taps the plate with his bat, gets set. He tells himself to see the ball. Know. Know its speed and spin, watch it now, and before his mind can form around the words *fastball inside, get around on it,* he snaps a line drive down the right field line. Sprinting now, he bows out at first, cleats digging, nips the inside of the bag, runs down to second, pulls up, a double. He puts his hands on his helmet, both feet on the bag, breathes deeply, looks into the stands. There she is, the girl, the one who's been calling him. She's sitting next to Mercer's girl. James is glad she came tonight: he's four for four.

Her name is Barb. She's wearing tight jeans and boots, a cotton shirt that hugs her torso, lets James know even from out on second base that she's thin. She's got lots of hair, thick, parted just off the center of her head. Every so often she pushes that hair back from her face, tilts her head back when doing so. She's doing this now, and James just watches.

Okay, the pitcher is ready to go to work on Jefferson. The first pitch is on the outside corner for a strike. The catcher, though, gave position away and now James signals this to Jefferson. Look inside. Sure enough, a fastball, which Jefferson smacks into left field. James sprints to third. Gil has moved down the line, is waving him home. James digs, everything working toward running, and when he gets to the plate Goodie is there holding his arms up in the air, the sign for *stand up, you've got it made.*

Back in the dugout—this is the part he loves—James walks up and down the row, slapping hands and banging forearms. "Yeah, baby," Metz says. "You are the man!"

Vince, down at the end, nods. "Way to go, cham-peen," he says.

God, James thinks, the man is green. Big circles under his eyes, dark as eye shade, his body all slouched over as though the air were heavy. At least he's not smoking.

"You're really the star," Barb says.

James doesn't know what to say. They're in her car, a little Honda Civic, rattling down Woodward on their way to meet Mercer and his girlfriend at a bar in Birmingham. He listens as the empty Diet Coke cans and Rolling Rock bottles roll about on the backseat floor. There is a discarded lipstick tube at his feet. He breathes in the car's heady aroma of perfume, beer, maybe a hint of tobacco, and is a little taken aback, almost made dizzy, by his good fortune, here in this car, with a beautiful girl who seems really to like him. He doesn't even have to say anything. She's happy to keep talking.

"I mean, you were really great. Great! We just knew when you came up that you would hit it, that something good was going to happen. And it did! I was like, never Susie Cheerleader, you know? Don't take this the wrong way or nothing, but I was more likely to hang with the guys in the smoking lounge. But that game was really fun, really. I enjoyed it. And you were great."

James feels the heat in his face. Jesus, he thinks, I'm blushing.

"You don't say much, do you?" She glances at him, then turns back to the windshield.

"I think I'm just out of practice."

A tenth of a mile of silence rolls by. They cross an intersection, pass a fancy restaurant where James sees a red-jacketed valet take off running to retrieve a car.

"Yeah, well, what was I saying? Oh yeah. I really liked that. The game, all you guys running around. It was cute."

"Cute?"

"Yeah. You know, the effort and all. It was nothing too . . . too sophisticated. Just win or lose. Boyish. Cute."

Cute, James thinks. Cute?

———

In the dim twilight of the restaurant Mercer pulls James aside and whispers in his ear, "Don't worry, I'm paying." James doesn't argue. He could never afford this place. Besides, James doesn't argue with Mercer, about anything.

Before they eat, they sit at the bar. There are men in suits here, though both James and Mercer wear slacks and short-sleeved shirts, clothes they changed into in the parking lot in Pontiac. Some of the guys are down at the clubhouse, but, this being a weeknight, attendance is not mandatory. Mercer orders drinks, white wine for the women, a Scotch for himself. James wants a beer—he's dry, for one thing, and he loves beer—but he also asks for a Scotch, because Mercer ordered one.

There is small talk now, about the game, the area, the restaurant. James watches the women. He's not sure what to make of Emily. She always seems to be tired, or bored. Her hair is short and blond, her clothes different, somehow baggy but able to accentuate her shape. James prefers Barb, who talks more, looks more interested, dependent.

"Yep, the kid hit the ball tonight," Mercer is saying. "Then again, he always hits the ball."

"It was a lot of fun, that game," Barb says. "I was surprised."

"She thought she would hate it," Emily says.

"I did not. That was you."

"It was?" Emily says. "Oh, I guess it was."

It's comments like this that make James wish Emily away.

"Sorry you hated it," Mercer says, sounding not at all concerned.

"I didn't say I hated it. It was . . . interesting."

The drinks arrive. James, thirsty, takes a large gulp. He feels as if a fire has flared up inside of him; his head seems to be glowing from the heat. How do people drink this stuff?

James glances behind the bar, where the spirit bottles stand, as though at attention. He likes this, all this order and style in the service of pleasure. He looks at himself in the mirror—his eye is still bruised, but the swelling is down—and sees that he fits here, doesn't look lost, a kid out of place. This is a relief. He's dreamed about a night on the town, women and drinks, good times, and here it is.

Later, James squirms when the bill arrives. He watches as Mercer digs into his pocket, fishes out a silver American Express card, flicks it onto the bill's leather case as though he were a blackjack dealer. He doesn't bother to look at the bill. James wants to be able to do that, to have that ease and control, that nonchalance and freedom.

Later still, James finds himself parked on the street in front of his apartment, in another panic. Do I ask her up? His mind is indecision and embarrassment. He wonders, briefly, where is his cool, where is that wonderful stuff that lets him slow down the moment when the ball leaves the pitcher's hand till it crosses the plate, let's him see the world in a different light, relaxed and fierce, ready for anything?

"There's not much up there," he hears himself saying. "I could give you some coffee. It's instant."

No, he thinks. Not like that.

She looks at him. Okay, this look he understands. He leans over to kiss her, leans gently for a quick, light kiss, when she grabs him and pulls him toward her, over the automatic gearshift, to her mouth. Her lips are soft but she is pulling him tight, her tongue is firm, insistent. Again he feels the heat inside him, everywhere.

They separate. He breathes deep and she lets go of something, a sigh or a giggle, and says, "I'd love to come up." Then, a beat later, "No, no. Maybe we should . . . no, it's too early, no need to rush, don't you think? You're very sweet, Luke. I want to know you, know you better. Don't you think? Did I say how much fun I had tonight?"

"You said."

"Well, I did. Maybe we could do this again. I mean, I know you're busy and all. Maybe next weekend. Oh God, I hope that's not too forward."

"We've got some games—"

"You are busy, of course. Of course. Really, it's no big deal."

"I've got one game Saturday, two on Sunday. But Saturday night, that's good."

"Saturday night. Oh, well. Yes. What time?"

"I should be done around five or so."

"So how 'bout eight? You need me to pick you up?" She is eager to pick him up; this he can tell.

"Yes," he says. "I need that."

"Then it's a date," she says, punctuates the remark with a shake of her hair.

Upstairs James fumbles with his keys, finally opens the door, drags himself and his duffel into the apartment, turns on the bathroom light, leaving the room dark and shadowy, just right for standing in front of the mirror. He stands, head-on at first, then turns left out of habit—he shadow-swings from this side—but his eye is bruised and he finds it unpleasing. Why, he asks, did this happen to me now, when finally I need to look good? He turns right, exposing his left to the mirror, not his best side but better tonight. The side Barb sees when he is riding in her car. He is wearing a pair of khakis bought at a secondhand store and a summer shirt that Barb complimented him on. He tilts his head, looks into his own eyes, says "Hi" aloud. Then he turns slightly, speaks again, alters his stance, runs through twenty positions, each a variation of the one before, each punctuated with a spoken greeting—*hey there, hi, how ya doin', what's up, hey*—each an attempt to look his best. Then he practices nodding at the mirror in the way he has nodded at Barb all night. He adds an occasional "uh-huh," but in the end he is too embarrassed to continue, but also too worked up to sleep. He changes into his shorts, grabs his practice bat, and shadow-swings. Not for his baseball but for his mind, swing after swing, till his arms ache and he can finally go to bed.

IX

Gil is back on the road again, this time to meet Alfredo Schuster. This is something they do from time to time, not to conduct baseball business but because they have known each other as boys, gone to the same schools, played on the same sandlot teams, traveled around and learned the game in the same flat landscape, among the corn and beet fields and the little fac- tories in those not-quite-small Michigan towns, lined up like beads on a string that stretches from Detroit to Chicago. Gil had been in the office that morning when Schuster called. As usual, Schuster suggested Jackson, but Gil negotiated Ann Arbor, the midpoint between Jackson and Detroit, a fair compromise.

Gil has chosen a place called Le Chateau, which is really a basement restaurant in a building on Ann Street. A fancy place, with dim lights and a long mahogany bar. Gil stands at the en- trance till the room fades into focus. The place is packed, prac- tically every table filled with Ann Arbor's business crowd, never so visible as here, in this dark restaurant, at roaring noon. Gil scans the room again, but Schuster has not arrived. When the hostess gives Gil the option of waiting at the table (he has, luckily, made a reservation) or the bar, he chooses the bar.

"Drink?" asks the bartender, a tall blonde with hair that curls under to touch her neck. Her manner is a little too curt for Gil's liking, but it's also attractive. Challenging.

"Scotch," Gil says, surprising himself. He hasn't ordered a Scotch in thirty years.

"What flavor?" she asks. She points to a row of bottles, each filled with a woody-colored liquid.

"Which do you suggest?"

"Me? I'd go with Bushmills. But it's not Scotch, it's Irish."

"Not that different," Gil says.

"As long as you're not Scotch or Irish."

She pours him the drink, sets it on a napkin, slides it in front of him, then walks down the bar to fill an order for a waiter. She comes back and places a ticket by his drink. Gil turns over the ticket. A Bushmills costs five bucks at Le Chateau.

Gil sips the whiskey. Now he remembers why he hasn't had a drink of whiskey in all these years. It's amazing, he thinks, what people develop a taste for.

The bartender strolls back down to his end of the bar. "Well," she asks. "What do you think?"

"It's good," he says.

"I think so." She takes a towel and begins polishing a series of wineglasses from the back counter.

"You a student?" Gil asks.

"Used to be."

"What did you study?"

"Art history."

"I was a student here," Gil tells her.

"What did you study?" she asks him, but before he can answer she moves down to the other end of the bar and prepares a tray of drinks. Gil watches, is impressed with the quick and effortless way she mixes and pours, so smooth and easy, like the play of a good infielder. She looks to him familiar. He's seen her before. Or maybe he just thinks he has. She's that easy to look at. He wonders about her boyfriend (she must have one), and thinks of a line he once heard, about youth and beauty being wasted on the young.

"Well," she says when she returns. "Let me guess. Business."

"What?"

"Your major. I bet it was business." She picks up polishing.

"You're right," Gil says. He feels heat in his face.

"My parents would have liked that. They like practicality."

"Most parents do. Mine insisted."

"Well, I got my degree."

"What will you do with it?" Gil asks.

"I'm assistant manager for an art gallery. I just work here twice a week, 'cause I make more here in four hours than I do at the gallery in a day and a half."

"Makes sense. So, is that what you want to do? Run a gallery?"

"Own a gallery," she says.

"Is Ann Arbor a good place to do that?" Gil asks, but again she is gone. He watches her work.

"Ann Arbor's okay," she says on her return. "Not a bad place to start. A lot cheaper than New York. Not as many artists, though, and not enough art lovers. At least not a lot with money. Scalpers can get people to pay five hundred dollars for a football ticket, but we usually can't get them to pay just a little more for a great work of art."

Gil sips his whiskey, which he considers a good alternative to trying to respond to her remark. Then a response comes to him.

"Do you have a card?" he asks. "Maybe I'll stop by the gallery."

Again she is gone, this time to pour two drafts. She returns and sets a card in front of him.

"Funny," she says. "I had you pegged for the guy paying up for the football ticket."

"Emily Hayden," he says, reading the card.

She smiles, and Gil feels a hand on his shoulder. He looks in the mirror behind the bar and sees Alfredo Schuster, in a blue-and-white seersucker suit twenty years old, fully half of Schuster's dressy wardrobe.

"What's this?" the scout says. "You're having a drink. It's a red-letter day. C'mon, I got us a table over here."

Gil slips the card into his shirt pocket, thinking for an instant that maybe he really should stop by the gallery—it's just up the street and she's a very pretty girl—but he knows he won't. She had him right. He turns and follows his friend to the table.

X

Mercer stares at his screen, fidgets with his Motrin bottle, watches the prices dance. Concentrate, he tells himself. He's got two new research reports on his desk, plus the stuff he's dug up on that bank the puppy told him about. He needs to call some clients, sell some stock, generate some commissions.

Instead the image of Lisa comes into his mind, the shine of her legs, like polished cedar. He bumped into her this morning on his way into work, and somehow they'd agreed to have lunch. No, not somehow. Tell it like it is, he says to himself. She looked fabulous, those great legs, the promise of her thin cotton dress, the wonderful way it took its shape from her body, her smile: that was the somehow. When he asked where she wanted to go for the meal, she said she'd cook him up something at her place. It was only a block away. "No crowds," she added.

Now, an hour into the trading day, he wonders if he should cancel. He has sworn himself off other women, will make a go of it with Emily. This is what he says he wants, what he thinks he believes. How, he wonders, can I believe this and then go to some girl's apartment for lunch and God knows what? Just look at the situation. Time stolen from work. A clandestine meeting. The dress. Take one step, the sins multiply.

He swallows a Motrin, dry, his seventh today. His elbow is not getting better.

Mercer punches the phone, dials a client. The best way to do it, without too much thought.

"Hi, Sheila," he says to the secretary when she answers. "Ben Mercer here. You play last weekend?" As in golf.

"Yep."

"Break a hundred?"

"One oh two. Can you believe it?"

"Close. So close."

"Maybe this week. Let me see if I can get him."

The line clicks and WJR comes on. Mercer decides this may be the world's most boring radio station. This and some of those local access signals, down at the end of the dial. While on hold, Mercer turns to his screen and checks on a couple of bank stocks, sees how they're trading. A voice comes through.

"Ben, what is your firm peddling today?"

"Forget about that, Jerry. Let's talk about what I'm peddling."

"One of those, huh?"

"Now, what is that supposed to mean?"

"What you got, Ben?"

"You ever heard of Burwell-Craine Financial?"

"Never."

Mercer goes into his spiel, one not that different from the puppy's. He knows Jerry Gillens, knows Gillens will find this company irresistible. Gillens is a hard-core Republican—likes Kemp, loved Goldwater—the kind of guy who believes in a strong positive correlation between moral turpitude and poverty. A company that charges usury rates to bankrupts will strike him as inspired.

"What's it trading at?"

"Eighteen and seven-eighths. Year high was twenty-three and change. Low was seventeen. You know banks are cheap now."

"You own it?"

"Long at eighteen." A lie, but Gillens likes winners.

"Trading ahead, eh?"

"I like the stock. Unofficially. As you know, Merrill does not recommend it."

"What now, is the SEC tapping your line?"

"Jerry, please."

"I'll take seven thousand shares."

Mercer types in the order. Twenty seconds later he says, "Okay, Jerry, you paid seven-eighths for seven thousand shares. You want to hear the official stuff?"

"Old news. What's the ticker?"

"BCFG."

The line goes dead.

Mercer calls Bart Symons, a history professor at the university. Symons once garnered a bit of fame, at least for a history professor, by taking part in Ann Arbor's annual marijuana legalization rally known as the Hash Bash. He was arrested for possession, spent the night in jail, found his picture on the front page of the *Detroit Free Press.* This he confided to Mercer the first time Mercer took him to lunch. At the time of the lunch Mercer found the story impossible, but now, with age, it doesn't seem as far-fetched.

"Isn't that a bit predatory?" Symons asks following Mercer's sales pitch. "I'm not sure I want to invest my money in a company that does business like that."

Mercer expects this. It's so typical of Symons. The man sold his Exxon on moral grounds because of the Alaskan oil spill.

"Well, Bart, I think you've got to look at this from the other side. These people have no credit. They need their cars. You know how bad public transportation is in this country. It's pathetic. So what's a poor person supposed to do? They need those cars to get to work. No car, no income. No income, no credit. No credit, no car. They're really in a catch-22. Now, here comes Burwell-Craine. It says, Hey, we'll take the risk. You get a car and a chance to establish your credit. But we've got to get paid to take the chance on you. No different than when you buy a risky stock: you expect a bigger upside. We can't make these kinds of moral judgments in a vacuum. Till Burwell-Craine, these people didn't have a hope. Now, it's win-win."

A silence, then, "Sell five hundred shares of Citicorp, buy a thousand shares of this. That sound wise?"

"I like Citicorp, but you already own a good chunk. Your way is a good way to get into this stock."

Also, that's more commission.

Mercer fills the order, takes a deep breath. Two for two. That's good, even for two of his more impulsive buyers. He likes this stock. Sells itself. He makes calls for another half hour, sells almost five thousand shares more. The price moves to nineteen and three-eighths. Hey, Mercer thinks, I'm moving this stock.

But back to Lisa. No, he decides. Have some willpower. Show some discipline. He fishes through his wallet, finds her number on the back of a Visa slip, dials.

"Hi," she says.

"Lisa, I can't make it. The boss has some bigwig lunch, wants me to go along. Trying to land a big client."

"That's too bad. Maybe after—"

"Lisa, let me call you back. I gotta run."

He punches off his phone. His arm is on fire and his forehead leaves a stain of sweat when he wipes it on his shirtsleeve. Calm down, he tells himself, half regretting the call already, the missed opportunity, a lunch and a roll with a very pretty girl. It's a portentous sign, desire and youth lost to fatigue and an apparently twisted sense of duty. He wonders why it doesn't feel more as if he's done the right thing.

XI

Driving. The whole world is driving. Gil rolls down I-94 in the after-work twilight, exhausted, running on caffeine, cruise control, and the Tigers on WJR. Detroit is already twenty-seven games out of first place, with a week yet to August. This, Gil thinks, is the tragedy of baseball, the long span of a losing season.

He gets off the highway an exit before the nursing home, drives a lap around the Jackson prison, a building oddly comforting, its old stone wall majestic compared with today's world of strip malls and glass towers. Here there is a palpable past. Gil wonders what has become of Lefty Wardwell, remembers the utter shock when Gil hit the man's pitch. Now those thrills are provided by his players, especially James, sent to him from this old place, such a provident find that Gil sometimes feels he willed James into being out of all the glories and frustrations of his youth. Now, having circumnavigated the prison, Gil heads off to Mapleshade, where his father has taken up residence— briefly, Gil hopes—before going back to Pineridge.

He dreads running the gauntlet of the wheel-chaired, palsied patients who will be placed, he knows, in the glass-ceilinged lobby. When he enters, though, the lobby is clear, the building quiet save for the faint, bubbly rhythm of a television and the hum of the lights. A nurse appears, looks at Gil as if to answer his question before he asks it.

"Where is everybody?"

"It's late," she says.

Gil glances at his watch. It's eight-thirty, the sky above the entryway still light, one of summer's endless days. He heads off to the second floor, where Morris lies.

He hears the coughing but it's not familiar to him at first. It's a raspy hack. He thinks, Someone should help that poor guy. He finds himself zeroing in on it, walking now farther and farther down the hall, checking room numbers, till there at the end he finds his father, eyes closed, on his back, coughing. Each exhalation rolls through the man's small body, a wave of terrible effort. Gil is repelled, wants to turn and run, catches himself and approaches the bed.

"Dad," he says. "Dad, Dad." He takes his father's cold hand, but there is no response. The man doesn't even open his eyes, just keeps coughing. Gil rushes off for a nurse.

"I don't understand," he says when he finds one. "How could this man be let out of a proper hospital?" He follows the nurse back to the room. She turns Morris on his side. The old man keeps his eyes closed, but his expression changes, he squints and frowns, agony. A tear rolls down his cheek. Then, a cough.

"He's an old, old man, Mr. Davison," the nurse says. She appears to be about twenty, with frizzy blond hair that overwhelms her nurse's bonnet.

"Can't you make him more . . . comfortable?"

She looks at Gil as though he's getting on her nerves, which perhaps he is. "I try," she says, and begs off, reminding him that there are many patients in her wing.

Gil is alone again with the coughing. "Dad," he says again, and still there is no recognition. The man's face is visible pain. The tears are heavy now, rivulets line his face. "Dad," Gil says again and again, and still he gets no answer, till he finds that for the first time in their lives, they are crying together.

XII

"It's important," Vince tells his wife, but she refuses to have anything to do with the money—that is, the lack of it. Vince knows his plight is next to futile and yet certainly essential, and so he pushes on, against her and her mind that she has set hard against listening.

"Vince," she says in a silence. "Do you remember how we met?"

"We went to the same high school."

"But you're older. I was in junior high when you were there."

"I played ball with your brother," Vince says, remembering Harry, killed in the Pacific, so long ago. Harry, Vince's best friend, what would he say about his sister's life now? Vince promised him that she would be happy, a promise that he felt it more important to keep than had he made it to Ellen alone.

"Yes," she says, "but when we first met."

"It was then," Vince says. To him his life before Ellen hardly seems to exist.

"No. You came over to our house to play catch with Harry. When you were twelve. I was seven. I watched you from my room, upstairs. Harry said you taught him how to throw a curveball. He said you had all sorts of good pitches. I told him you looked nice. You were so quiet, so reserved. The next time you came over, I sat on the grass. You said hello to me, so I knew then that I was right, you were nice."

"Really."

"Harry told me that I should marry you. This was later. He said you were someone I could depend on."

"Harry was my friend."

"He thought the world of you, Vince. When you came over

to the house after the war, then I knew why. Lots of people came, but you . . . you were so sad."

Vince lets her words hang, sips his coffee. It is morning, not the after-dark hours most people reserve for remembering.

"How," he asks, "did Harry tell you I was the one to marry? You were too young."

"He sent me a letter. He said that he'd met all kinds of guys, from all over the country, and that he knew what he was talking about. And I wasn't too young. I was eighteen. Which, back then, wasn't *too* young."

"How come you never told me this?"

"You never asked. You never talk about old times, Vince. You never do."

He knows she's right about that. He's always had a coach's mind, one bent on planning.

"El, what about our finances?"

"You handle it," she tells him. "Like Harry would."

XIII

"Well?" Hagenbush asks. "I mean, he's old. And soon he won't have Vince to help."

"He's not going to quit," Mercer says. "No way."

"He's not young."

"He ain't *that* old," says Kohn.

"Gil Davison will die on a baseball field. We'll be too old to play before he gives it up," Mercer says. He waves for a waitress. It's Saturday night. Mercer sits at a table with Jefferson,

Hagenbush, Goodstein, and Kohn. The restaurant is Goodstein's call, the Parthenon III, in Greektown, Detroit. It's a
meeting of the team's old-timers, a dinner planned back in May.
In seasons past they got together all the time, but then they aged
and developed careers and now what surprises Mercer is that
they get together at all.

"I don't know," says Hagenbush.

Mercer wishes Hagenbush weren't grandfathered into this
group. The guy is negative, can't ever seem to let things go, or
find any humor in them. Mercer wonders if maybe it's having a
wife and kids that does that to a man. Goodstein hangs out with
a stripper and he's the easiest guy in the world to be around.
Kohn, too. And Jefferson, well, he's a one-man party.

"Four o'clock," Goodstein says, giving directions. Each man
shifts to look to Goodstein's right. There's a brunette there,
standing from her table, in a black leather miniskirt and a tight
white T-shirt. Long, cherry-colored legs. Yes, Mercer thinks,
Goodstein has always had a good eye.

The waitress arrives and the men order, moussaka all around.

"I think Merc is right," Kohn says. "Gil's not leaving the field
till they carry him off."

"What do you think, Les?" Hagenbush asks.

"Well, a man gets older, his priorities change. At least that's
what my old man says. My guess is that Gil's going to decide
when he's ready to go, and then he'll go. It's a lot of work,
coaching. He must get tired of it once in a while."

"What do we do if Gil decides to call it quits?" Kohn asks.

"That will be it for me," Jefferson says. "I'm not going to
start up with someone new."

Mercer watches the brunette standing up by the hostess stand, apparently waiting for her date. He becomes aware of the clinking of silverware and the trickle of water in the fountain. No one at the table is talking.

"I'm done, too," Goodstein says finally. Kohn and Hagenbush concur.

"Well," Mercer says. "I hope Gil keeps at it, because I'm going to miss you guys if he doesn't."

"When are you going to quit?" asks Hagenbush.

"When my arm falls off."

The food arrives. Minutes pass before a word is spoken. Mercer likes this about eating with men, how they get down to business, no random small talk needed. Again, it's Goodstein who breaks the silence.

"Ben, what exactly did James do?"

"When?"

"To get thrown in prison."

"He killed a guy that was messing with his girl. You knew that."

"No, I didn't."

"With a baseball bat."

More silence. The players around the table just chew and nod. End of subject. Mercer figures that they feel as he does, that it's not exactly something you can condone, not really something you would do, and certainly not something you want to talk about. But taking a baseball bat and going after the guy messing with your girl, well, you can't blame James for it, either.

XIV

Barb is playing a Bob Seger song for James as he drives her car with his newly renewed driver's license, a piece of crisp paper folded into his wallet. In the song grass is as good as carpet, anyplace will do, and later people are cruising on Woodward Avenue, which is indeed where James is driving, north now through Birmingham, when Barb has him pull into a liquor store to buy a bottle of wine.

The night is warm, even fragrant. Right away James knows that this is not the kind of liquor store that lives in his memory. First, the store is part of a restaurant; its entrance is a modified cask of enormous proportions, musty enough that James thinks it must be real. All patrons pass through this barrel to enter and exit the store, and James enjoys this, reaches out to touch the darkened wood, savors the oddness of the moment. Inside is all manner of gin, Scotch, Irish, rum, and the exotics, too—aquavit, slivovitz, kvass—the variegated shelves enough to make James's head spin, as if he's already a little drunk.

"Red or white?" Barb asks. James shrugs, as if to say, Whatever you want. She wants white.

At the counter she pays and James confronts his poverty and her easygoing generosity. The clerk seems never to take his eye off James, who wonders if the man suspects larceny or underage drinking. But James knows he is innocent, that he doesn't have to prove anything.

He holds the door for Barb, and she flutters her eyes at him as she enters the cask. It's a coquettish move. "You're so well-mannered," she said to him once, which made James beam—he could feel the heat of pride flush in his cheeks—and remember the training his mother had given him. She wanted him to be a gentleman.

Still in the darkness of the cask, he bumps into a patron who is entering. Then, before recognition or comprehension, James is pushed.

"Lookie here," says the pusher, who turns out to be Johnny Langston, five to eight for armed robbery. Inside, Johnny L. took a special interest in James—Johnny L. considered himself exceptionally knowledgeable about baseball and life—and insisted on barraging James with advice and, when he felt respect was lacking, an occasional fist. "Don't let them mess with your girls or your money," he was always saying, "'cause when they mess with your money, they're messing with your girls." James had neither money nor girls—hell, they were all in prison—but Langston wouldn't leave him alone.

Now, Raheem Smith is with him, grinning that eerie grin of his, nothing happy about it. Smith, James can see, has let some hair come in, rather than stick with the shaved head he had inside.

"Who's this?" Langston asks, meaning Barb, whose eyes are looking to James, who has lagged too far behind, so that Smith and Langston stand between them.

"Don't mess," is all James can manage to say.

"Well, you've learned something," says Langston. He is a tall man, hair the light-brownish color of autumn leaves, a brow that folds over his eyes and gives him an odd look of sadness. James knows better.

"What they got in there?" Langston asks.

"Huh?"

"How many clerks?"

"One, I think," James says, looking at Barb, wishing she would just keep on walking.

"Cameras?"

"I don't know."

"You don't know?" Langston points to Barb, or maybe just to the brown bottle bag she is carrying. "You paid for that?"

Out of Langston's ensuing laughter comes a fist. James sees it, sees also a flash of metal, sees it too late to stop it or duck but early enough to know he will be hit, as he knows sometimes that a pitch will hit him, that he is dug in too deep and there is nothing to do but sit there and take it. He tries to turn away and is blinded by pain, familiar as the darkness that follows.

XV

Loose, sweat dripping from his nose, down his face, his shirt wet against his chest, Mercer hitches up his pants, which gives his fingers a dab of goo. Krauss drops a single finger and Mercer waits, waits till he gets the single finger again, the sign that the wet one is coming and be ready. There are three outs yet to be gotten, and Mercer will have the win and Koch and Sons the league title. Mercer is not about to take any chances.

The batter is so far in front of the pitch—Mercer takes a little off—that he would miss it were it straight. The way it dives and leaves the batter stumbling records not only the strike but a measure of the batter's hopelessness. The crowd—O'Rourke's parents, Hagenbush's wife and two sons, Goodstein's and Kukla's girls, the other faithfuls—hoot it up. The next pitch is hard and away, swung at for strike two. The third comes up and in, just about chin music, and the batter is so surprised or scared that he swings and Mercer has one away.

In the zone. Mercer is there, so tuned, focused, that nothing can stop him now, not the pain in his elbow, not the Motrin and its incandescent burn in his gut, not a girl who won't be true, and not a game that means nothing—if you take the long view, the view Mercer himself once had, say, at seven, when he possessed the little-boy dreams of playing big-league ball, dreams that never really die in a man, dreams that are maybe worse now that he has been there and yet is back in a league for has-beens and wannabes. It's almost embarrassing that he still dreams against everything he knows to be true, that maybe he could get back, get another two weeks, or more.

The next batter hits the first pitch on the ground, right side, and Kukla slides over like a panther, scoops up the ball, and flips it to Hagenbush at first, a play of such ease and fluidity that Mercer must admit that here is a kid who could play big-league ball, maybe. He's young—Mercer envies him that—and he's got talent and the clean-cut looks that put scouts and managers at ease.

The faithful are on their feet now, yelling and stomping on wooden bleacher slats like an amen corner. Mercer stands at the back of the mound and rubs the ball, his elbow feeling as if the bone at the joint has turned to gravel. He watches the batter rasp his spikes in the batter's box, digging like a pit bull. Mercer doesn't like hitters to get too comfortable or dug in at the plate, so he lets loose with a fastball aimed for the brim of the batter's helmet. The batter dives out of the way, throwing his body down but leaving his bat hanging in the air, and the ball is drawn there, so that everyone can hear the ping and the umpire must declare the pitch a foul ball. The batter stands and dusts himself off. Strike one.

The opposing coach is out of the dugout now, demanding action. "He threw at 'im, he threw at 'im," the man says. The umpire lifts his mask and meets the coach halfway between home plate and the dugout, a look of resignation on the umpire's face. Coaches must complain and umpires must listen—it's the way of the game—and then do nothing, for a pitch can get away from anyone and if asked Mercer will say just this, Hey, it got away, why would I want to put him on, I'm one out away here, I'm trying to throw strikes. Better, too, if the batter must worry about your control, you don't want him to think you always know where it's going, because wildness breeds fear in a way that a brushback pitch from a player on top of his game never can. The next pitch is a spitter—Mercer respects the hitter, played a full season in St. Louis, a swinger and he's pumped—and sure enough the guy is out in front and over the top of the ball, which lands on the back rim of the plate and bounces into Krauss's chest protector. Strike two.

Now the crowd is hollering, the dugout is on its feet, even Vince, who stands at the end, holding on to the cinder-block wall. For him, watching the league championship game—or maybe just standing—requires all the strength he can muster.

Mercer feels he can hear the man think—c'mon, cham-peen, nothing too good here—and Mercer delivers a fastball low and away, for ball one. What Mercer wants to do now is throw another fastball, fan the guy on the hard one, but he can still hear Vince thinking, because pitchers think alike, and when you think like a pitcher and not a yahoo—not like a batter— then you've got to come with some junk away, because this guy is a fastball hitter and strong, and you don't tempt fate. Mercer decides on a slow curve. Snapping it off sends a shock of pain up his arm, and it is just as this is registering in Mercer's brain that the batter reaches out, trying to hold back, and hits a soft-and-easy poke job to right field. And then things get interesting.

Brattenburg is in right field because James has yet again gotten the shit kicked out of him in a parking lot. What is it with this guy, Mercer can't say; the kid finally gets a date, his face is almost healed, and he takes it on the noggin, a kind of warm-up for a couple of thugs who hold up a liquor store in Birmingham, of all places, surely one of the most notorious crimes ever in the city of Birmingham, which was a reasonably safe place till Luke James started calling it home.

So now Mercer watches Brattenburg start back, then lumber forward, so out of place in that great expanse of outfield, Mercer's mind calculating, the dropping ball one side of the equation, Brattenburg's labored sprint the other. And then—and things go this way, they really do when things are going right— Kukla yells, "Mine!" and dives, dives out into right field, his back to home plate, makes the catch, lands on his belly, and bounces and slides at Brattenburg, who has the presence of mind to hurdle him.

The players jog to the mound to congratulate Mercer and each other, not a wild, romping celebration—it's only the league championship—but one with the subtle tone of assurance of a team that knows there are many more games to be won.

XVI

Vince sits with Gil in the dark, leathery interior of Gil's car, its windows down and motor off, only the summer-night sounds of crickets, cooling metal, and a Tigers game broadcast from Kansas City, low-volume background music to a conversation which is, of course, about baseball.

"Mercer ain't so young," Vince is saying. He tries to use his wise-old-man voice, the one that every once in a while will get Gil's attention. "Rest him more. Pull him sooner."

"He went the distance tonight."

"Barely. The season. It's wearing him down."

"Me too," Gil says.

"Brattenburg doesn't hit well enough to play right field."

"Agreed. But I wanted to use him. He's restless. We need two catchers, in case. I'm going to work him this week." The team has practice games against the Canadian national team, which is coming through on a tour, a warm-up for the Olympic Games next summer.

A pause. Crickets, and a foul tip from Missouri.

"You're looking better," Gil says. Vince looks over through the dark interior of the car to Gil, who is staring back through his glasses. They are parked in Vince's driveway. Vince glances through the windshield to see Ellen peering out the kitchen window with an expression of concern. He knows she wants him inside, where his health—he knows she thinks like this—can be protected. His health. It's not better. Last night, three hours' sleep, most of the night spent watching high-torque motor sports on ESPN2, the inhaler gripped tightly in his hand, and often in his mouth. Ellen knew he was up and held it against him, as if sleepless nights were the cause of his illness and not the result of it.

"No," he tells Gil. "The truth is, I'm not better. In fact, I'm beat. Couldn't sleep last night."

"Hang in there. Another day, we're in August. We need you for the tournaments."

"You know what to do in the tournaments." Vince opens the car door, steps out as quickly as he can, shuts the door against the car's interior light. Then he leans back in through the open window.

"I know," Gil says, "but I like to hear you tell me."

Vince smiles, stands upright, takes a deep breath of night air, then another, till he feels buoyant enough to face Ellen.

XVII

James remembers the day his mother fetched him from school in a borrowed pickup and drove him to a house in the country, where on the asphalt driveway sat a La-Z-Boy chair, one arm cat-scratch-frayed, the rest of the chair shabby and sad in the harsh daylight. The owner watched from the front door as James lifted the chair into the back of the pickup, and James remembers feeling that the owner of the chair was somehow putting his mother down by selling it to her. People did that, separated themselves by wealth. Now, convalescing, his head still dulled by concussion, the bruise, the pain-killers, he is glad to have the chair, its extendable bottom that lets him put his feet up and sit like an astronaut while he watches the Tigers play the Rangers on cable. His mother is there, too, sitting on another secondhand chair, her feet resting on a steamer trunk that serves as an ottoman.

They are in the middle of conversation, pausing now for Alan Trammel to bat, a conversation about James's future. His mother wants him to go to college—he got his GED in prison—what with his baseball skill even the University of Michigan might want him—there are, she says, kids who work in her office who make more than thirty thousand a year their first year out of college. Once you have that degree, she points out, no one can take it from you, because when you're older no one but you will care if you played ball, look at your father. But James remembers that people did care that his father had been a ballplayer—it was, it seems, all they remembered—and one day he just up and left. James was twelve, which wasn't so bad. What was bad was not having a story. So he told kids his father worked on an offshore oil rig in Nigeria, because he'd once heard they had oil rigs there and he didn't really know where Nigeria was, so he figured the other kids wouldn't, either.

Trammel takes a ball low and outside, a good pitch though not, in James's opinion, a strike. The umpire gives the pitcher the call.

In truth, James's father was killed in an auto accident on I-80, outside Cheyenne, Wyoming, the man's expired driver's license providing the clue that brought the news back to Jackson. News got out, but no one ever challenged James on his story, Cheyenne being as remote as Lagos or Abidjan.

Trammel hits a lazy fly to center, an easy out.

James looks to his mother. She was, he knows, once beautiful, lean, with high cheeks and color, sinewy arms that she bared at his Little League games, back when he had a mother and a father (like other kids) and played so well that everyone wanted to be his friend. His mother is still lean, but in a desiccated, world-weary way. She cleans for a living, and James knows there is nothing she prefers to do less. When he lived in her apartment he was forever wiping down counters and sweeping floors, not wanting any filth to suggest thoughtlessness, or worse, the loss of hope. If he doesn't get some money soon . . .

"What I don't understand," she says, "is how these guys can just hit you for no reason. Did you do something to them in prison?"

"They're bad guys, Mom."

"Yes, but why?"

Cecil Fielder hits a line drive caught by the shortstop, end of inning and start of the beer commercials.

"No one should hit you," his mother says.

He looks at her and she back at him. He knows what she is seeing, bruises on bruises, two beatings in as many weeks, the blues and purples of pain and an insistent past.

XVIII

Arm wrapped in ice, much Motrin and a little beer in his veins, Mercer wakes to the trill of his phone. It's two-thirty. He answers, does not speak.

"Hi," says a voice. Emily.

"Em."

"Well?"

"Well what?"

"I'm available."

"Emily, I've got to work in the morning. Early."

"I tried earlier. You weren't home."

"I told you I had a game."

"You always have a game."

"I don't think I can tonight. I'm zonked."

"'Twenty-four, seven, three-sixty-five.' Sound familiar? It's a promise you made."

"Emily."

"I thought you meant it."

"I did. I mean, I do. But, Em, you don't work in the morning."

"I told Doug we—that is, him and me—we're through."

"What?"

"You heard me."

"Tell me more," he says, thinking—now that he has what he asked for—Oh, shit.

"I told him we were no longer a couple. I'd still be his friend, but no . . . you know."

"Wow."

"You're the guy," she says.

"When did this happen?"

"Today."

"What did he say?"

"Not much. He wasn't happy."

Silence, but for the phone-line buzz.

Mercer thinks about tomorrow. No big earnings announcements, no GDP numbers, nothing of import. He could call in sick. For the first time in his life.

"Give me ten minutes," he says, rising now, groping for his clothes.

XIX

Vince sits in his backyard, listening to the birds, trying to get comfortable in the lawn chair. He could use some more sleep. Sleep! He missed it last night, with his coughing so bad that Ellen called 911. The ambulance team gave him oxygen, wanted to take him to the hospital, but he would not go. Lord only knew what they'd do to him there. When people in his condition go into hospitals, they often don't come out. Ellen pleaded with him to go, and when the men left she broke down completely, wailing in that way she has, heaving shoulders so bad that he grabbed them, felt in them the beat of her sadness. His cough was gone, and he pleaded with her, please, please, please, but she could not stop. She locked herself in the bathroom and stayed for an hour. He went downstairs and fixed himself a drink. An hour! Half a ball game of time she spent brooding in a room designed for the least-glamorous functions of the body. It made a kind of sense, and when she reappeared, she had calmed. She downed two quick snorts of vodka, which she never, ever did, then went to sleep, soundly, as if nothing had happened. Vince started to cough; he went downstairs so as not to wake her. Now he sits perfectly still in the backyard, where he will watch for the sun over his neighbor's red tile roof—about as out of place in Michigan as a palm tree—and wait for Ellen to wake and make him a cup of coffee.

He has spread bread crumbs at his feet. There are finches that will come to feed. It amazes him the joy this brings, feeding birds that are hardly starving. He likes the way they hop about his feet, how even they are used to his wheezing, they don't flee when he gasps, just hop away a few feet, quick to return, forgiving. The birds are landing now, hopping around, looking at him, heads tilted, and this makes him smile. He is still good for something. One of the birds hops onto his shoe, a thick-soled athletic shoe called a cross trainer. The bird performs another hop forward, then jumps up and alights on his knee. He can feel its tiny claws, though the bird is light. Vince proffers a hand with bread crumbs resting in its creases, and the bird hops onto the hand, grabs the largest piece, and flies off. Boldness has been rewarded.

It is still early. He pulls out a cigarette—a Camel, what a funny name for a cigarette—and smokes it as lustily as his lungs will allow, long drags, smoke rings, each movement carefully registering in his mind. This is pleasure and he doesn't want to miss it. Then he pulls from his pocket a cigar, given to him by Lane Gittry, owner of the tile roof, father now of a baby girl almost a year old. It's an old cigar, then, this one, saved in a Baggie in the trunk where Vince stores his baseball paraphernalia, all the old team pictures, the clippings, old wool uniforms, a glove from 1938, a ball used in a shutout game he pitched in Double-A. He meant to save the cigar till season's end, to smoke it in celebration of winning the national championship, but years of not winning have made him wary. He doesn't have much time, and so the league championship will have to be reason enough.

The smoke is fragrant. It gives him a sense of well-being, almost a sense of health. He thinks of the tasks that remain and decides they are easy enough. He must coach baseball and persuade Ellen to learn the household finances (which are simple: all sorts of idiots pay bills with checks). The thought of money reminds him that he must still call his agent and write Gil in as a beneficiary of his life insurance. His debts will be settled.

He finishes the cigar. When his neighbor finally starts up the Buick with the throaty muffler, Vince decides to shower, brush his teeth, and get Ellen to cook up some breakfast. He is actually hungry this morning, and giving Ellen a task usually helps her mood.

The exertion of the shower leaves him winded. He towels

himself slowly, staring at the plump model in the Renoir knock-off that Ellen picked up at a garage sale and hung above the toilet. Then he notices the small black bowl on the sink counter. It's a product of the Hopi tribe, brought back from Arizona by Johnny Granger, the last and final time he attended a professional spring training. The bowl is small, with a few engraved lines. Ellen uses it for a pill box. Vince is struck by the odds and ends that have made their way into his home. Things pile up in a house till your whole life seems to bury you.

Clean, dressed in a terry-cloth robe, as hungry as a ballplayer after a game, he heads off to find Ellen, who, pill or no pill, should be up by now. The bedroom is still, excepting the movement within dusty shafts of light that slant through the white gauze that Ellen calls drapes. Vince takes a deep breath, as deep as he can. He needs oxygen; his head is light. He walks to the bed and puts a hand on Ellen's hip, the one tipped upward, as she is lying on her side.

"C'mon, El. Let's have some breakfast. It'll be noon before long." He gives her a gentle nudge.

It is the nudge that makes his heart skip, his breath quicken. There is only give in the hip, none of the resistance of life.

"El?"

He hurries around the bed. The air is thin. He struggles with his breath, the blankets. Ellen's eyes are closed, her face drained. He touches her skin. It is cold, the damp cold of thawed meat.

"El! El!"

He sprints across the room, heading for the downstairs and the phone. All the years they lived in this house, he has never felt it worth the expense to put a phone jack in the bedroom. He tries to run down the stairs, but can't make his feet keep up with the gravity, till he trips and finds himself spread out on the landing, halfway to the ground floor. He is suffocating, gasping, struggling for air, each breath as elusive as it has ever been. His mind suddenly flips to the perfect game he missed in Cuba, the ugly confusion of the brawl, then to a game down South in which he curved a number nine hitter and the guy knocked in the winning run, then to a fastball he threw in Glens Falls, New York, that the batter hit practically to Canada. The memories come at him now, rapid-fire, the high, out-over-the-plate fastballs and every hanging curve, a lifetime of bad pitches. And then his mind turns to Ellen and his efforts to help her till he is choking on the futility, struggling, aware suddenly that the pressure has come off, he feels a kind of giddiness, as once when he was brought in to get the last out of the game and the guy hit a grand slam, at some point there's just nothing left to worry about, and he knows that he is there, aware for one brief instant that the moment he has long expected has finally arrived.

AUGUST

I

James feels a steady calmness on these streets, with their feltlike lawns and trimmed hedges, their shiny black driveways. He doesn't spot one car up on blocks; there are no old toys lying about the yards, no fast-food wrappers cartwheeling in the breeze—none of what he remembers from his neighborhood, where he grew up, what seems like a century ago. Someday he would like to live in a subdivision such as this. It surprises him to realize that he does, in fact, live here, even if he's crammed into a third-story apartment with no closets and a hot plate for a stove.

He walks, his feet pinched in an old pair of black shoes with two buckles, shoes his mother saved for him. The suit, too, dates from his high school days, double-breasted, light beige, with a brown tie, an outfit purchased by his mother at a thrift store. He leaves the jacket unbuttoned to make it easier to move—the shoulders are a bit tight—and the front panels flap with each stride. He moves purposefully, as he is late and it is still over two miles to Koch and Sons.

The funeral home stands on Woodward, among the fast-food joints and discount stores. James has seen the building many times before, on his way to the clubhouse or cruising with Barb, an enormous white Georgian affair with Greek pillars and large lights that illuminate the entranceway. In front of the building is a patch of grass, perfect as a putting green, a small sign planted in its middle. KOCH AND SONS, the sign says, without any other explanation. Along the side of the building James sees the parking lot. There he spots Gil's Continental, Mercer's Beemer, Metz's Sunbird, Jefferson's Ford, the whole lineup of cars he normally sees at the games. He buttons up his jacket and heads to the entrance.

The front door—heavy, a door he associates with the castles of fairy tales—closes off the light and noise of Woodward. James sees dark rugs, then tables that appear to exist only as resting places for flowers. As his eyes adjust to the light, more detail comes into view: paintings of verdant countrysides, gold sconces holding light bulbs in the shape of flames, creamy walls the color of James's suit, and then a sign, small, in the Koch style, with an arrow to the right for "Paklos," and an arrow to the left announcing a different death. James spots a man standing by the sign. He is a large, solemn man, with a dark suit and a carnation in his buttonhole. He nods. James heads right.

He walks down a long hall lined with more countryside paintings, another flower-laden table at its end. To the left two French doors open into a long room where the Koch and Sons baseball team is milling about in suits, except, James notices, for Metz, who wears his brown UPS uniform. Gil stands to one side, looking grim, talking to a large man James does not recognize. Mercer, Jefferson, and Krauss chat nearby. The other players—Kukla and Goodstein, Hagenbush, Kohn, the whole team—seem to be conversing quietly while keeping their backs to the far end of the room, where two mahogany caskets rest, each one half open to reveal Vince and his wife. Even from this distance James can see Vince's cheeks, that they are a pink color unlike the green pallor he had in life.

Metz looks up, sees James, nods. It is something, James thinks, to see Metz act restrained.

James has, of course, heard the story, how Vince died of a heart attack trying to help his wife, who had died in her sleep. It didn't exactly come as a surprise to hear that Vince had died—he'd seemed half dead to James the day they met—but it was a shock nonetheless, the way death is always a shock. James moves forward, drawn now by the bodies at the front of the room, the idea of paying respect in his head.

As he navigates the room, nodding and saying low-volume hellos, he is struck by how nice everything is. The room is nice, what with the chandelier, more landscape paintings and flower-filled tables, fine woodwork on the walls, a stone fireplace, several plush couches, ornate lamps. The people (his teammates, mostly) are nice, well dressed, proper. Even the carpet below his feet is first-rate, plush enough to put a bounce in his step as he moves forward through the crowd.

Vince's wife was not, James decides, an attractive woman. Certainly not at the end, and looking at what the embalmer had to work with, James feels she probably never was. She wears a navy dress, a mask of beige makeup with highlights of rouge. Her dyed hair is carefully combed, each strand perfectly in line.

Vince's expression is unlike anything James remembers seeing. In life the man had a perpetual wince, even on the rare occasions when he laughed. James understood this to mean that he expected everything to hurt. Now, though, he appears calm, almost bored, like a man who has fallen asleep watching television.

James's eye travels about the casket, over its fine wood exterior to its silk insides, then over Vince's suit, charcoal and neatly pressed, past the blue tie to the baseball that rests by his head. It's tawny from infield dirt, dry, an old ball. James stares back to see if anyone is watching him; no one is. He wants to take the ball, his hand is moving now, about to reach when he feels someone at his side.

"Pretty amazing, huh?" It's O'Rourke, a college boy, the other guy—at least one of the other guys—the scouts come to see.

"He looks good."

"They fix 'em up nice here," O'Rourke says.

"What's with the ball?" James asks.

"It's from some shutout he pitched in Cuba. Gil says he wanted to be buried with it."

Such a request deserves some measure of unspoken consideration; James does his best. Then he pumps O'Rourke for information.

"Who's the guy Gil is talking to?"

"That's Mr. Koch. You should introduce yourself."

It has never occurred to James that there is a Mr. Koch. But there he is, a large man, his barrel chest wrapped in a dark suit, his face deeply lined, as though a lifetime as a funeral director has left him with a permanent expression of grief and consolation. He holds his hands behind his back, his shoulders forward, so that he appears to be leaning over Gil, who is looking up and nodding at what Mr. Koch is saying. James approaches.

"Luke," says the coach, "meet George Koch."

Mr. Koch shakes James's hand, tells him how much he's heard about him. "I'm sorry we had to meet at such a sad time," the man says.

"This is a very nice place," James says, immediately embarrassed by the comment. He wishes words came from him with more ease, especially the right ones. He envies people who can talk in the clutch.

"We do our best. My father started the company in 1933. That was the worst year of the Depression."

Mr. Koch looks around the room, as if to impress upon James just how much he has now. James nods, but doesn't venture a comment.

"How'd you get so banged up?" Mr. Koch asks.

"You heard about the Cork and Barrel robbery?" Gil asks. "Luke was there, coming out of the store when the robbers went in."

"That was terrible. I've lived with my family in Birmingham all my adult life, and even today I'm shocked that such a thing could happen here. It makes me wonder what kind of people are just out there, walking around."

James waits for Gil to make the appropriate comment. The silence that comes instead makes James want to bolt from the room. Luckily, Goodstein comes up to say hello to Mr. Koch. Goodstein, clean-shaven, in a dark suit, some sort of grease in his curly hair, looks like a distant relative of the guy James knows from the field, someone higher up the evolutionary scale. It amazes James how guys like Goodstein can transform themselves, while James feels even more out of place than usual. He fidgets, then excuses himself when Goodstein does. Now he is again at a loss. He wanders around the room, finds himself running his hand along the long, smooth top of a wooden table. He comes to a small ashtray, oval, the glass so fine and pure that it appears to be its own source of light. It is beautiful, this ashtray, just the type of object he covets, that he has never had in life. He wants nice things: a sleek black compact disc player, a leather couch, crystal wineglasses, a twenty-seven-inch television, and now an ashtray of heavy glass. He eyes the one before him. He wonders if he could sell it—he needs money, too. He looks around, is sure he is unobserved, lifts the ashtray—it is surprisingly heavy—and slides it into his front pants pocket. It hangs there, the weight pulling at his belt. He looks down. His jacket covers the bulge. He moves along, finds a second ashtray, and drops it into his other front pocket.

He walks now through the crowd, weighted, toward the coffins. He is unsure what to do, so he keeps going, doesn't want to seem strange. Soon he arrives at the pink-cheeked Vince. Think, he tells himself. He decides he has been foolish. For once in his life he is seeing trouble before it happens. He must take steps to avoid it, as a coach might bunt along a runner to avoid a double play. He knows he needs to get rid of the ashtrays—how would he explain them?—but he wants them, too, wants one nice possession. Vince is offering no help. James wonders what Vince used to say to pitchers when they got in trouble. James remembers once, earlier in the year, when Vince went to the mound to visit Kindle. Just the walk to the mound badly winded Vince, who put a hand on Kindle's shoulder, as much to gain support as to offer it. He said a few words, then walked back. What did he say? James wants to know. He would pay for those words now.

Staring at Vince, still hoping for inspiration, James spots the baseball. It gives him an idea. He'll leave one of the ashtrays with Vince. He reaches in his pocket, grabs the glass with his index and middle finger. Vince was a smoker, a heavy one—it killed him—and what could be better than sending him off with an ashtray? James slides it into the silky coffin.

Now he is weighted on one side. His instincts tell him to fight for balance, so that before he can think it out, he has placed the second ashtray in the coffin as well. Now he feels light, relieved, his troubles momentarily lifted.

"Hey, bud," says a voice. It's Mercer. He wears a dark suit, very neat and handsome, like a magazine model.

"Come back from the coffins," the pitcher says, "or people will start to wonder what you're doing up here."

Mercer places a hand on James's shoulder—lightly, not like the hand Vince placed on Kindle—and James feels himself being turned around, back to the team.

II

What bothers Gil is all of Mercer's busybody fidgeting. There was a time when this pitcher just took the sign, rocked back, and threw. Mercer never even shook his head, just stared the catcher down till the guy flashed the sign he wanted. It was beautiful, all economy and power and purpose. Now he looks as if he has fleas.

Still, he's setting them down, really pitching. Gil has Kohn charting pitches, and all the marks show that Mercer is hardly using the fastball at all. Gil has been on Mercer about this for years, telling him it's not speed but the change of speed that hurts the batter. So there is some pleasure in watching him mix it up now. Mercer throws an off-speed pitch, a slow curve that has the batter lunging forward, then swinging down, so defeated that he doesn't bother to run when the ball hits the dirt (it's a third strike), just stands there while Krauss scoops it, tags him, and throws the ball down to Goodstein at third, then pop pop pop, the ball goes around the horn, and now there are only four more outs till Koch and Sons wins the district.

Gil glances at his watch. It's just half past two. With luck the game and postgame shenanigans—trophies, a speech by the district leader—will be finished by four, and maybe Gil can get from Pontiac out to Jackson by six-thirty to check on Morris. The old man is hacking, coughing and coughing, a symptom, Gil is told, of an old person who has fluid in his lungs. He appears to be in awful pain, but the doctors give him little in the way of medicine, because he doesn't ask for it (he can't) and pain-killers just might slow down his breathing to dangerous levels, when, as Gil has pointed out, they might actually have to put him back in the hospital. Where, Gil knows, at least insurance would cover it.

The batter pops up. Kukla waves the others off. Gil can see O'Rourke and James jogging in through the wavy heat of the outfield—good to have James back in the lineup, the team missed his bat—and then the ball drops into Kukla's glove. The inning ends. Three outs till the district championship.

"Attaway, attaway," Gil shouts as the team comes in, his players loose and smiling, confident. Mercer passes, and Gil asks him about his arm.

"Fine." The pitcher puts on his jacket.

"Yeah, baby," says Metz, walking by in his helmet, bat in hand.

Gil thinks of the drive, what time he'll get home. Is it really worth it, five hours total in the car, just to walk in, see the man, leave, without ever being noticed? For a moment it strikes Gil as an inane compulsion, but then Metz slaps a line drive to right center and scoots into second with a double, the hit erasing in Gil's mind any sense of doubt. Man, he thinks, the team looks good. He turns to the corner of the dugout for affirmation and is momentarily shocked when he doesn't find Vince nodding back.

———

With the game tucked away and the road rolling by, Gil has time to think of Vince, of how they first met twenty-seven years ago, when Gil had Vince's kid on his Little League team, the first year Gil coached, Rick's first year of baseball. Gil had been out of the game long enough—eleven years—to feel estranged from the fraternity found on the field, from the experience shared by players and coaches. When he first talked to Vince, the man's forearms resting on the perimeter fence, a cigarette smoldering in his fingers, Gil felt as if he'd been admitted back into the club.

"Where'd you play your ball?" This was the first thing Vince said to him. No hellos, no how-do-you-do's. Vince could spot a ballplayer.

Soon they were trading baseball résumés. Vince had jet-black hair then and a bounce in his step, and he'd played all over the world, and it was nothing for Gil to ask and Vince to agree that Vince would help coach.

Gil remembers that first year, when he and Susan tried to entertain Vince and Ellen, or at least see them socially, but those nights turned out to be dreadfully long and uncomfortable. Vince and Ellen were from the East, had never been to college or a play and rarely read a book, all of which was fine with Gil but did not go over well with Susan. Baseball was a proscribed topic on those nights, and yet without it long silences hung over them, as if they couldn't talk for fear of revealing some terrible secret.

Vince's son turned out to be a lousy baseball player. A ballplayer without a ballplayer for a son. Well, Gil thought, it can happen. The boy didn't return to play the next season, but Vince was there, ready to coach. At the time Gil found this amazing, that you'd just coach these kids when one of them was not your own. When Gil's family fell apart and Rick stopped playing, he understood. He and Vince moved up to the Class A league. They had something going.

Now what will Gil do? Where will he turn for advice, for banter? Gil remembers something his mother once told him when he was a boy, one of those little comments that for some unfathomable reason a man never forgets. In life, she told him, you have to find kindred spirits. Well, now where would he find one? Baseball, Gil realizes, was the key. He thinks of all those years he and Vince talked about the team, how they tossed ideas back and forth on the roster and the lineup, on each player's coaching needs. Then on the game itself. Baseball. It was their only subject, and they were faithful to it.

Gil passes the Grass Lake sign. He is getting close to Jackson, where Morris waits, oblivious. How Gil wishes he could talk to his father about baseball. Nothing profound, just some chitchat about the game, so that, as with Vince, there could be some spark between them.

Late that night Gil slides his Continental into his garage, slow and sure, as though he were docking a boat. He eases the door open, smells the familiar smell of the musty wooden wall against which he has opened the doors to various Lincolns over the last twenty-five years. He walks out into the drive, then over to the small patio area behind the house's rear door, sits in the seat where he once sat with Vince, who knew better than to smoke in Gil's house. The air is filled with the sounds of summer life: bleating insects, a car horn, in the distance a stereo thumping out rock and roll. Gil rests his head back and just listens. His father was as bad tonight as Gil has ever seen him. The nurse said he might need a tracheotomy. Gil thought this meant a tube down the old man's throat, but it turned out to be even worse. They may actually cut a hole in the man's throat, through which he would breathe. Gil never thought of Vince as a lucky man, but at least Vince never had to live with that.

"How long would he have to have that before he recovered?" Gil asked. The nurse lowered her eyes, and Gil understood that no one expected Morris to recover, that what they were doing now they did because they could. It seemed then quite logical to Gil that his father would choose an illness like this, one full of filial burdens, without the possibility of hope.

III

Mercer wakes with a sharp pain in his lower back, finds that he has fallen asleep on a bottle of Motrin. He can see that next to him, beneath the sheet, Emily lies asleep on her stomach, her right knee pulled up even to her waist. He thinks to wake her, but it's already a quarter to six and he has to get ready for work. Besides, she won't be civil for several more hours.

In the bathroom he unwraps the ice bag he attached to his elbow the night before and empties the water into the sink. He holds his arm to the mirror, grimaces at the way it is swollen, at the way it burns, at the way he has four or five more games to pitch this season. And what about the next? How's he supposed to keep pitching if his arm keeps acting up? He has always been so meticulous in the care of his arm. How did this happen?

His morning jog takes him through the arboretum. He follows the Huron, its waters especially still. It is a warm day, fragrant with the smell of trees and grass and damp soil. Get me through this season, he thinks, a prayer to the god of baseball, or at least of pitchers, a god in whom he really doesn't believe. He has had this problem before—whom to pray to—and faith would solve it, but he can't accept that any god who watched over him and his sport would allow passed balls and fielder's errors, bad hops, and especially infield hits and Texas Leaguers. These are items of a god with a perverse sense of humor, one too cruel to deserve respect. In the end Mercer just prays, without thinking too much of the implications.

On his way to work he decides to grab a bagel—he skipped dinner after the game, had just a beer and a few french fries with Emily at the Old Town—and it is while he is waiting at the counter that Lisa walks up behind him.

"Hi!" she says, her exuberance all out of scale for the time of day, especially for a woman who was recently stood up for lunch.

"You're up and at it early," Mercer says.

"I like the mornings in summer, when it's warm."

Mercer smiles, and she smiles back, a wide and happy grin. She is wearing a simple pastel shift, thin and light. Her hair is boyishly cut. He is stirred, affected in the way this woman has always affected him.

"When are we going to do that lunch date?" she asks.

Mercer pauses, then suggests today. He knows he shouldn't— he may not be engaged or really living with someone but it's close—but he wants to do this. He is a novice at fighting temptation. Who am I kidding? he thinks. He knows that he is tempted now, that he will be tempted later, that each missed opportunity will build and build, as demoralizing to a man as men left on base to a ball club. And for what? He will either go crazy or settle in and accept it, which is its own kind of insanity. To the voice that asks him about Emily he answers that he feels for her as strongly as ever, this has nothing to do with that, it means nothing to him if it happens and everything if it doesn't. A rationalization, he knows, and not even an original one, but he never claims, as most people do, that he is unique. Never. Nothing unique about wanting to sleep with a beautiful woman.

"Benjamin?" she asks.

"What about today?" he suggests again.

She smiles. It's as simple as that.

IV

"You should talk more," Barb says.

"About what?" It occurs to James that since Barb has telephoned him, she should carry the burden of the conversation. She seems to have in her mind an improvement plan for him, as if she were running a finishing school.

"About whatever's on your mind. It's not polite never to talk."

"When I have something to say, I say it."

"I'm talking about social small talk. Or with me. I always talk to you."

"I like it like that."

"Well," she says, "I want to know what you're thinking. Like now. What are you thinking?"

"I'm wondering what I'm going to talk about."

"What about before I brought it up?"

He pauses to consider what he should say, and then decides to tell her the truth, knowing he'll probably regret it. Tell the truth. Small children are taught this. For an adult, it's usually a bad idea.

"Baseball," he says.

"Baseball. Good. What about it?"

"I'm thinking maybe I should move up in the box against lefties, on account of breaking balls, 'cause that's pretty much all I see from lefties. And I should go to left more with these pitches, 'cause a lot of times I'm just swinging without thinking, and if I tried to take these pitches to the opposite field, I'd hit them harder."

"Uh-huh," Barb says. She breathes, seems to be thinking of what to say next. "You really love baseball," she adds.

"I do."

"Why?"

"I just do."

"Don't you have a reason? What do you like best?"

"I like hitting best. I like being outside. I like playing on a team, being with other guys. I like winning."

"Men are so funny about that."

"About what?"

"Winning."

"It's better to win. Woody Hayes said, 'Show me a good loser, and I'll show you a loser.'"

"Who's Woody Hayes?"

"A football coach. From Ohio."

"Now we're on football," Barb says.

"He hated to lose. So do I." James wonders if she's teasing him.

"That's it, Luke, isn't it? Men hate to lose. I don't think they care as much about winning as they hate to lose."

"Maybe."

"And your team, it wins all the time."

"It's a good team."

"What are you going to do when the season ends?"

"What do you mean?"

"No more baseball."

"I'll work out. Work at my job."

"And then?"

"My probation is up next April," he says.

"And then what?"

"I'm hoping to be drafted."

"Drafted? Into the army?" she asks.

"Into baseball. Pro ball."

"Then what?"

"Then I get a contract, and a signing bonus, I hope. The money would be great. And then, next season, I'll play pro ball. You know, in the minors, to start."

"Where?"

"I don't know that yet."

"What about us, Luke?"

"That's a long way off, Barb. And you can come."

"Do you want me?"

"Sure I do," he says, wondering, even as he speaks, why he is saying that he does.

"What about my job? What would I do? Where would we live? I mean, I can't even imagine it."

He tells her that it will be great. "Mercer lived in a town where they went waterskiing almost every day. Everybody loved the team; the guys got invited to dinners. . . . Krauss played in Knoxville, Tennessee. Kohn pitched in Texas. I've never been to any of these places. And there's always the chance you move on. Can you imagine playing in a big-league stadium?"

"What if it doesn't work out?"

"That's what my mother always asks."

"Well?"

"It has to work out, Barb. It's the only plan I've got."

"I see," she says.

James feels something slipping by him in the silence that follows.

V

We're back, Gil thinks, sitting in the dugout at Battle Creek, watching Mercer scrape his spikes at the dirt in front of the rubber as a horse might rasp its shoe on the ground. There's almost a frown on his face, the worried look of a pitcher. Goodstein and Metz stand next to each other at deep short. They field grounders tossed by Hagenbush, while in the outfield the ball loops between O'Rourke and James, at this distance a slow and dreamy arc. Yes, Gil thinks. We're back.

For the first game of the regionals Koch and Sons has drawn a team from Escanaba, Michigan, its players having made the long trip in a chartered bus Gil noticed out in the parking lot. They wear white uniforms with caps and piping the creamy red color of Cambpell's tomato soup. It is probably lucky to draw a team from the Upper Peninsula for the first game; with snow from October to May, the UP is not known for its ball teams. But this is a tournament, two-game elimination, too late for lackadaisical play, too important to play sloppily or poorly, even against a weak team. Every pitch of the season counts, coaches are always saying, but watching Mercer warm up, Gil can feel his stomach tighten, which tells him that the pitches now count more.

Mercer is still fidgeting on the mound—Gil hates this—
when the first batter steps up. The crowd starts clapping in
beat. The stands are filled with local people who are clearly
on the side of Koch and Sons. Gil has watched how this
amazes his players, especially the new ones. Amateur baseball
teams do not normally attract the passions of those who do
not know the players. Except here. People love this team,
love it, and Gil realizes that Vince was right; he always said
that they love the team not only because it wins, but because,
in the end, it loses. All that failure right at the end has pulled
at their hearts.

Now, Mercer sets, both feet on the rubber. He stares at
Krauss. The moment slows. This, Gil thinks, is life, his best
pitcher on the mound, his best team on the field. Mercer
rocks back, his leg rising now, his back arching, the lanky delivery, like a whip—the images come fast now, almost over-
take Gil, he wants to win so bad. Here we go, he thinks, here
we go.

"Hey, way to hum it out there!" he yells after the pitch, a
called strike. "C'mon, let's hear it!"

"Hey, you got him now, you got him," Metz yells from shortstop. Metz is always good for a comment. He bangs his glove
with his throwing hand. Kukla, too, shouts encouragement.

Another strike, then a pop-up. The next two batters go as
easily.

James and O'Rourke hit back-to-back doubles in the bottom
of the first, and Goodstein follows up with a single. By the top
of the fifth, Koch and Sons is ahead by six runs. Cruising.

"Hey," Gil says to Mercer, who is about to head out to the

mound for the top of the sixth. Now that Vince is gone, Gil must do all the talking to the pitchers. "How you feeling?"

"Fine, Coach."

"Why the ice between innings?"

"Same old elbow stuff. I'm okay."

"You need help, let me know. Don't pitch yourself into a hole."

"Relax, Coach. Look at the scoreboard."

Gil knows that Mercer gives you nothing, but something is up. Mercer is a different pitcher now, a busybody. Gil watches, the hand pulling up the belt, tugging at a shoulder, his cap, again the shoulder, and finally the pitch. The batter is Escanaba's best, and when Mercer gets him to chase a breaking ball down in the dirt, a thought enters Gil's mind. The arm trouble, the off-speed stuff, all the new junk—these items line up in Gil's mind, are totaled into an unbelievable sum. Mercer, doctoring the ball? No, no, Gil thinks. The kid's a power pitcher, straight-edged and clean-cut. Not the type at all.

VI

Mercer's elbow is still numb when he enters the room. The joint feels as if it were encased in ice, distant, for once inviolable. Lately he has come to think of his arm as some separate being, a difficult partner, capable of power and beauty and betrayal. It has not betrayed him yet, though he suspects that it might. He knows he has been fooling it with a steady regimen of ice, pain-killers, and junk pitches. He has kept it off-guard, and, as it were, by his side.

He scans the room, plain vanilla even for a Ramada Inn in the Midwest: two double beds separated by a wall-mounted nightstand; a television with an A-frame card atop it announcing the premium cable offerings; a painting of a duck hunter rising from behind a blind as ducks fly against a candy-pink sky. The door clicks and Mercer turns to see Emily enter, barefoot, a bucket of ice in her hand, as if she knows he'll be needing more.

"You made it!" she says. She moves forward and kisses him, then sets the ice on the dresser, opens a drawer, and produces a bottle of Bushmills.

He loves the crinkle of a new whiskey bottle when it is twisted open. Emily twists open the bottle now, her blond hair falling over her face. She flicks it back, then tucks it behind her ear.

"Who's your roommate this trip?" she asks.

"Jefferson, like always."

"What's he say?"

"He doesn't care."

"So you can get away with it."

"Sure," Mercer says.

"Like everything else, Ben. You always get away with things."

"I don't know what you're talking about."

"Just that you get whatever you want," she says. "You're very lucky."

"I wouldn't say that."

"Oh yeah? You live in a nice place, you've got a good job, drive a nice car. You want to sneak away from your team for an assignation? No problem and no consequences. And you've got women falling all over you—"

Mercer starts to counter this—deny, deny, deny, it's always worked in the past—but Emily raises her hand as if to scold him. He doesn't speak.

"I know you, Ben, better than you think. No bullshit now, just listen. You've got everything now, even me. Think about it. What don't you have that you want?"

I'd like another shot at the major leagues, Mercer thinks to himself, because if I had a second chance I wouldn't waste it, I'd do whatever it took to make it work. I would fear nothing.

"See?" Emily says. "You get whatever you want. It's amazing, really, your luck. I was thinking about it on the way out here. I've never met anyone like you."

"Because I get everything I want?"

"Yes."

"I wish my life seemed as good to me as it does to you."

"It should, Ben." She sips at her whiskey, the ice tinkling in her glass. "It should. Because if it did, you might be able to settle down and enjoy it more. Not push things all the time."

He sips his whiskey. It's good, though he wishes it were Scotch. He wonders what she means by "push things all the time," but he doesn't ask, because she'll probably tell him and he finds all this talk about his good fortune depressing.

"So," Emily says at last, "did you win today?"

"We won."

She smiles her I-told-you-so smile.

"You won," she says.

He grins at this, at her understanding of a pitcher's win, as distinct from the team's win.

She looks around the room, says, "Baseball takes you to some pretty romantic places."

"If you're lucky, we'll win this tournament. Then we can come back here the next week."

"Two Battle Creek vacations back to back," she says. "What about some variety? I hear Kalamazoo is nice."

"We could be playing this tournament in Gary."

"Not you," she says. "You're too lucky for Gary."

Later, entangled in bed, resting, he is startled when she speaks, having thought her asleep.

"Are you happy?" she asks.

"Huh?"

"Are you happy?"

"I guess. I mean, you told me I am. Or should be."

"I told you that you were lucky. And you are. But that doesn't mean that you're happy. That was the whole point. You said you wanted this, right? Now it's just us and I want you to be happy."

"Have you really stopped with—" The words "the puppy" come to his lips, but he forces them back down. "Doug," he says, a separate sentence.

"Yes, yes. And I don't miss that now. He was much stronger, you know, than I thought. We really are friends now, but all that other stuff, it's so nice to have it out of the way."

She maneuvers her body around, puts her head on his chest. "I can hear your heart," she says.

"What's it like?"

"It's very slow."

He doesn't answer.

"So, are you happy?" she asks again.

"Yes," he says, intending never to explain.

VII

James knows, even now, that this game will be left up to him. He sits in the dugout, hefting his bat, watching Goodstein stand outside the batter's box and rub dirt into his batting gloves. It's only the fourth inning, and Koch and Sons is ahead by one, a lead that, if held, will give the team its sixth consecutive regional championship. James closes his eyes and sees himself coming to the plate, feels the pressure of the moment, sees the ball coming at him, feels the sublime wonder of contact, a vision so real that Metz must poke him—*Hey, you playing this inning?*—and then his eyes pop open and he sees the dust from his teammates' spikes as they jog out onto the field, sees Goodstein standing by short, waiting for Metz to bring him his glove and cap. The inning is over. James follows.

In the top of the sixth, the opponents—a team from Bad Axe—score two, on a walk and, a sacrifice later, a home run. The ball is hit over James's head, and he knows even as he sprints back to the fence that the ball is gone. He watches it land on the grass knoll beyond the field. Already two young boys are sprinting along the right field fence, on their way to retrieving the ball. James jogs back to his position. He looks past Booth, who is rubbing a new ball, to the opponents' dugout, where the bodies are still moving, all cheers and high fives, and he thinks, Yes, it's going just as I thought.

The last inning arrives. James is climbing the dugout steps when Gil stops him. Metz is on second base. Kukla is about to be intentionally walked.

"Hey," the coach says.

James nods.

"Get a good cut at a good pitch."

"Yeah, Coach."

"You're the guy I want up there now."

"Me, too, Coach," James says. He walks up to the plate, glances for a moment back to the grandstands—not an empty seat in sight—then to the foul-line fences, and then to the granite sky. Okay, he tells himself. Here it is. The pitcher starts him off with a fastball in the dirt. The ball hits the catcher's shin guard and rolls off to the left. Metz and Kukla advance. Now the winning run is on second base. James can hear his own bench whooping it up, but he doesn't glance over. This isn't about cheers. The pitcher is a lefty, a stocky guy. His pants are stretched tight over his thighs. He is sweating, constantly wiping his right arm across his face, trying to clear his brow. The first time up, James hit a low fastball into the dirt, a ground out. The second time he hit a first-pitch fastball well into right center, but the ball carried on the humid air and the center fielder ran it down. The third time up he walked. Now, the pitcher settles into his stretch. James stares him down. The pitcher puffs out his cheeks, and James can see in this that the pressure is weighing on him. This pitcher wishes he hadn't given up the hit to Metz, or allowed the runners to move forward with the pitch in the dirt. James clears his head. He wants a mind without words, with only perfect animal clarity. The pitcher pivots, the whip of the arm, the spin on the ball, away, low—a curve!—and James does not bite. The pitcher comes with the same pitch again, this one over the plate, and James hits the ball, feels the contact. He catches sight of the ball, a liner to left, curving away from the fielder, who was shading toward center. The ball drops, fair by two yards. The crowd roars, as Metz and Kukla sprint home.

"You see," the scout is telling James, "it's different now than when I was a player. Time was, a team was like a family. You lived with 'em, ate with 'em, put up with 'em. Hell, a whole organization was like that. Now it's a business and you're just so much raw material, like some piece of steel to GM. Money did that, some guys getting so much. It made the whole thing change into a kind of lottery. I know, you want some of that money, and, by God, I believe you're going to get it. But you also want some of the old-style ball club, too, a team that's a team. That's why we want you to take a serious look at us, because your play has impressed a lot of our people. I know Freddie Schuster damn near sprung you from prison, but you're out now and you're going into a whole organization. Once you sign, Freddie's just one guy you won't see again. You follow me?"

James nods. He doesn't want to give anything away. He

wants to be wanted, but he isn't going to dismiss Alfredo
Schuster. Never. Not after Mr. Schuster stuck by him all
those years. It amazes James that he received help like that,
no matter how good he is at baseball. When his father was
around he was good at baseball, but James still couldn't get
the man's attention, except on those rare occasions when his
father showed up at one of his ball games and cheered his
lungs out on each of James's hits, attention more embarrassing than not having a father at all. James watched other boys
for clues to how life was supposed to be. He remembers leaving a ball field once—he was maybe ten or eleven—and
watching the father of one of his teammates put his arm
around his son's shoulder as they headed out into center
field, toward the parking lot. They just walked like that, as
though they did it every day. James remembers the droopy
way the boy's pants hung over his sanitary socks and stirrups,
how the kid had his glove tucked under his outside arm. The
kid wasn't a very good player. When James got to the parking
lot he found a seat on one of the cement parking barricades
and waited for his mother to come for him. He hoped that
she would take him to McDonald's or the A&W. He hadn't
had lunch, and he was thirsty, too. Down the way the boy
with the droopy pants got into his father's Cutlass. As they
drove by, the boy waved. James could see that the boy was
drinking a Faygo red pop. His father must have brought it
for him. It occurred to James then—in a startling, world-
expanding way—that other fathers loved their sons whether
they got hits or not.

Now he watches as his teammates are clearing out of the

dugout, jostling one another with good-natured jibes, as ribbing is less embarrassing to a ballplayer than full-front praise. James acknowledges Metz, Jefferson, O'Rourke, Brattenburg, Kohn, celebration alight in all of their eyes.

"Good, then," the scout is saying. "Make sure you stay focused." The man hands over his card. James sticks it in his back pocket, where it mingles with the machine-washed remains of some other scout's card. This scout smiles and heads off, his head pivoting. James wonders who he is looking for. Kukla? O'Rourke?

"Hey, bud," says a voice, low, subdued. Mercer. James turns. "Nice job," the pitcher says. "Looked to me like you hit a good pitch."

"I guess."

"Tommy Raymond tell you how he was going to look after you better than your father would?"

"My father wouldn't," James says.

"You know what I mean. Keep your head. You're close now, you know."

"I know."

"Maybe you could leave Barb out of this week."

"You talk to Barb?"

"Via Emily I do. My point is, limit distractions."

"Everybody keeps saying that. I can take care of myself."

"It's just friendly advice," Mercer says.

"How'd you sleep last night?" James asks, bothered now by the meddling. When Mercer says that he slept fine, James lets a smile come to his lips, just to let Mercer know.

VIII

I-94. Gil drives toward the sun, away from Dearborn and a day of work. Long shadows from the cars ahead of him stretch back into his path. It is practically seven-eighteen, the time, the station told him, his piece would air.

At present there is an ad for an Italian and Greek restaurant on Gratiot, then a brief pause when it ends.

"This past week," the deejay says, "an unprecedented baseball feat was accomplished in our midst. The Koch and Sons Baseball Club of Pontiac won the regional Class A Amateur Baseball Tournament for the sixth consecutive year. The club beat its own record and made itself the only team ever to attain that level of excellence and constancy. We asked Coach Gilbert Davison how he accounted for the team's success.

"'We stress the fundamentals, even at this level of play. We try to do the little things well, the basic things.'

"Indeed they do. Next week the team will take on teams from around the country in the national championship, to be held at Memorial Field in Battle Creek. If you want to see baseball the way it was meant to be played, without artificial turf, sky boxes, dancing chickens, inflated salaries, rapacious owners, or coddled players, call 616-389-2929 for ticket information."

Then an ad for Buff Whelan Chevrolet.

Gil plays back the piece in his mind. A heat rises up his back when he thinks of the sound of his voice, scratchy, gravelly. He tries to remember what he said. Something about fundamentals. All coaches say that. He wishes that the right words rolled off his tongue when he needed them to, that communication in all its forms could be facile.

But no, in this regard he is truly his father's son. The old man has lived what most men would consider more than a lifetime and he's barely lined up three consecutive sentences. Well, there isn't much hope for anything more, what with a hole in the man's throat. Not a bad trade for Morris, who certainly must prefer breath to talk.

It is a dark, full-throated summer night when Gil cuts the engine in the hospital parking lot. He stands for a moment next to his car, listens to the crickets and the thousands of other insects whose names he cannot guess at. The metal of his car clicks as it cools. He sniffs cut grass—a ball field smell—and thinks, Almost made it. One more tournament now. Please, one more.

Inside, the sight of his father shocks him. The man lies on his back, eyes closed, a bandage around his neck, out of which sticks a clear plastic tube half the length of a man's pinky and about as thick. From the tube a frothy mix of blood and spit and the old man's insides bubbles and then spurts whenever there is a heavy breath or cough. There is plenty of coughing. The coughing spews the mixture—dark, a color not unlike that of a sloe gin fizz—down the man's body and onto the towel that has been laid on his chest. Morris's expression is one of pain, a crinkled brow, cheeks sunken, a toothless keyhole mouth. He does not respond when Gil speaks, nor when his son takes his icy hand. This, Gil knows, can't be right, for Morris to work and struggle for almost a century to end up like this. Where are the doctors? Are they not duty-bound to relieve suffering? Gil fetches a nurse.

"I don't understand," he says. "This was supposed to make it easier for him to breathe."

"It's working," the nurse says. "That's fluid coming from his lungs. He was drowning before."

"He's not comfortable. Look at him. He's in pain."

She looks, but does not speak.

"Can't you give him something?" Gil asks.

"We're doing what we can."

"The man is in need of pain relief. Morphine, or something."

"Morphine slows the body. I have instructions not to give him any additional morphine. For a man like your father, it might shut him down altogether. We can't take the chance of slowing his breathing."

Gil looks at the froth bubbling at the tip of the tracheotomy tube. He wishes Vince were here. He would know what to do, or at least he would have an opinion. Gil watches as a cough projects bloody phlegm across the towel and bedsheet. Breath, the nurse calls it.

IX

Waiting, Mercer takes in the red, white, and blue bunting that now hangs from the grandstands in Battle Creek, along with a large banner announcing the national tournament. In the out-field, new cereal advertisements hang from the fences, all the familiar names, a battle of raisin brans.

Okay, two more innings. Mercer has yet to allow a run. Koch and Sons is on its way to winning the opening game. But Mercer's arm is burning, scalding, and the inning hasn't yet started. Krauss crouches and Mercer delivers, his first warm-up pitch of the inning. There is a pop and immediate pain.

Krauss jogs to the mound, armor clanking.

"What's up?" the catcher says.

"I got stiff. Let me get loose." Mercer doesn't have to think to say these words. He is a pitcher, knows them by heart.

Krauss turns toward the dugout and nods. Mercer follows his line of vision till he sees Gil waddling out across the foul line. The players wait.

"Well?" the coach asks.

"Arm's stiff," says the catcher.

"I'm okay," says Mercer.

"Sure," Gil says. He signals for Kindle.

"I meant it, Gil."

"Hey, you pitched a great game. We need you for others."

"I'm talking about now."

"I need to talk to you," the coach says.

Soon they are sitting in the dusty air of the dugout, in the remote corner. The pitcher's corner. Down the row Mercer sees Brattenburg sitting in Vince's spot, the scoreboard on his lap. Kohn and Booth are whispering to each other. Mercer leans back, breathes deep. The air smells of old leather and sweat and the earth. The baseball smells.

"Your junk is working well," Gil says.

"You told me to mix it up."

"What about your fastball?"

"What about it?" Mercer asks.

"Still got one?"

Mercer stares.

"I knew a guy," Gil says. "This was in Japan. He played pro ball for the Browns after the war. Jim Foley. Big righty. He got arm trouble, so he joined the navy."

Kindle throws his first pitch, a strike.

"Played on the base team. Had a sinker no one could touch."

A curve, strike two.

"What's the point?" Mercer asks, impatient now, tired of coaches who tell stories to make points.

"Somebody shot him. In Hawaii. We all knew he was doctoring the ball. No one said anything, though."

A ball. The batter steps out of the box and stretches. He is tense, this batter. Mercer can see it. Come inside on this guy, he'll never get around.

"Somebody killed him for throwing a spitball?" Mercer asks, chuckling. "Then I'm okay, 'cause I still got my fastball, and I'm not throwing spitters. Safe, you might call me."

Strike three, on a lame, pathetic swing.

Gil jumps to his feet. "Attaway," he yells. "Way to hum out there!" He sits back down and says quietly, "I'd want to know if things weren't kosher. I've got almost sixty years in this game. I've coached close to thirty. This is my whole life. I want to go out the right way."

"A winner," Mercer says.

"A legitimate winner."

So that's it, Mercer thinks. Legitimacy.

X

For James the tour is something of a revelation, the long planning and careful steps of baking, splitting, and baking corn
till in mechanized wonder whole phalanxes of cornflakes
boxes come streaming out of the assembly line, all of it sug-
gesting a world far more orderly and planned than anything
James has imagined. It is his idea, this tour. Metz told him
about it. He hadn't thought of bringing Barb; she just appeared in Battle Creek and James, not knowing what else to
do, invited her.

They approach the tour's end, where young women, girls really, blond and hale, hand them boxes of cornflakes fresh off the
line.

"I came out here, Luke, to tell you not to call me again." This
is Barb talking. James is not sure if he is hearing her right. "Not
that you really planned to. Your future isn't going to include
me, so we might as well cut it right now."

They emerge from the building into the parking lot and a
light drizzle.

"You want to break up?" he asks, wondering if she really
means it.

"In a word, yes."

He feels his stomach clench.

"I think it's best," she is saying. "You've got a great future in baseball. Everybody says so. You're going to be moving on and I'm not part of that."

He can't speak. He feels that old feeling coming back. Alone, but also relieved. "C'mon," she says, "I'll give you a ride back to the hotel."

He refuses. He could do a number of things right now, but getting into Barb's econobox is not one of them. No amount of her asking will change his mind. She catches on to this last point quickly.

"Fine, then," she says. "Walk." And she is gone.

He stands a moment longer, feeling angry. It is several minutes before he awakens to what surrounds him, aware first of the light rain and the late-summer dampness, of the smell of dirt and pine (trees line the lot), smells that for him evoke the days of his early youth. He sniffs the cornflakes, still hot from the oven, the aroma rising from the steaming box, and it sets him back to the summer he was eleven, the last summer he saw his father, when his friends worshipped him and he sometimes ate dinner with both of his parents and the world was still held together in a way he could understand. When the tears come he is shocked—he thought he was beyond tears—but they keep coming, a sadness and yearning over a box of cornflakes and a world that he's not sure ever existed.

XI

It is late, past ten, when Gil pulls into Mapleshade. He'd planned to be here by seven, but the team lost its first game of the day and had to stay to pull out a last-inning nail-biter—James, again, got the winning hit, cool as ice, pure clutch—to reach the finals, to be played tomorrow against a team from Georgia. Both the Georgian team and Koch and Sons now have one loss in a double elimination tournament, so tomorrow's game is the deciding one. He has rushed from today's game, having changed but not showered; he rubs one forearm with a free hand and feels the rough grime of infield dirt, realizes he is literally wearing the field. Tired, weary but awed at what lies before him, he is close, on the verge, dizzy when he lets himself imagine the win, so close his mouth goes dry in contemplation of it.

The parking lot is unusually full, and he cruises the near rows before giving up and driving to the back, where he parks and stands, licking his dusty lips, thirsty.

"Hey," a voice says. "Look."

Not ten feet from where he has parked, two nurses stand, heads tilted back, eyes on the stars. It is impossible to resist such posture, so Gil, too, gazes upward and notices, for the first time in years, stars—yes, the first time since the navy, when looking at the night sky was required. Stars. Millions of them.

"See it?" asks a nurse.

"See what?"

"The comet!"

He follows the line of her finger. His eyes dart from star to star and then he sees it, a bundle of lighted fuzz, as if some kid were holding a Fourth of July sparkler in the heavens. He watches and watches, transfixed suddenly by the hugeness of what is happening, this bubbling comet. He stares, in contemplation for the first time of such vastness, oddly joined together with these two nurses. *Did you see that?* he wants to say, to let them know that he has.

"Wow," says one of the nurses, a tall, hefty blond woman whom Gil recognizes as usually working the downstairs station. "Wow."

Inside, the building is quiet. Gil is ready to sweet-talk his way up to his father's room—it's after visiting hours—but no nurse appears to stop him. He takes the stairs to the second floor. As he approaches his father's room he can hear the hack, a kind of beacon that draws him to the room and at the same time tightens his stomach. He turns into the open door just as his father spews an enormous glob of phlegm and blood out the tracheotomy tube and across the sheets.

Sickened, tired of witnessing endless agony, Gil replays in his mind the conversation he had with the doctor not two days earlier. It took seven phone calls to get the man on the phone, and when Gil did, he wanted to know just what was the prognosis. Gil couldn't see where the tracheotomy was leading, if all they were doing was moving Morris out of the hospital, back to Mapleshade to hack away his final breaths in misery. He asked the doctor if this was the best that could be done.

"Your father is a very old man," the doctor said. "We can't very well change that."

"So why the hole in the throat? The tubes? It's not making him better."

"He is alive," the doctor said, his voice arch, as if maybe Gil hadn't noticed, as if this simple fact made his argument—whatever it was—unassailable. And Gil, angry and somehow cowed, lacking something—expertise, authority, power—did not demand anything more, did not ask where was hope, healing, relief.

Now he stands over his father's bed.

"Dad?" he says.

There is no recognition. Morris's eyes are shut tightly, as if anything might be better than opening them.

"Dad?" Gil asks again.

Only hacking.

C'mon, Dad, Gil wants to say. One more day, one more day and we just might win it all. Finally, your son will be the champion of something. If you can make it one more day.

More hacking, lines of pain across the man's forehead, his face leeched, even his lips the color of the bedding.

Gil looks up, sees a plain of acoustical tiles a few feet above his head dotted with the odd sprinkler, but he is looking beyond. He is not a religious man, but if there is a God, he demands an audience now. What, he wants to know, is right in this? Here is a quiet, humble man (and an impossible one, too), who has worked hard his whole life, and kept to himself. How can you let him suffer so?

Gil remembers a sermon from Rabbi Kirsch, in Jackson, back when Gil took his father to High Holy Day services. The rabbi said that you don't appeal to God for favors. He exists for guidance and judgment. It is up to you to act. Gil never forgot that because it sounded so much like the old coach's line, about making your own luck.

"Dad," Gil says. "We need some luck."

Stillness. Gil realizes he is talking now to his father as he talks to Laurence in the cemetery. It's an easy connection to make, this and talking to the dead. Hardly a difference, except that Laurence has some peace. Gil knows he must act, knows in a way that is so shocking and sudden that he can't find its source; it is deep instinct, natural and compelling. He looks at his father. This is as close as he and his father will ever get. Yes, for the first time in his life he knows what to do with his father.

He takes a deep breath, breathes in the hospital smells, chemicals, staleness, sees the anonymity of the darkened room, the empty chair, the wall-mounted HVAC unit, the shades drawn to the night sky. He knows this could be a hospital room—or, for that matter, a hotel room—in any city in the country. This saddens him. A dying man deserves more.

Gil walks to the hallway and looks, then listens for signs of life. The linoleum floor shines, even in the dim lighting. There are only the normal building noises of air and water moving through hidden ducts and pipes. Otherwise, all is still.

Gil walks to his father's bedside. The old man's body still shakes with each cough. Gil grabs a washcloth from the bathroom, then returns to the bed, reaches down, and pinches the tracheotomy tube. After a slight delay, the old man's body jumps. A breath is forced up out of his mouth, which gapes open, fishlike. For one brief moment Gil feels doubt, but then takes his free hand and grabs a pillow, clamps it down on his father's face. The man's body is in revolt now, and Gil is shocked and terrified by the force of life left within the man. The body is bucking, but Gil, having chosen his course, persists. The body shakes, bucks, shakes. Suddenly, it is still.

Gil removes the pillow. One of his father's eyes is open. Gil gasps for composure. He wipes his face with his forearm; this leaves the hair on his forearm matted, sweat-soaked. He folds up the washcloth; he must hide it. He stuffs it in his pocket. He looks again to his father. There is no more hacking, nor is there an agonized look, though Gil would hardly call it peaceful: bothered is the right word. Gil feels his stomach flip. He dashes to the bathroom, wretches, nothing but bile; he hasn't eaten all day. He splashes cold water on his face. He is winded, heaving, as if he'd just sprinted up a five-hundred-foot hill. The bathroom spins, and he grabs onto the sink with both hands and holds on, till the spinning finally stops.

He emerges from the bathroom, studies the room. Satisfied that it looks normal (what could look more normal than this room?), he walks out. He is full of composure because composure is now demanded. He must make his own luck. He tells himself he must be hard. He is a rock. At a rest area just west of Jackson he stops and disposes of the bloodied washcloth. It is quiet here, save the rush of traffic from I-94. He looks for the comet but now finds his vision clouded, and then the tears come. And come, as they once did and sometimes still do for Laurence, the last death in the family.

XII

James wakes. The room is quiet, except for the hum of the air conditioner and Metz's sleep-heavy breathing. James swings his legs out of bed, walks to the window, pulls back the plastic-lined curtain. Already the sun glares off the windows of the cars in the parking lot, off the asphalt. Looks to be a scorcher.

James dresses in Koch and Sons shorts and a Koch and Sons T-shirt and heads to the gym to stretch. That hotels now have gyms is one of the signs of progress that James has noticed, like cable sports channels (he remembers when you could almost never get a game), and phones without wires (a technology whose use never fails to startle him). In the gym James lies on a mat, kicks his legs over his head to stretch his back. He thinks about the game. Today they are facing Kyle Gertsen, a tall lefty who pitched four seasons for Montreal. Yesterday Alfredo Schuster told James that Gertsen was the best pitcher in the tournament. James wanted to know if this meant better than Mercer, and Schuster had nodded a solemn yes. "Hell," the scout said, "Montreal didn't let him go, he quit, on account of his getting older and feeling he didn't want to hang on. He's got a little boy who's real sick—crippled, actually—and he didn't want to be on the road all the time." And then, as if Schuster could read James's mind, he added, "And the guy's got money. Real money. The Gertsens own half the real estate 'round Atlanta, mosta which they bought back when General Sherman got done with it and nobody thought it was worth much. Ain't often you get a ballplayer from money like that."

James thinks of all that can get in the way of a baseball life, and he knows he will never let it happen. Never.

Schuster says that Gertsen has a rangy motion and a three-quarter delivery that lets him curve a lefty so that the batter chases balls outside or bails out on strikes. James knows he must hang in against this guy, keep his shoulder and weight back and drive the ball to left. Everybody's always waiting for Gertsen's fastball. It, too, is a good pitch, though most batters think they have a better chance with it. This is a weakness of batters, that almost all prefer to hit fastballs. Gertsen knows this, and makes them chase bad balls, throws off their timing by changing speeds. James thinks that Gertsen must be good because he can think as hitters do, knows their desires and fears, and then crosses them up. So James must hit the breaking ball, because it is exactly the pitch he is not supposed to want to hit.

Standing now, his knees straight, his palms flat on the mat, James allows himself the fantasy that always creeps into his baseball dreams, the full stands and rich green of big-league stadiums, a life of baseball and promise. *You've impressed a lot of people,* Alfredo Schuster told him yesterday. *Oh yes, a lot.*

And then he feels an ache inside that he cannot really understand, a sense of joy that reaches around almost to panic. All is well, he tells himself. All is well.

XIII

Mercer glances up at the sun, the glow so directly overhead that there are no shadows. The team is paired off, playing catch, but

Mercer is watching, his elbow wrapped in ice. This morning when he woke he noticed a golf-ball-sized lump protruding where there should only have been smooth muscle. He has not told Gil about the golf ball. The coach plans to use him for relief, and Mercer wants this chance, the chance to win, finally, a chance to redeem for last year, when he got thumped in the penultimate inning of the season, and had to live through the last, and then a whole year—yet another year—with the loss.

"It's an oven," Gil says. He winces at the wavy outfield heat.

"Yeah, but they say it's supposed to go down to fifty-five tonight. Cold front's coming down from Canada. It'll be football weather before you know it."

"I'm just concerned with today, Ben."

"Today is today. Tomorrow you'll be working on next year's roster."

"I wanted to talk to you about that."

"Yeah?" Mercer says, interested. Gil has never asked his advice about personnel.

"You ever thought about coaching?" the coach asks.

Mercer laughs. "I'm not cut from coaching cloth," he says. "Don't have the patience, don't want the worries. You need an assistant, get Goodstein or Jefferson. They'd be good."

"I'm not looking for an assistant. This is it for me, Ben."

"Gil, this is what you do," Mercer says. He looks at Gil, sees a man who looks tired, with dark, drawn eyes and slumping shoulders. When Mercer first met Gil, Gil had a stare and a sharp jawline that made him look every inch the coach. Now his jaw has disappeared, his eyes often seem teary, his walk is stiff, and he looks like somebody's grandfather. But he can't stop coaching. It's in his blood. "You've got to coach," Mercer adds.

"This is the year."

The two men stand, not talking, listening to the pop of baseballs into gloves.

"My father died last night," Gil says.

"I'm sorry to hear that," Mercer replies, thinking it the source of the quitting talk. "That's terrible, Coach."

"My father was a very old man, and very sick."

"Still."

Gil says nothing more. Mercer glances at him out of the corner of his eye, realizes that he didn't really know Gil had a living father, that after all these years he still hardly knows Gil at all.

XIV

It took till three in the morning for the home to call. "I'm so sorry," the nurse said. Gil asked how his father had died and she told him the man's heart "just gave out," and Gil found that the tears came all over again. He'd never lived without his father, a man who always seemed certain how life should be lived. Even if his rules were ridiculous, they stood as a guide. Now Gil would have to make up his own rules, serve as his own conscience. This made the world new, and a little scary. There was also the sudden lack of duty. That he would never again have to drive to Jackson to pay bills seemed sad, even monumental, and though he knew he'd always hated it, he felt a little wistful now. He liked to drive, after all, liked cruising through the countryside in a big car. What, he wondered, would he now do with his time? Who would need him?

After Gil heard from the home, he called Rick, told him his grandfather was dead.

"What do you need me to do?" Rick asked. His voice sounded surprisingly clear, given that he was being waked in the middle of the night.

Gil said there was nothing he needed to do, but he thought there must be something.

Rick said that his grandfather had been an old man, one whose time had come. "He was born before there were really automobiles. Think of that, Dad."

Gil thought, but couldn't really imagine what it meant.

"Listen, Dad," Rick said. "I'll come in tomorrow. Visit. Help you make arrangements. Maybe spend a few days. I can take the time."

"I'm in Battle Creek," Gil said.

"What for?"

"The national tournament."

"The national tournament? Now?"

"We play the finals tomorrow."

"The finals! Why didn't you tell me?"

Gil said nothing. Why had he not told his only son? He had no idea.

Gil tries all morning not to think of his father at all, and most of the time it works. But there are lapses. Sometimes he gets a vision of his father's last seconds, of the fight and kick Gil felt in his hands, and this memory makes Gil's hands shake and his bowels slacken and he must sit down. He can't tell when the vision will haunt him, so he attempts to sit on the bench as much as possible (as Vince did at the end) or never to stray far from it. Also, there is an argument running through his head, a dispute his brain seems to be having with itself. How could he do such a thing, it wants to know, and how could he not?

And then there are the memories that catch him off guard: his father standing in the driveway of the old house wearing a sheepskin coat Gil had bought him, waiting, as always, for Gil; his father walking out to start the car when Gil was a boy; his father leaning over a bowl of soup during a visit Gil made from the navy; his father sitting with his mother on their old couch, listening to the radio; his father lightly licking his thumb, as he did every time he intended to flip the page of a newspaper; his father in his last bed; his father standing with his hands on his knees in his old living room, Laurence at his feet.

At the start of the fourth inning, Gil glances up to the stands to find them aflutter. Everyone seems to be waving something—programs, hats, cardboard food trays—anything for a breeze. He even spots Rick, amazing, given how packed the stands are. Rick wears a blue Koch and Sons T-shirt, and seems to be chatting with O'Rourke's father. Yes, Gil thinks,

Rick can get along anywhere. Gil appreciates that Rick has come to Battle Creek on such short notice. It's more than Rick has to do, but Gil realizes that Rick feels duty-bound to him the way Gil felt duty-bound to Morris, that Rick's coming to Battle Creek is little different from all those trips Gil made to Jackson. And this saddens Gil, because he never wanted his sons to be raised like that, full of old-world duty and guilt.

Gil turns back to the game. Along the foul-line fences he can see rows of fans in lawn chairs; others lie on the upper edge of the knoll that rises beyond the outfield fence. The scoreboard is out there, too, all zeros except for the inning.

Metz leads off, walks. He tries to steal second—on his own—but Kukla fouls off the pitch. Then a ground ball to deep short. Gil watches as Metz goes into second high and sideways, a cross-body block three feet behind the base. The second baseman is caught in midair, throwing, and, in the slow, frame-by-frame time that humans inhabit when they leave the ground, he spins and cartwheels, the sun glinting off his spikes, his cap in the air, and then he drops, onto his left shoulder. Gil can hear him grunt. Kukla beats the throw at first, which is weak and up the line.

A cry goes up from the crowd. The opposing coach comes running from his dugout. His name is Darryl Clutterbuck; Gil knows of him, knows that he played in the Cleveland organization, never got out of Double-A. Clutterbuck now owns an Acura dealership in Marietta.

"Hey, blue," Clutterbuck yells at the umpire, "c'mon!"

Gil watches Metz trot down the dugout steps, clapping the

dust from his hands. Gil thinks he sees a smirk. Metz is normally a smiling, happy-go-lucky guy, but, like all good athletes, he can be a mean son of a bitch, too. He plays with a reckless abandon that makes Gil proud. Clutterbuck is arguing as if he'd just been shortchanged at the bank. Gil realizes he must go out. He doesn't know this umpire. He's standing with his hands on his hips, looking short, florid, damp. Gil just wants him to do what almost all umpires do about plays around second base: nothing.

"It's second base," the umpire is explaining to Clutterbuck when Gil walks up. This is the right answer to any question or statement Clutterbuck might have. Clutterbuck gives Gil a quick glance, full of disdain, as though Gil were the umpire's lawyer.

"It ain't right," Clutterbuck says, his voice low now, more Southern. "Just 'cause they're the hometown team, to favor 'em. It ain't right."

"That's way out of line," Gil says. "We play two and a half hours from here. We beat teams from this town to get here. That's way out of line."

"I'm just calling it how I see it."

"So am I," says the ump. "Let's play ball."

"I'll be watching you, blue," Clutterbuck says as he backs away. "Watching to see if you got just an ounce of guts."

James bats next, and he slaps the first pitch into right field for the game's first hit. Kukla never hesitates at second and soon pulls up into third. Gil is using Brattenburg to coach third; the player/coach pats Kukla's fanny, chats up his player. C'mon, Gil thinks, look over here. Kukla does. Brattenburg does. Gil crosses his right leg over his left, resting the ankle on his knee, and straightens his cap. Brattenburg relays the sign, and on the next pitch James steals second, gets such a good jump that the catcher doesn't risk a throw.

Now a noise rises up from the stands as might come from big-league stands, a collective roar. Second and third, and one out. O'Rourke at bat.

The pitcher goes back to a full windup, and throws a pitch that passes an inch from O'Rourke's nose. Next thing Gil knows, O'Rourke is in the dirt; the player's bat rolls all the way to the backstop. Now it's Gil's turn.

"Hey!" he shouts, trotting now toward the home-plate umpire. "He threw at him! He threw at him! Plain as day!"

"He didn't hit him, Gil," the home-plate umpire says. Gil knows this guy. Chet Burdick, works at one of the cereal plants.

"You watch it," Gil says. "You'll lose control of this game. A boy can get killed."

Now Clutterbuck arrives. "Hell," he says, real Southern. "He didn't mean to throw at him. He's got runners in scoring position. It's too risky."

"He's got first base open," Gil says.

"C'mon, Coach," says Burdick.

There is, as in family squabbles, no end to this, only ritual. One coach must complain, the other defend, the umpire listen. Gil walks back to his dugout doing his best to look indignant. He has to hand it to Gertsen, this pitcher. Throwing at a guy with a man on third takes a lot of guts.

Three pitches later, O'Rourke lifts a fly ball to left, and Kukla scores on the sacrifice. Finally a one goes up on the scoreboard.

Gil studies that board as if it can tell him secrets of the future, studies it till he begins to believe that on a day like today, with Kohn pitching well and Mercer in relief, one run might be enough.

XV

James's eyes pick up the ball while it's still in Gertsen's hand, off-kilter to the throwing finger, and this sight, along with the twisted wrist, tells James a breaking ball is coming, tells him before it leaves the pitcher's hand. James follows it, watches the tumble of the laces, moves with it, and doesn't swing. Low and away. Ball one.

The pitch makes sense. The last time up Gertsen threw him a change-up, low and not quite inside, and James hit it hard to right center. James thought it a bad pitch to throw him, especially for an inside strike. A pitcher's got to come hard inside if he's going to come inside at all. This Gertsen was supposed to be the best pitcher in the tournament, but James is not impressed. Mercer is better. Kohn is better. Easy.

Now James decides that if Gertsen has half a brain he'll come hard inside or again try to make James fish outside on a bad, off-speed ball. James decides he'll come hard inside, for a strike, because it's already the sixth inning and Gertsen doesn't want to walk the leadoff hitter. And besides, it's best to challenge your opponent to do the difficult thing. So James looks for a fastball inside. He gets a curve, again low and away, but for a strike, called.

The inside fastball comes next, a little too inside, ball two.

James steps out. He feels the odds of this at bat tipping in his favor. He knows he will hit the ball hard, knows that he will take one more step toward his goal. Everyone has been telling him he will be drafted; next season he will be living in a minor-league town, with a signing bonus in the bank. Yes! he thinks. Yes.

Gertsen misses on the next pitch, another curve, a real roundhouse, with a wide and sneaky release. Ball three.

Three and one, a hitter's count. James looks for a fastball, figures Gertsen can't risk the walk and his control on off-speed pitches has not been good. James slaps the fastball off the right field fence. A double.

Georgia tries a pickoff play on the next pitch. The second baseman makes sure that James gets the tag in the teeth. James feels an electric bolt of pain, but it's fleeting. He's safe.

XVI

The seventh inning, still one to nothing. Kohn starts it off by throwing two balls. In the dugout, Gil turns to Mercer, asks him if he wants to get ready.

Mercer nods. Hell yes, he thinks.

Warming up, Mercer can tell that his arm is not good. Doesn't have the pop he'd like, but he won't need many outs. Six at most. He throws fastballs, three-quarter speed, works up his arm and body into a sweat, till drops roll off his nose and chin and splash in the dust of the bullpen. He tries a few curves, then goes for the goo, and is surprised and pleased by how nicely the ball moves.

Brattenburg, who is catching him, stands and says, "It's a tough pitch."

Mercer nods.

"If they don't see it coming," the catcher adds.

Mercer nods again, knows that in baseball the most important things are left unsaid, that superstition and common sense tell players never to discuss ongoing events. No one ever speaks of no-hitters or hitting streaks, or phantom tags and certainly not of doctored balls, even if it's all plain as day. Some things you just don't say.

XVII

Remember this, Gil tells himself, knowing that he will not do it again. Remember how it looks, with one inning to go, three outs to the win. Remember the people standing with their fingers hooked through the metal fence, remember the milky blue of the stadium paint and the similar color of the sky. Remember the cereal ads hanging from the outfield fence, and the sound of practice grounders rolling across the infield and the jumping dust in their wake. Remember that your son has driven in from Chicago to witness it. Remember your dry mouth and constricted breath, the thump in your heart. Remember the eerie silence. Remember the ache of being close.

XVIII

"Hey! Hey! Hey, hey, hey!"

James is jogging out to right field when he sees the kids, two of them, waving pieces of paper like hankies. Young kids, maybe ten years old.

"Hey!" they yell. They ask for autographs.

"I've got to warm up," James yells back.

"C'mon. Pul-leeeeez."

"After the game, come by the dugout."

"All right!" they yell. They sprint away, bounding and bumping into each other like puppies.

"Hey!" Now it's O'Rourke, calling from center field. He throws James a ball in a long, looping arc. James returns the throw, then looks for the kids, wishing he hadn't put them off.

XIX

It's on the third strike, the one that has the batter lunging, swinging after a ball that bounces on the plate—with Krauss knocking it down, pouncing on it, then tagging the batter as he stumbles out of his follow-through—that the answer comes to Gil. Grease. Mercer is throwing spitters. No doubt about it.

My God, he thinks. He feels the anger building, born from a career as a hitter. All hitters think that pitchers have enough of an advantage already, standing an eye's blink from the batter, who knows neither the mix of pitches nor their speed, with eight other players positioned to take away what little success the poor man might have. And now Gil has a pitcher who is a fraud, a cheat—his chosen successor, the player in whom he has the most confidence, in whom he trusts most to get the job done, the right way. Gil misses Vince now more than ever. Vince would know what to make of this. Yes, Vince would know.

Gil wants to pull Mercer. He wants to win, but on the up-and-up. He decides he must be sure. He calls time, then waves Krauss over to the dugout. The catcher clatters over, lifts his mask. Sweat is beaded up on his face like water on a glass.

"He's throwing a spitball," Gil says.

"Who?" the catcher asks, without surprise or question in his voice. He looks down to where his shin guards lap over his shoelaces.

Gil thinks, These guys must think I'm blind. "Okay." It's a low utterance, almost a groan. He can say nothing else.

"Coach," Krauss says. He looks out to the field, then down again, speaks low, through his glove, the way players do when they don't want their lips read. Gil can barely hear. "Relax," Krauss says. "It's a good one."

XX

The pitch leaves Mercer's hand and he feels the pain in his elbow. Something in there is tearing, he knows it. The golf ball is now as big as a plum, and about the same color, covered in

Koch and Sons royal blue, so no one will notice. He meant to start this curve more to the outside, but he didn't, and now he watches as it sails in over the plate. Mercer doesn't have to wait for the ball to be hit, he knows even now, in that split second it takes for the ball to travel sixty and a half feet, that this ball will be well hit. And so it is, up onto—no, beyond—the knoll in left center field, the people jumping from their blankets, ducking, rolling out of the way.

The Georgia bench erupts and Mercer must endure a long wait on the pitcher's mound. He rubs the new ball, and plots his revenge. In the battle between pitcher and batter there can be no question who is in control. The gods of the game gave the ball to the pitcher for a reason. He must dominate or be crushed. So Mercer puts the next pitch in the batter's ear.

It knocks the batter's helmet off, leaves him in the dirt. The helmet spins, slows, like a top coming to rest. The opposing coach, some used-car shyster from down South, comes running from the dugout. Other players sprint to their fallen teammate. Then a man in Bermuda shorts and a golf shirt arrives, a first-aid kit in his hand.

Jesus, Mercer thinks. He's never hit a batter in the head before. Shoulders, ribs, the small of the back, once on the kneecap (the ball bounded all the way to the first base dugout)—Mercer knows the routine for these beanballs. Normally, a hush comes over the crowd as the batter lies in some awkward position in the batter's box, as if he's fallen from the top of the backstop. Then he gets up, brushes himself off, and trots to first, trying not to look relieved that he's alive. (But this one is not trotting off anywhere. He isn't even moving.) Mercer has always loved the beanball, the power and fear it creates. Getting hit is part of the game. The good hitters know this. They respect a pitcher who tries to move them back. There is a rule against hitting someone intentionally, but it's one of those rules that's impossible to enforce.

The used-car guy thinks otherwise. Mercer waves for Krauss to walk up the first base line, so Mercer can keep throwing, keep his arm loose. The smelling salts aren't having much effect on the batter, but they seem to have livened up his coach. He berates the umpire, who finally decides to walk out to the mound. Mercer watches him come, then sees that Gil is also heading for the mound. Krauss joins in—catchers think they have a right to be in on everything. The used-car salesman tries to gain admittance to the meeting, but the umpire won't allow it.

"What happened?" the ump asks.

"It got away," Mercer says. As he speaks he begins to feel innocent, what he says makes so much sense. "I meant to pitch him high and tight. He stands too close to the plate. Obviously I didn't want to put him on. Game's tied, last inning. I don't want the winning run on base."

"His control is normally excellent," Gil says, which, it seems to Mercer, is not an argument in his favor, but he lets the coach run with it. "This one just got away."

"Pretty good coincidence," the umpire says, "right after a guy takes you downtown."

"I've been downtown plenty of times," Mercer says. "I'm no yahoo kid. I'm thirty-four years old. I got nothing to prove."

Finally, back at the plate the batter is helped to his feet, then guided back to the bench, held by his elbow, as if the pitch has left him blind. A pinch runner jogs out to first.

"Watch it," the umpire says quietly. Then he belts out a "Play ball!" and walks back to the plate.

"You're letting him stay?" the opposing coach shouts. "You gotta be kidding."

The umpire is now bent over, a fanny as wide as a Caprice facing Mercer. The ump sweeps the plate. "Play ball!" he says when he stands.

Gil is still at the mound. "You're not who I thought," he says.

"I only meant to knock him down," Mercer says.

"That's not what I mean."

"What, then?"

"Spitters."

Mercer says nothing. He feels odd, caught but not really caring. As if he's finally grown up.

"I don't want to cheat," the coach says.

"Then yank me," Mercer says, knowing that Gil would never. Never.

"Let's go!" the umpire shouts from home. "Let's play ball!"

Gil says nothing, just walks back to the dugout.

XXI

Gil knows he should pull the son of a bitch, right now. But he needs two outs—James leads off the bottom of the inning and it would be great if they only needed one run to win it—and

Gil is not going to let anything get in his way. Not even the rules. He has to put these things out of his mind. Vanquish doubt. He must be hard. So he leaves Mercer in, and he gets his two outs.

XXII

James threads his bat between his arms and lower back and twists to loosen up. On the field the Georgian catcher is throwing the ball down to second and the red team—it's how James thinks of them—snaps the ball around the infield. A breeze has started to blow, and on it James can feel the hint of a storm, lightning-charged and severe, a mixing of hot air and cold. The stands are quiet—there's too much tension, a one-to-one game in the bottom of the last inning of the last and deciding game. James taps his cleats, gets ready to step into the box, then becomes aware of something he hasn't felt in years: he's happy. Yes, happy.

He sets his back foot up in the box, positioning himself close to the plate. He's sure Gertsen will make him hit a curveball. An inferior pitcher would start him off with a fastball, not wanting to fall behind in the count. No one wants to walk the potential winning run, but Gertsen is not inferior. Maybe not great, but he's got guts. He knows hitters prefer to hit fastballs and James knows he knows this, so James looks for the curve. As Gertsen reads the signs, James inches up in the box even more. He wants to get as close to the mound as he can, so as to cut off the angle of the ball.

Okay, he tells himself. Keep your shoulder in, drive the ball to left. Be ready. Hang in on the curve. Own the plate.

His eyes flare as he searches for the ball in the pitcher's lanky fingers.

XXIII

Mercer is wrapping ice on his arm—not only did Gil not pull him, the coach told him to be ready to go extra innings—when he hears the sound, like a ball well hit by a wooden bat. What the hell, he thinks, knowing everyone in this league uses aluminum. He turns to see what has happened, but the whole bench has jumped up, and his view is blocked by a wall of Koch and Sons uniforms.

XXIV

Gil sprints, sprints as he has not sprinted since he was a player, sprints to where James lies in the dirt. He saw it coming, Gil did, knew that Gertsen might throw at James, send a message after Mercer's shenanigans. As Gil runs he sees that the third baseman has fielded the ball and is throwing it to first. But Gil knows that ball didn't hit the bat. No. He once saw a boy get beaned in a sandlot game—no helmets—and the sound had the same stunning tone. Benny Schwartz; everybody liked Benny, but he was never right again, spent half a year in the hospital, just trying to relearn how to talk. Then his folks sent him to a special school in Grand Rapids, and that was the last Gil or any of his friends saw of him. Ted Redding, who hit him, didn't play ball much after that. When Gil heard, years after the accident, that Redding had been killed in Korea, Gil felt relieved that the story had ended, even if it was all bad hops.

When Gil reaches James the player is still shaking, eyes rolled halfway up in his head, his batting-gloved hand shaking in a palsied way. Though his blue batting helmet is still on it's easy enough to see where the ball hit him, above and to the outside of his left eye, where a welt has already formed and is still growing, red and angry, glowing with ever deeper reds and purples, as if there were an ongoing explosion beneath the skin.

"Hold on, son," Gil says. "Hold on."

There are calls for an ambulance. The Georgian doctor who treated last inning's casualty instructs that James should not be moved, as if someone had the idea. The doctor produces a tiny flashlight that looks like a pen and shines the light in James's unseeing eyes. Gil feels his heart constrict, the muscles of it tight, straining.

"Shit," the doctor says.

In minutes the ambulance enters through a gate in the right field fence, then bounces along till it reaches home plate. Its back doors swing open and two paramedics jump out like commandos. Gil looks into the face of one. He's young, wears a patch with a serpent and staff, a symbol that has always made Gil think of magic.

One of the paramedics grabs for James's wrist.

"Faint, irregular," the doctor says. "Get him out of here."

And they do. It's a matter of seconds before they have James strapped to a stretcher and shoved into the back of the ambulance.

"Anybody coming?" asks a paramedic.

Gil knows he should go, but the game's not over. He can't go now. He must be hard. He sends Kohn. Kohn has pitched already. He's done for the day.

XXV

With the field cleared and settled, Mercer can see that Gertsen is cold, stiff. He stood motionless the whole time it took to send James on his way, and now that he's warming up Mercer can see it's not going well. It's hard to start up again after so much downtime. Especially when the wind is carrying a cool breeze. Especially when you're no longer young.

Mercer remembers a pitching coach he knew in Double-A, a guy named Bernie Snick. A mean son of a bitch. "Death is an occupational danger of hitting," Snick told him. "And it's your job to make sure that hitters never forget that. I mean, it's goddam hard, really, to kill a man with a baseball, or to hurt him, even if you're trying. The trick is to make the guy think you're not trying to kill him, but you might not be able to help it. He doesn't know where the ball is going. That's a bit scary. But if he thinks you don't know where it's going, well, that's terrifying. You know what I'm saying?"

Mercer did.

"One thing I love about the DH rule is that pitchers can't throw at pitchers. Used to be, you throw at a guy's teammate, he'd stick one in your ear. That was something of a deterrent. Now, why, the other guy can only throw at your teammates, and no matter what a guy says, putting his friend at risk ain't the same as putting himself there."

And so now Mercer knows what Snick meant. Mercer himself has never thought of baseball as a life-or-death issue. He's always just loved the game, which is, he believes, how a player should be. Don't analyze. Just love the game, the way you loved it when you first loved it, at six or seven, long before you ever thought to ask why. Eventually you figure out that it won't love you back, that it doesn't give a damn about you, and that will be all right. When James gets back on his feet, he'll understand that, and it will be all right. It's all right with Mercer now. In fact, in that odd way that rejection can work, it makes Mercer love the game that much more.

XXVI

Gil whispers instructions into Booth's ear. He's using the pitcher as the pinch runner for James. This is no time to take chances with mixed signals, especially with a pitcher. Go on the second pitch, he tells the player. And you damn well better make it.

Make it. Gil thinks these words about James. Gil is not a religious man, but he is praying now. Please, God, let him make it. All the medical gear they got now, how could he not? All the way that kid has come, You've got to let him make it.

Gil has never had a life-threatening injury before. He's had pitchers get sore arms that never got better, career-ending injuries that seemed pretty serious but weren't about dying. Gil wonders what James ever did to deserve this. Gil thinks of the murder, but then thinks, no, James has already been to prison, and besides, the world doesn't work that way. A guy gets hit by a pitch, it doesn't mean a thing, other than a guy got hit by a pitch. You can't live your life worried about payback that may never come. You've just got to go out and take your cuts.

O'Rourke takes the first pitch. The second skips into the catcher's glove, and the kid makes a nice play to get the ball down to second with something on it. But Booth slides in ahead of the throw. Then he stands and points a finger back at Gil. Done, that finger says, just as you wanted.

Three pitches later, O'Rourke has walked.

Now, with men on first and second and nobody out, Gil must decide if he wants Jefferson to bunt. This would take away the double play and put Koch and Sons in position to win on a fly ball. Except that Jefferson is a horrendous bunter, so Gil nixes the idea. He could do nothing, just let Jefferson hit, but the kid is none too fast and thus an easy double play. So Gil decides on a play that is a bit risky, but that fits nicely into the situation. He turns to run it by Vince, then remembers. Vince no doubt would like the play. It's the kind of thing Vince was always begging him to do.

So on the first pitch Jefferson squares around as though to

bunt. Gil watches the third baseman. The kid doesn't charge.
(Sometimes they do, and then the play works the easy way.) As
the ball is delivered to the plate each runner breaks for the next
base. Jefferson, meanwhile, pulls back his bat, and stands as tall
and big as he can be—he is a big man—so that the catcher must
step around him to throw to third. Booth dives headfirst: a
rooster tail of dust, the tag, the breast stroke of the umpire. Safe.

Now the stands are rollicking—second and third, no outs,
one run needed. Gil is up on the dugout step. He glances
back at the fence that runs from the backstop to the dugout,
and his heart skips. There, among the spectators, pressed to
the chain-link, is his father, a short, little man wearing a cardi-
gan sweater over a shirt and tie, a fedora on his head. No, Gil
tells himself, no. It's just some little old man come to see the
game. Just some little old man. This part of Michigan must be
full of them.

Gil turns back to the game. Concentrate, he tells himself.
Concentrate. He watches as the Georgia outfield jogs in: they
have to make a play at the plate. The infield plays in as well.
Gil can feel the compression, of the game, the tournament,
the season, a life squeezed down and beating through him, as
palpable as his pulse. A premonition comes to him. For the
first time in his life he knows something will happen before it
actually does. He knows that it will work out. Yes, it will.

It happens like this: Jefferson fouls back the first pitch. The
crowd swoons. The Koch and Sons players shout encouragement. Then Jefferson lifts a fly ball that carries on the new
breeze; it floats out toward the cereal signs. The outfielder

sprints back, positions himself, catches the ball, and throws it home, but Booth, having tagged, sprints across the plate well ahead of the throw.

Gil finds himself carried along by the rush of the team. His steps are almost weightless, as if in a dream, carrying him out to home plate, where the team mugs Booth and Jefferson, a tumble of white-and-blue uniforms. Gil finds himself in this tumult and then lifted above it by shoulders and cheers, held aloft, finally, victorious, conspicuous, uneasy.

XXVII

"Ben," says Patty, one of the secretaries, "Jerry Gillens on forty-six."

Mercer is standing, trying to get out of the office.

"Okay," he says, "I'll take it." He straps on his headset, pulls the mike close to his mouth—he doesn't like others to listen in when he sells—and punches the blinking light.

"Ben!" Gillens shouts. "You wonderful SOB! You missed your calling. Absolutely missed it. You ought to be a fund manager."

"What are you talking about?"

"Burwell-Craine. Burwell-Craine!"

"What about it, Jerry?"

"Hey, I know you've been out for a week, but surely you read the stock tables when you're away."

"Actually," Mercer says, "I try not to. Otherwise, why be away?"

"Pull up Burwell on that computer of yours."

Mercer sits, and taps at his keyboard. His screen tells him that Burwell-Craine is trading at seventy-three and a quarter. "Wow," he says.

"You just added a third of a million bucks to my net worth and probably a little jake to your own. I'm downright grateful. And you, Ben, you are blessed."

It takes an hour to drive to the suburbs of Detroit. Mercer passes fields of high corn and another he knows to be a pumpkin patch. There's the Domino Pizza headquarters, also a huge cemetery, then the town of Plymouth. He scoots north, then east, past Farmington and Orchard Lake, on across 696 till he gets to Royal Oak. Pulling into the lot of Koch and Sons he expects to find the usual lineup of cars, but the only one he recognizes is Gil's evergreen Lincoln, uncharacteristically dusty and mud-splattered.

"Where is everybody?" Gil asks when Mercer makes his way inside. Mercer can only shrug. He looks about the room, the same room in which Vince and his wife were displayed. There is a funeral attendant standing beside a large mirror; a woman hovers up by the casket, which is closed. There's a priest nearby. Otherwise the room is empty

"Everyone *knows*," Gil is saying. "I called them all."

"Who's the woman?"

"That's Mrs. James."

"I'll pay my condolences," Mercer says

"Good," Gil says. He purses his lips. "Go ahead."

Mrs. James looks almost starved, with sunken cheeks and deep half-moons of charcoal beneath her eyes. Mercer introduces himself. "I knew Luke fairly well," he says. "He confided in me. He was a great ballplayer, and a good person. He meant well."

"That's what I used to tell folks," she says, "but no one would believe me after what happened."

"It's what you know in your heart that counts," Mercer says.

"He was a good boy."

"Yes," Mercer says, thinking that deep down each mother must believe this about her son. Has to.

"Do you have children?" Mrs. James asks Mercer.

He shakes his head.

"Are you the boy who played for the Orioles?" she asks.

"Yes, that's me."

"I recognize your name. Luke talked about you."

"He did?"

"Sure. He admired you."

Mercer feels something rise up inside him; he identifies it as pride.

The priest approaches, and says, "Shall we?"

Mercer turns around. Kindle has arrived, and Jefferson, Goodstein, Krauss, Kohn, and Metz. They look a bit startled, or confused, as if they think they could be in the wrong place. But they're here. It's not a great turnout, but it's a Tuesday after the season, and about as good as one can expect.

XXVIII

Gil drives alone to the graveyard, a short way south on Woodward. Koch and Sons, in a last bit of sponsorship, picked up the funeral and burial. James will lie in the westerly area of the same graveyard where Laurence is buried, in newer, Christian ground.

Gil stands in the parking lot and notices the gray sky, thinks it appropriately solemn, though he also remembers his mother's funeral, on a brilliant day of sun that still felt no lighter than this one. Today there is a coolness to the air that sometimes arrives at this time of August. Mercer falls in next to him and together they walk to the gravesite, which turns out to be little more than a hole in the ground in a garden of low, polished granite.

"Maybe," Gil says to Mercer, "you could say a few words. After the priest."

"What?"

"Just something quick. From one of his friends. For his mother."

"Okay," Mercer says.

The priest's ceremony displays an economy Gil had not anticipated, so that moments later Mercer is talking.

"I've played organized baseball since I was eight years old," the pitcher says. "Now I'm thirty-four. I don't know why I started playing. I guess it was because everyone played. I do know why I still play. Because I love the game more than life. I think Luke loved the game like that, too. Why do I love it so? Why did Luke? I doubt he knew any better than I. The thing about love is, why doesn't matter.

"There is no good why to explain what happened to Luke. I wouldn't even try to explain it. I think I'll just try to remember how Luke could hit a baseball. It was beautiful. If you ever saw him do it, you'll never forget it. That's something. People forget most things that they *think* they will remember. I mean, I know it seems odd that such a thing as hitting a baseball can be eternal, but it is.

"Now the seasons will go by. Great hitters will come and go. You'll see some on your televisions. Remember that for every talent that succeeds, there must surely be many of equal gifts who don't. It's not only talent and sweat that create greatness, but luck, too. So when you watch these great players, whoever they'll be, remember that you could be watching Luke James, but for a little luck."

"Amen," Gil says, seeing in a flash his greatest players: Wood and Kravic, Rocci and Stein, Mercer, and James. All that talent, but so little ultimate greatness. God, he thinks, someone is due.

XXIX

Mercer is walking back to his car when Jefferson catches up with him.

"You ought to be a preacher," Jefferson says.

"Not a talent of mine."

"Like hell. You were great."

"No faith."

"You could work around that."

They stop beside Jefferson's Taurus.

"Gil asked me to help coach next year," Jefferson says.

"What did you tell him?"

"I said I'd do it. Didn't he ask you?"

"Yeah, he did."

"And?"

"I told him no," Mercer says.

"Why?"

"Coaching's not a talent of mine either. Did Gil say he wanted you to help, or to take over?"

"Help, of course. I mean, he's still gonna be the man."

"You sure?"

"Yes, I'm sure. Maybe you're right. He won't quit."

Mercer feels a smile pull at his face. To stop it he says, "We'll miss James."

"That kid," Jefferson says. "You just had to look at him and you could see the hurt. You know what I mean?"

"I suppose."

"I know you want to play forever," Jefferson says, "but you ever think about quitting? I mean, just contemplate it. Maybe spend more time with that blonde?"

"Every pitch," Mercer says.

"So why don't you?"

"'Cause I still get people out."

"Yeah," Jefferson says, a chuckle rumbling up from his belly. "I can't quit, either."

———

XXX

Gil eases the Continental into the left lane, then merges from M-14 to I-94 west. Ahead the clouds are breaking, and the sun is evident in the gargantuan light shafts that slant to the ground. As he drives past Dexter and Chelsea he can see that the fields are full with corn, and he thinks of fall and the old harvest markets that once sprang up, long ago, during the war, when there was no gas and the farmers brought their goods right into town on horse-drawn carts.

The cemetery lies in what is now a residential neighborhood to the east of Jackson. Gil exits the interstate and snakes through the cement streets till he turns up one that is blind, where at the end what once was a view of the gravestones is now blocked by a tall wooden fence erected to thwart the vandals who had been defacing the stones. The graveyard itself is small and old, a Jewish cemetery in an area of few Jews, a square of land no bigger than any of the neighborhood's backyards. Perhaps twenty bodies are interred, including Gil's mother, dead now for more than thirty years.

Jim McQueen, who lives in the adjacent house and caretakes the cemetery, is standing in his driveway when Gil pulls up. That must be something, Gil thinks, to have a cemetery for a backyard.

"Hello, Gil," McQueen says. "They're all here, inside."

McQueen leads Gil into the living room, which is small and thus crammed with people, almost all of them strangers. There are three old codgers, Pineridge types, sitting on folding chairs, plus five kids, Babe Ruth League age, standing about. Gil notices one kid in particular, a redhead tugging at his collar, a good-sized kid, rugged, not unlike the Brinsen boy, who played Triple-A ball in the St. Louis system, someone Gil hasn't thought of in years.

Then Gil sees the rabbi—a young one, no more than forty—sitting with Alfredo Schuster on a couch. The couch is low, with soft cushions, so that the men's knees are high, their pant legs hiked up, their shins white, exposed. They look as uncomfortable as hell.

"Fredo," Gil says. "You didn't . . ."

"Yes, I did, Gil." He climbs from the couch by half-crawling up the armrest. The rabbi has an easier time standing.

"Dad," says a voice, and Gil turns. There, over in the corner, near a stand with an open Bible, is Rick. Gil hasn't told Rick about the funeral—didn't want to bother him, or deal with him, either—but Rick is no dummy. There's only one Jewish funeral home in Jackson. The information was easy enough to come by, if you were looking.

Rick comes over and Gil has one of those awkward moments, like those he's had with Rick ever since the kid hit high school. What do you do with your grown son? Hug? Shake hands? Rick takes the initiative this time and lightly cuffs Gil on the shoulder. Rick is wearing a charcoal suit, white shirt, a navy-and-yellow silk tie. He's clean-shaven and he's done something with his hair that makes it look smooth and neat. Rick was always a good-looking kid, but today he looks like a movie star. Gil realizes he is glad Rick has come, and he wishes he had simply given him the details. He wishes that family details were actually simple.

"It's just a little service," Gil says, meaning, I didn't tell you about it because it's no big deal.

"Gramps wouldn't have wanted it any other way."

Soon they are outside, where the rabbi runs through the service. Morris's coffin—a pine box, per the old customs—lies in an open grave. Gil has never been one for religion, but when the Kaddish arrives, he can recite the ancient words as though it were the day of his Bar Mitzvah. He has long imagined this moment, and now that it has arrived he thinks of the long final years of his father's life. Gil wonders what kept the old man going. Was it the life of his son, his grandson, the satisfaction of having created a legacy, however meager? Or maybe Morris just had no choice. Maybe he didn't expect an outcome, or some final, game-winning hit that confirmed that all the sacrifice that had come before was worthwhile.

The service finishes and the mourners turn from the grave. The day is fading. Shadows are long, and Gil notices a hint of rust in the top leaves of an oak—yes, it's an oak—across the street. It is the time of day when everything changes, when people leave work, when ball games commence or friends meet for drinks, for company. Gil can hear the traffic from nearby I-94, and he can feel, it seems, the actual turning of the earth from the sun, and the loss of light and heat.

"*Alav ha-shalom,*" says one of the codgers, shaking Gil's hand. Peace be upon him.

Jim McQueen has opened the gate in his new fence, and the boys are already walking out to the street.

"I hope you didn't mind the age range of the minyan," says the rabbi. "But we are a small congregation, and so many of our congregants are working, or too old to travel. The boys, they're from my confirmation class. They're all Bar Mitzvahs."

"I had no doubt," Gil says.

The rabbi expresses his condolences, then leaves. Jim McQueen walks back to his house, and Gil is left in the yard with Rick and Alfredo Schuster.

"Gil," Schuster says, "I need to talk to you for a second. Whenever you feel up to it."

"Sure, Fredo. I'll meet you at your car."

As Schuster retreats, Gil turns to Rick. "I didn't see your car out there."

"It's there, but up the block. I didn't really know where I was going. The last time I was here, I think you drove. We were visiting Nana's grave, a long, long time ago. I don't think I had my license yet."

"I remember," Gil says.

"Anyway, I parked up the block. You probably passed it on your way in, before you would have thought to look."

"Probably," Gil says.

"Anyway, Dad, I've been thinking about your last visit."

"And?"

"You weren't as bad as you thought you were. As a father, I mean. You weren't bad at all. Laurence dying, that's really what screwed everything up. And you can't blame yourself for that."

"It happened," Gil says, thinking, Sure you can. You can blame yourself for everything. But Rick is giving something here, and Gil is glad to have it. A little pat on the back, such as he never got from Morris.

"It is what it is, Dad," Rick is saying. "What I want to say is, I could have made it easier on you. I guess you don't know these things till it's too late."

"Amen to that," Gil says. "And thanks."

"That's what I'm trying to say, Dad. Thanks."

Gil stares at Rick, at his fine dark suit. Gil doesn't know what to say, and for once Rick saves him.

"Dad," Rick says, "usually after a funeral there's a reception, you know. People eat and whatnot. You got something like that going?"

"No. Like you said, your grandfather wasn't much for parties."

"Yeah, well, it's not a party for him. What do you say we break some bread, you and I. Get a meal. You got plans? It's just about dinnertime."

"Sounds good," Gil says, and it does. He tries to remember the last time he and Rick had dinner alone, wonders if they've ever had dinner alone. Sure, they must have. Gil just can't remember it.

"How 'bout Gilbert's?" Gil suggests. A fancy place where Jacksonians have been eating steak and potatoes throughout the generations.

"You know, Dad, I was thinking, we should eat at Bill Knapp's."

"Bill Knapp's? I thought you hated Bill Knapp's."

"I don't think I'll go there again, but tonight it's a farewell. I'm thinking that tonight I just might enjoy it."

"Yeah," says Gil, chuckling. "I just might enjoy it, too."

Rick takes several steps toward the street, then turns. "Fredo's still standing out there waiting," he says. "I'll go ahead, get us a booth."

Gil agrees to this plan, and himself heads toward the street. He notices that the leaves of the oak are darker now than they were moments before, though he can still see the rustle in them. Beneath the oak a man is working on his hedges by the day's last light. From down the block Gil can hear a kid yelling, "I'm open, I'm open," and ahead, leaning against the rear fender of his Buick, is Alfredo.

"I'm sorry about your father, Gil," he says.

"Thanks, Fredo."

"Why didn't you tell me about the funeral?" Schuster asks. "I had to call Bernie Salzman, who gave me the name of the nursing home. They knew about it there. You didn't have to have strangers here today. There were plenty of people who would have come. People from Jackson. People you've known all your life."

"You mean people I used to know," Gil says. "People who didn't really know my father. You know, sometimes you just don't feel like making a big deal out of things. I didn't even tell Rick. Because I knew he would come. And it just wasn't necessary. He came when his grandfather was alive. That's what was important."

"Looks like he wanted to come."

"He did," Gil admits.

"So, what's a minyan, anyway?" Schuster asks.

"A group of ten men, who get together for the purpose of prayer. A proper mourning, with the Kaddish prayer, requires one."

"Half of the minyan looked like Little Leaguers."

"They were old enough to pray."

"As long as you're happy, Gil."

"James didn't get a minyan," Gil says.

"How was it?" Schuster asks.

"How could it be?"

"I couldn't go, Gil. I mean, I didn't think I could take it. I went to the state pen all summer for almost five summers. I don't know what to say. A kid of that promise."

"You spotted that promise, Fredo. You can feel good about that."

"Hell, anybody could have spotted that promise. Anybody. But I couldn't watch them put him in the ground."

Gil wishes he hadn't had to watch it. Boy, does he wish that.

"So, Fredo," he says. "What do you need to talk to me about?"

"It can wait. This being your father's funeral and all. It can wait."

"Just tell me what it is."

"A player," Schuster says, having let slip a moment of silence. "Can you come look at a kid next week?"

"Where?"

"Ludington."

"Ludington? That's a haul. Besides, I'm easing my way out. I've made Jefferson assistant coach. Give him a call."

"But this kid is special. I wouldn't ask if he wasn't. Only seventeen. Throws ninety-seven. A real live arm. Pure talent."

"I don't think I believe in pure talent," Gil says.

"Please, Gil."

"I'm tired, and Rick is waiting for me."

"Please. It's important to me."

"Fredo."

"Yes?"

"Why do you keep doing it? You want me to keep looking at players, but you get nothing back."

"You know why," Schuster says.

The corners of Schuster's mouth turn up, ever so slightly. It's a trademark Schuster look, mischievous and spry, and even in the dim light Gil can see it. It's as close as a look gets to being ageless, the look on a man's face when you see him as a boy, just as he was fifty years before.

Why doesn't matter. Mercer's words float through Gil's mind. Schuster is begging, and Gil knows not to fight it. And so he reaches into his breast pocket for his pen and notepad, then leans close to Schuster, as though he were to be passed a secret, and jots down the route to Ludington, and the time, careful to get the details right.

For essential help with the manuscript, the author
wishes to thank Herbert Barrows, Andrea Beauchamp,
Deborah Lasser, Jennifer Rudolph Walsh, and Rob Weisbach.

ABOUT THE AUTHOR

Scott Lasser received his M.F.A. from the University of Michigan and his M.B.A. from the Wharton School, and is currently the treasury bill trader at Lehman Brothers. He has written for the PBS nature series *Wild America*, and his short stories have appeared in *The Missouri Review*, *The Mississippi Review*, and other literary journals. He lives in New York with his wife and two children.

ABOUT THE TYPE

This book was set in Simoncini Garamond, issued in 1958–61 and designed by F. Simoncini and W. Bilz. It is a variation of the classic Garamond typeface originally designed by the Parisian type cutter Claude Garamond (1480–1561).

Claude Garamond's distinguished romans and italics first appeared in *Opera Ciceronis* in 1543–44. The Garamond types are clear, open, and elegant.